AF328059

The Concert Made in Heaven...

As Gloria passed the performance from her CD recording over to us "earthly performers," the audience was mesmerized and groovin' to the soulful sweet pocket of the ending vamp. And, just when no one thought we could go any higher, Stevie Wonder, who I thought had left after his last number, came up on stage. We passed him the lead vocal mike and away he went and away we all went.

I really felt that the whole place was going to be transported to Gloria's stage—it was ridiculous! Stevie was "blowing" rifts from heaven, the background singers were singing phrases never rehearsed, and the band and I were laying a heavenly carpet of sound for all to float on. The jam lasted almost 20 minutes, and the ovation that followed another 20.

When the applause died down, I grabbed the microphone, looked up to the sky, and said, "That was for you, baby! I love you eternally. Do well!"

The Song That Never Ended, page 160

Also by JOHN NOVELLO

The Contemporary Keyboardist (1986)
The Contemporary Three-Part Keyboardist Video Series (1991)
Stylistic Etudes (1995)

THE SONG THAT NEVER ENDED

A Jazz Musician's Journey to a Love Beyond Life

John Novello

New Paradigm Books   Boca Raton 2003

NEW PARADIGM BOOKS
22491 Vistawood Way
Boca Raton, FL 33428
Tel.: (561) 482-5971/Toll-Free: (800) 808-5179
FAX: (561) 852-8322
Email: <darbyc@earthlink.net>
Web Site: <http://www.newpara.com>

**THE SONG THAT NEVER ENDED:
A JAZZ MUSICIAN'S JOURNEY TO A LOVE BEYOND LIFE**

Cover design by Peri Poloni, Knockout Design
<http://www.knockoutbooks.com>

Cover photo by Dick Zimmerman. Photo illustrations No. 6 ("The author sings with Stevie Wonder at the life tribute concert for Gloria Rusch-Novello, April 27, 2000") and No. 7 ("The author tames the promordial beast") by Neal "Chaz" Bowie.

First New Paradigm Books Quality Paperback Edition: June 15, 2003
New Paradigm Books ISBN No. 1-892138-09-3
Library of Congress Preassigned Catalog No. 2003100726

10 9 8 7 6 5 4 3 2 1

This book is dedicated to all those who have lost a loved one.
May they, upon reading it, come to believe that
the song has not yet ended.

Table of Contents

1. Gloria Rusch as Coretta Scott King in *King*, performed at the Barnsdall Art Theatre, Hollywood, January 7-28, 1985; 2. Gloria Rusch, aged 14, in Los Angeles; 3. In her early 20's; 4. In Asia; 5. With Isaac Hayes, 1995; 6. The author sings with Stevie Wonder at the life tribute concert for Gloria Rusch-Novello, April 27, 2000; 7. The author tames the primordial beast; 8. Gloria Rusch-Novello in the 1990's

Acknowledgements

I would like to thank my father and mother, John and Menga Novello, and my sister, Patti Esper, for their continued love and support through all these years. For their support, I would also like to extend my thanks to: my brother-in-law, Bob Esper, for his long-distance medical assistance; Gloria's daughters, Rachel and Ileane, and their husbands, Eric and Patrick, for their help during Gloria's journey; John Chambers and the staff at New Paradigm Books for believing in me and for their hard work in helping me tell my story; Daveda Lamont, for editing the original manuscript; Terry Parr Williams, my business manager; Gloria's auditor, Jolie Marsh; Susan Watson and everyone at Celebrity Center International; and the Religious Technology Center and the Flag Land Base.

For their wonderful contributions to Gloria's life tribute, I would like to thank: Michael Roberts, for his masterful hosting; Mario Feninger, for his superior piano performance; Michael Norris, for his wonderful one-man act; Geoffry Lewis, Geoff Levin and Betty Ross from Celestial Navigations; musicians Pat Torpey, Ritchie Kotzen, Glenn Hughes, Melvin Davis, Randy Drake, Eric McKain, Donald Hayes, Linda Griffin, Amy Keys, Joey Diggs, Allen Chang, Connell Moss, and Larry Hopkins; and Stevie Wonder, for his matchless gift of song at my wife's life tribute.

Special thanks also to Gloria's mother, Dorothy Allen, to Gloria's sister, Marguerite, and her brothers, Neal and Kenny, to Dick and Patti Zimmerman, to Izzy and Mary Ann Chait, to Mark and Donna Isham, to Isaac Hayes, Paul Haggis, Kevin Burke, Bruce Wiseman, Craig and Sally Jensen, Ritchie Acunto, Arlo Gordin, Chick and Gayle Corea, Ron Moss, John Cerullo and everyone at Hal Leonard, Barb Quinn at Warner Chappell Music, Eveyln Brechtlein, Billy Sheehan, Dennis Chambers, Kevon Edmonds, Babyface, Barb "Jersey Girl" Simpson, Mike Faley, my partner at Lunatek Music Alan Howarth, Aajonus Vonderplanitz, and many more who supported us in our time of need.

And a very special thanks to my granddaughter, Naomi, who has filled my life with love and the spirit of play.

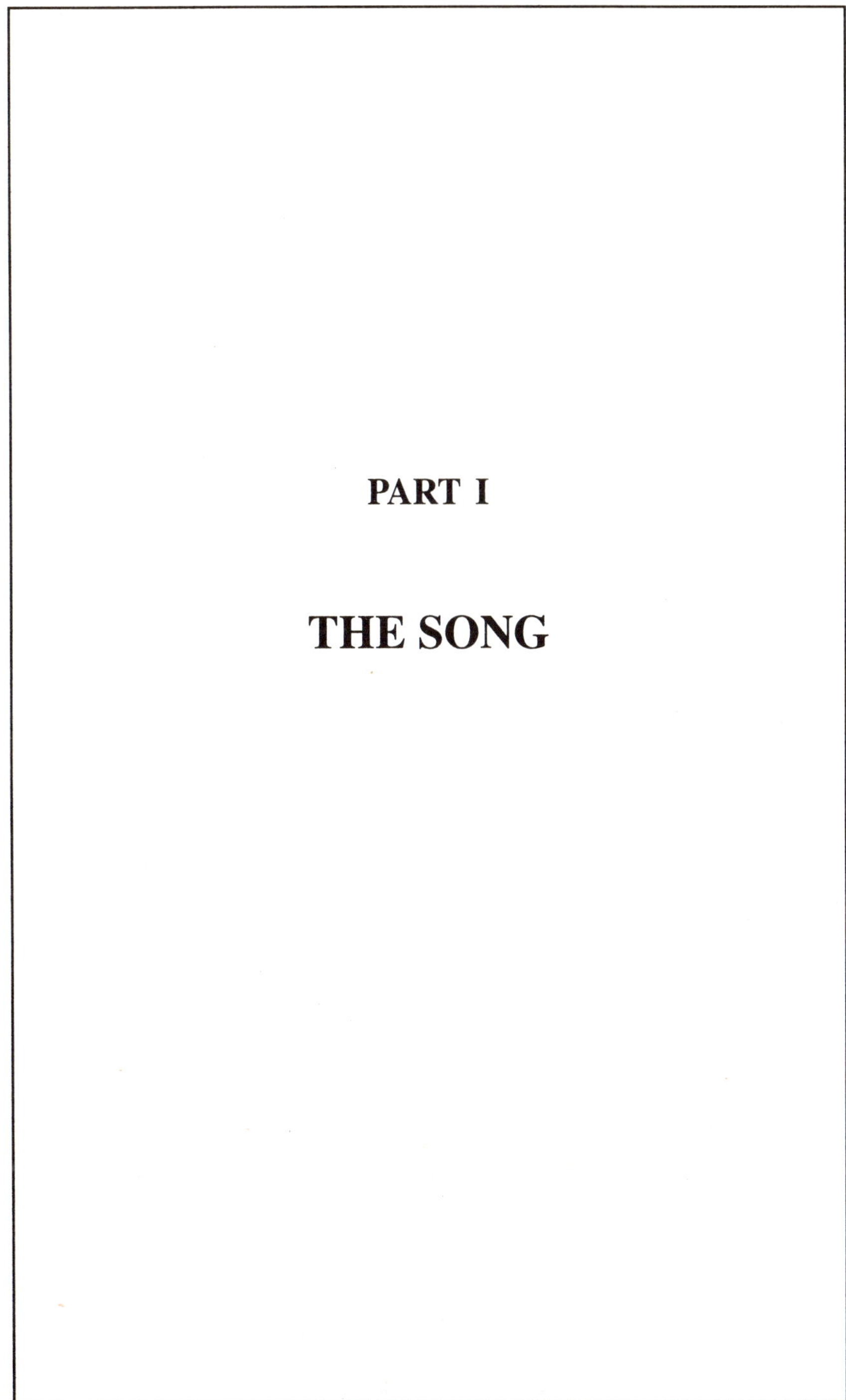
PART I

THE SONG

Prologue

On January 28, 2000, at 3:00 in the morning, my wife, the talented and beautiful jazz singer Gloria Rusch, died of cancer.

But she did not die.

At 5:00 A.M., just before they took her away, I uncovered her body and looked at her beautiful face for the last time. I had first seen that face in a photo passed to me by a friend 22 years before. I had fallen in love with her then, and I had never ceased to love her. Now I bent over Gloria, kissed her on the lips, and said my last good-byes. To me her body, even lifeless, even ravaged by cancer, was still a work of art. Gloria had always had the ability to look good under the most trying of circumstances, and she was looking good even now.

Then they took her away. At 7:00 A.M., her brother, her sisters, her mother, my stepdaughters—the family all left for their homes.

I looked around at our once-beautiful house. There were signs of battle everywhere. The house was strewn with medical equipment— hospital bed, medicine, food supplements, oxygen tanks, bed pans, blood-pressure devices, inhalers, wound dressings of all types—and now, no Gloria!

I collapsed. I broke into convulsive sobbing. I realized I was horribly exhausted. I probably hadn't had a good night's sleep for over eight months. I had a recording session to go to at 11:00 A.M.— three hours away—and I absolutely had to get some sleep. I made my way wearily to the bedroom, pulled off my clothes, fell into bed and closed my eyes.

And then something wonderful happened.

My mind filled with Gloria's voice. It was crystal-clear. It was as if she were right in the room with me. She began to talk to me just as she normally talked:

John, I'm all right. It's just like you said. It's just like in the movie <u>*Ghost*</u>*. I'm right here. There's no more pain. I'm free. It's true. We do still exist after bodily death. This is unbelievable. Wow!*

I sat up and started to cry, tears of joy as well as grief. "Baby," I said, "I hear you! I hear you. Keep talking."

I'm right with you. It's all right. I love you. I really do. Thanks for our earthly 21 years together. They were fantastic. But we can still be together. It'll just be a different relationship.

Through my tears I made a joke: "You mean we used to have an interracial relationship, and now we have an interdimensional one? I don't know if my heart can take it!"

Then Gloria started to rattle off so many communications that I could hardly keep up with her. When she'd had a body, she'd always been going at warp speed. I guess that after more than a year of being sick and not being able to work as usual, she was making up for lost time. She started giving me instructions about how to continue marketing her book on vocalizing, about her vocal exercise tape, about her vocal school, about remodeling the house, about dividing up her possessions, about my not being hard on myself for not being able to help her more with the cancer, about my career, about her family and friends, about my promise to finish her solo CD, and about the memorial tribute to her life that I was planning.

I lay there in total amazement. I knew for sure that this was not my imagination. I knew Gloria and the way she spoke and operated. I knew this was unmistakably her!

Our conversation went on for about an hour, each of us talking in turn. And then I told Gloria that I was absolutely exhausted, that I had to get some sleep. And so, that night—that early morning—Gloria slipped away, into the place where she now dwelt, and I slipped away into sleep.

As one day followed the next, I would discover that what I thought was an ending was only a beginning. For Gloria would speak to me again, and again, and again, and she is speaking to me even as I write this line. I know now that I had been prepared, ever since I was a little boy, for the ravishing sound of Gloria's voice in a song that will never end. I know now that her cancer was the crucible in which our earthly love was refined to so powerful a flame that she will speak to me forever just as she is speaking to me now.

This is my story.

Here is my song.

Chapter One

My Inner Voice

The first time I became aware that my life was being guided, or that I had some special intuition or precognitive abilities, was when I was three years old. I was born in Erie, Pennsylvania, a small, all-American hamburger town—hardly a city known for the arts. I was sitting in front of the TV and I saw an accordionist, the famous Dick Contino, playing. I think it was *The Lawrence Welk Show*. An inner voice said, "That's it!"

I immediately pointed to the accordion on the TV screen. My mother, Menga, took this to mean that I wanted to play the accordion. She was almost correct as, yes, I wanted to play—but not the accordion. What I really wanted to do was play the piano! But, at three years old, I wasn't quite articulate enough to make the distinction. All I knew was that I wanted to play those black and white keys.

I didn't start playing until I was nine, though, so I guess I'm a late bloomer. And even then, until I was 14, I only played the accordion. But I had wonderful teachers, first of all Moses Ronzitti, and then his son, Erie's own Basil Ronzitti, when Basil came home from the army. Basil used to do transcriptions for the accordion from the works of the great masters like Mozart, Bach, Beethoven, Stravinsky, Bartok and others. If you can imagine five accordions playing accordion chamber music, that is something I was exposed to when I was very young, and it was a most inspirational experience for me.

When I was 13, my sister Patti started to take piano lessons. And I heard my inner voice again, this time telling me: "Piano, stupid, not the accordion!" I quickly became fascinated by the piano and its differences from the accordion. I began playing it when my sister wasn't practicing, and soon I had fallen completely in love with it. I took piano lessons and not long after I began I got into my first band, first playing the Farfisa organ (The Doors had one) and then, somewhat later, the Hammond B3 organ. The keys of the Hammond B3 organ would come to be my favorite black and white keys.

I was a shy, skinny, introverted kid who loved mathematics and logic. This didn't run counter to my passion for music, since music at its foundation is very logical and mathematical. There are just twelve tones in Western music. If you want to make music, all you have to do is organize the tones in various linear patterns, throw in some rhythmic variety, and add a few different colors—i.e. instruments—and, presto, you have music! I marveled at how something as logical and mathematical as music could evoke such deep emotions in people. It seemed almost magical to me, and so, to the shopping cart of my dreams that already included my desire to learn math and logic, I added my desire to be a musician.

During all this time, my inner voice continued to communicate. The next major encounter took place when I was a young teenager gazing up at the starry sky one night. I had never been able to understand how outer space could be endless, and nobody at school could give me an answer to my question. The only thing my teachers ever told me was that space went on infinitely, my physics teacher adding that it was constantly expanding. But *why* was it expanding, I wanted to know? Who, or what, was making this happen?

And then, one starry evening, as I was gazing up at the sky, I heard my inner voice again, and this time it was answering my question. Or rather, it was communicating to me a feeling, which I didn't understand very well at the time, but which I would translate today as, "Yes, outer space is endless, because *you* are endless. You are co-creating it, this infinitude, because you are eternal."

I was entranced by the feeling that was communicated to me by this concept. I found it pleasurable to think about it—and also puzzling and thought-provoking. My inner voice had planted in me the seeds of a great and abiding interest in the pursuit of truth and knowledge.

By this time, listening to this voice had become perfectly natural for me. I thought everyone listened to an inner voice. I thought it was second nature for everyone, and that if you paid attention to your inner voice then everything would work out all right in the end. And, since I assumed everybody was having this experience, I never mentioned my inner voice to anyone.

Hearing this inner voice was not the only paranormal experience I was having. As a boy I had begun to have lucid dreams—dreams in which you're conscious that you're dreaming, but at the same time you're able to keep yourself from waking up. If you work at it, you can even consciously control the direction of the dreams you're having. In many of my lucid dreams, I was the only child who could fly around the neighborhood at will. This flying was extremely real; the details of the neighborhood seemed more vivid than waking life itself. This was amazing to me. It got so I actually looked forward to sleeping so that I could consciously attempt to go on these dream flights; and most of the time I succeeded. Sometimes I would wake up unexpectedly, but I wanted so badly to fly that I would immediately fall back asleep to resume my lucid dream.

One theory is that in lucid dreaming your "astral body," i.e. your non-physical body, leaves your physical body, and that it is this non-physical body that, for example, does the flying around. That's my own belief, and I believe that the non-physical body is the real "you." I now regard those lucid dreams whose course I could control with my thoughts as my first experiences of crossing into another, less dense and less physical, more thought-responsive dimension of reality.

This otherworldly level of communication was never absent from my life. The more I listened to my inner voice over the years, the more I noticed that, far more often than not, it told me the right thing. Whenever I was in a dilemma, I would ask it for advice or for outright direction. I found that, if I had the courage to follow this advice and/or accept the answer, things very often worked out for the best.

There were times when I didn't listen to the voice and as a result made the wrong choice. It took a great many mistakes before I learned to trust this inner prompting. Eventually, I called it my "life's barometer." Whenever I heard that persistent inner voice, it was a kind of

Red Alert! It was time for me to do something, or not do something—and to do it quickly.

Quite apart from my inner voice, I had a very happy boyhood. I was reared in a good, loving and stable family. My father, John Sr., was a carpenter and sheet metal worker who played guitar by ear and often jammed with me when I played accordion or piano. My parents had no bad habits. They instilled in me a strong work ethic and a strong moral sense. They encouraged me toward my goals and supported me in everything I did, both then and now. I had an excellent private education. I was an honor student all through grade school, high school and college. Looking back on it now, I would have to say that I had a "storybook" upbringing.

My inner voice spoke to me a second critical time while I was watching TV. This time it was *The Ed Sullivan Show*. I was watching a band called Gary Lewis and the Playboys perform. The band finished a song and then, all of a sudden, I heard my inner voice say: "You can do that."

"Do what?" I asked.

"Have your own band and play and write music."

Up until then I had never thought of music as a career. In the environment in which I was raised, music was a hobby. Being a doctor, a lawyer or a fireman—that was having a career.

But my voice knew what it was talking about. For, some weeks later, out of the blue, a friend of mine who played bass in a band approached me and asked me if I wanted to play keyboards with the band.

At that time, I had entered my senior year at Edinboro College in Erie. I was majoring in math and science. There came a point in my senior year when I was asked to fill out an application form for post-grad school so that I could work on getting a doctorate in mathematics. I looked over the 25-page application form—I was in the dean's office at the time—and suddenly I started to laugh out loud. My academic advisor came over and asked me what was so funny. I replied: "This application form has absolutely nothing at all to do with me."

And then I tore it up, right before his eyes. He couldn't believe what he was seeing. I was one of his best students, with a 3.7 grade point average, and here I was "just throwing my life away!" But actually I was doing the opposite. I was taking my life back. I didn't go on to postgraduate school. I pursued my real love in this life: the creative arts, specifically music. And, ever afterward, when people have asked me how they can give up their day job and do what they love—e.g. follow a career in music like I did—without worrying about where the money will come from, I always tell them that it is only fear that holds them back from following their dream, that the money will somehow come, and that "Heaven" consists of doing exactly what you want to do and making a good living at it, while "Hell" consists of doing something you absolutely hate—and making a good living at it!

Chapter Two

Early Bands and Boston

I did play keyboards with that friend's band. And soon after I had a band of my own, The Jades. While I was still in Erie, I became the leader of two more bands, Symon Grace and The Tuesday Blues, and C.J. Bri.

It was while I was with the second group that I almost acquired some fame. Symon Grace and The Tuesday Blues had the good fortune to be discovered by a well-known record producer, Roger Karshner, who at the time had the hit single *Time Won't Let Me* with The Outsiders. Karshner was passing through Erie on his way home to Cleveland when he got caught in a bad snowstorm and had to put up at the Ramada Inn off Interstate-90 just outside of town. This was the very same Ramada Inn in whose lounge my band, Symon Grace and The Tuesday Blues, was playing that night. Roger Karshner came into the lounge, listened to us play and signed us up to a record deal on the spot.

We recorded a single with Mainline Records, *You Won't Keep Me Working*, that made it to Number Seven on the tri-state charts and seemed about to break nationally. To make a long story short, right about then our lead singer, Mike Kuber, was drafted into the military, and the record company dropped us because we were a vocal band and too risky an investment for them without our lead singer.

This devastated me. "*Why?*" I asked my inner voice. "Now what? First, you tell me to give up graduate school and follow my musical dream. And now it appears my dream just went up in smoke. What gives, man?"

The answer I got was very specific. "You were not ready for this success. For what you're destined to do in life, you need to move away from Erie and experience being on your own. You also need to get fully trained as a composer, arranger and keyboardist. And you need to learn about your spiritual roots. None of this will you be able to do here in Erie."

I'll never forget that answer. It was clear, precise—and even a little spooky. But it made sense. I had been through the belief systems of conventional religion, which didn't work for me, and I had gone about as far as I could as a bandleader in Erie. But moving away was a big decision. Where in the world would I go? And when? What in the world would I do?

What happened next was actually quite astonishing. It must have been about six months later that one of my best friends, Eddie, who was an organist like me, called me up and told me he would be playing in Erie that night, at the Saegerbund Club. He said he'd been away studying music in Boston at the famous Berklee College of Music.

To be truthful, I'd never even heard of the Berklee College of Music. I went down to the club that night and listened to Eddie play. Since I knew he and I were about equal in musical talent, I was flabbergasted to see how much better than me he'd gotten. We talked, and he told me that he'd learned all this new stuff at Berklee and that the college was an amazing training ground for serious musicians.

Then he went back to Boston, leaving me to ponder my next move.

A few months later, Eddie was back in town. He called me up again, and I went down a second time and heard him play. At the end of the gig, I thought, this is getting ridiculous. He's getting better and better. I'd better get a move-on myself.

That wasn't all. When we got together after the gig, Eddie started talking about philosophy, not music. We ended up discussing many aspects of psychological and paranormal phenomena, from mental techniques for improving your ability to concentrate (something extremely important for a musician), to out-of-body experiences, to psychic ability, to life after death, to reincarnation, and much more.

Because of my own ongoing paranormal experiences, I had maintained a strong interest in these subjects. I had read numerous books in these areas. The more Eddie and I talked, the more I saw that he espoused the same beliefs as I did. More than that: He told me he'd gotten into these studies because, in Boston where the Berklee campus was located, there was every sort of esoteric philosophy society you could imagine, and on campus there was a huge number of foreign students who were into alternate modes of thinking that (at that time) were not very well known in America.

Everything clicked. I could see that Boston was the place for me. I decided that I would seriously study my musical craft at the Berklee College of Music, and that, while I was there, I would study whatever aspects of the paranormal and the "other-dimensional" I could. Perhaps I would thereby obtain some real insight into the nature of my own "inner voice."

That same year I worked two jobs, saved my money, and enrolled in the summer program at Berklee. To do all this wasn't hard, as I was aware that I had taken my life back into my own hands—that I was following my inner voice.

The Berklee College of Music is located in Boston's Back Bay area. It turned out to be a pretty amazing place. It is the world's largest independent music college, and probably it is the leading institution in the world for the study of contemporary music. In the mid-70's there must have been close to 3,000 students on campus, with 40 percent of them coming from as many as 70 countries other than the U. S.

I studied my craft at Berklee for only three semesters, but I hung out in Boston for about seven years. I had some amazing teachers during this time period, including the famed jazz instructor Charlie Banacas, who at the time was specializing in teaching bebop. Eventually, I would leave Berklee and Boston for Los Angeles; but, before I did, Charlie told me, "John, there's making music and then there's the music business. They're not the same thing." At the time, I didn't know what he meant. I do now.

I took away from Berklee College not only some fine training in the techniques of making music, but also a renewed interest in the classical composers, which interest had first been inculcated in me when I was nine and ten and listening to the five-accordian chamber music that my teacher Basil Ronzitti had transcribed from the works of the masters; that interest was reinforced when I was 19 and studying twentieth century composition with Dr. Paul Martin at Edinboro University. If it hadn't been for these two mentors, only God knows where I'd be now. While at Berklee, I would again become interested in a good many twentieth century composers, such as Penderecki, Stockhausen, Stravinsky, Bartok and Hindemith—and, also, I would become vitally interested in a new form of music, called fusion, which I wanted one day to compose and perform with my own band.

While on the subject of the Berklee School of Music: People often ask me (especially if they know I'm a teacher as well as a musician, and have written a textbook, *The Contemporary Keyboardist*) if I think a musician should even go to music school at all. My answer is that this is a very individual thing. Often, the more creative musicians never graduate at all. They go to a school, say Berklee, take some meat and potato courses—which they are generally able to get through in just three or four semesters—and then get a gig and then are out of there. I think that out of all the music schools Berklee still has the best contemporary program for any musician who really wants to make a full-time living in the industry. As far as how long to go is concerned, that really depends on the student and what he or she wants to learn.

Chapter Three

City of Angels

I had been diligently studying my craft in Boston for about seven years when one day I began to hear my inner voice tugging at me again. This time, the Red Alert was, "John, it's time to move. I suggest Los Angeles."

Initially, I found this odd; I absolutely loved the Big Apple and had been planning to go to New York. "*Why* Los Angeles?" I asked.

"You will not only continue your musical career and spiritual studies there, but you will meet someone very special."

I have to tell you that this communication felt very strange to me, especially the last part. The first part made some sense in that Los Angeles is not only a mecca for the music industry, but also at that time it was even more of a center for esoteric studies than Boston, and I had continued to pursue all my interests in the esoteric and in everything paranormal. And, as well as that, not only did the great majority of the record labels and sound companies and all the major film studios have their main offices in L.A, but the area had as well a bunch of other well-known attractions, such as mountains, deserts, balmy weather and foxy girls.

But the second part of the communication was even more confusing. I was already going with a very nice girl whom I'd met in Boston, and I was even living with her at the time. When I told her about my growing interest in moving to Los Angeles, perhaps in just a few months, she not only thought it was a good idea, but she wanted to accompany me! Interestingly enough, by the time we were ready to move, our relationship was beginning to show signs of trouble. But we were still very good friends and we both wanted to move to California anyway, so off we went together.

Never once during that time had my higher voice stopped telling me, "You need to go out to L.A., and quick. It's very important!" By this time in my life I'd had so many positive experiences following my inner voice that I thought I'd be a fool not to trust it now.

We arrived—and right away I hated the City of Angels. Los Angeles was buried in fog and smog during the summer (though in the fall and winter it could be beautiful), and so spread out that it was really a bunch of "little Los Angeles's," such as Los Angeles city proper, Beverly Hills, Hollywood, Santa Monica, Malibu, Westwood, Pasadena, Woodland Hills, Toluca Lake, Glendale, Burbank—the list went on and on. In this city of at least 100 square miles, your car could easily become a second apartment.

Moreover, when I started to get into the social whirl, the city seemed fake and plastic to me. Everybody seemed to be so pretentiously into health and exercise and boasting about their achievements. I attended "networking" parties—events I hated anywhere—where it was hard to find the real behind-the-scenes professionals with integrity and taste and the ability to actually give you a leg up. Los Angeles was an incredibly hard city for an aspiring musician to crack; my friends and I liked to say that it was a town where you needed an agent to get arrested, but you needed to get arrested to get an agent. In other words, you had to score a hot gig to get an agent to represent you—but you couldn't get a hot gig without an agent. It was a Catch-22 thing, for sure, though it is one that every person, musician, artist or athlete, has to crack some time in his or her career. And, in Los Angeles, it is probably harder than anywhere else.

But my guardian angel, or whatever force was behind that inner voice that always spoke to me in time of trouble and helped me out, was right there with me again. And not just with regard to my career as a musician. I'd only been in Los Angeles for a few days when, one evening, I strolled over to the famous Manor Hotel in Hollywood on a tour. In the lounge of the Manor I met a couple of musicians from Detroit, a drummer named Gordie and a guitarist named Chris. We got to talking. I suggested we go somewhere and eat.

Chris was reluctant. He wanted to go, but he "sort of" had a date.

For some reason, this made me very curious. I immediately began to interrogate him about this "sort of" a date.

"What's her name?" I asked.

"Gloria Rusch," he said.

"What does she do?" I asked.

"She's a singer."

I wanted to know: "Is she any good?"

"Yes, she's very good," he answered.

Then I asked him something that it was very odd for me to ask, considering that we hardly knew each other. "Is she your girlfriend, or is it just business?"

He hesitated. "Well, I'd like it to go somewhere, but for now we're just writing songs together."

"Cool," I said, "Do you have a picture of her?" It was most unusual for me to be so aggressive. I could hardly believe what I was saying.

"Yes, I do."

And he pulled a picture of Gloria out of his wallet.

I stared at the picture. I was looking at the slim face of a black woman in her mid-30's who was so luminously beautiful, and had so captivating a smile, that she could easily have been (and, as I would later learn, often was) mistaken for Vanessa Williams.

I immediately knew this was the woman for me. More than that, I knew that I had always known her and that I had always loved her.

Of course, I didn't tell Chris this. All I told him was that I would like to meet this singer someday, since I liked working with singers— which was certainly true.

I realized that my inner voice had been absolutely right when it told me that one of the reasons I had to go to L.A. was to meet somebody special. I knew absolutely that Gloria Rusch was that somebody special. I had found my "angel," and I had found her in the City of Angels.

Chapter Four

A Taste of Honey

But Gloria was a singer on the L.A. jazz scene who was on her way to becoming a somebody, and, as for me, I was still a nobody. I had arrived in L.A. with my funds severely depleted by the 3,000-mile journey. Two months had gone by and, though I'd gotten some work and was playing general business gigs, or casuals as they're called, I was down to my last several hundred dollars.

It didn't seem like I was about to strike it rich. "What now?" I asked my inner voice.

The reply was, "You need to promote yourself better."

"No shit, Sherlock!" I exclaimed. "Any idea how I can promote myself in a city as big as Los Angeles?"

The voice answered without hesitation:

"Go to the big music stores every week. Hang out and play the instruments. You need to see the latest keyboards anyway, and this way you'll kill two birds with one stone. All the major acts buy their touring equipment at these stores, so this is a good place for you to meet the bigger acts and get wind of what's happening in town."

This didn't seem promising to me. But at least it was an idea. I did as my inner voice directed. I started to hang out every Saturday at Guitar Center, a huge music-chain store on Sunset Boulevard. I would go down and wail away all day on the store's shiny new keyboards and synthesizers. One morning, as I was jamming on a brand new synthesizer, someone named Perry Kibble—he has since passed away, God rest his soul—came up to me and declared: "Man, you play with a lot of feeling! I have a band named A Taste of Honey and we've signed with Capitol Records and we have our first album coming out in a few weeks. We need another keyboardist/musical director to help us put our live show together. Are you interested?"

I told him I was interested and we exchanged phone numbers. I wasn't hopeful, though. It seemed as if every musician I met in L.A. had a big recording deal and lots of backing and was about to hit it big, and was willing to let you play with the band for no money at all because, obviously, you would soon be making millions with that band. I forgot all about Perry.

It must have been about three weeks later when I was awakened one morning by the sounds of disco music blaring from the radio. I yelled at my girlfriend, Carol, to turn the radio down. She had to get up early, since she had a straight 9:00-5:00 job. Being a musician, I got up much later, which was one of the reasons why our relationship was on the rocks. Perhaps it was just as well we weren't on good terms, though, since I'm sure she'd turned the radio up on purpose, knowing I'd be annoyed. And, as it turned out, this was one disco tune I absolutely needed to hear.

I was getting up myself to turn the radio down when the music ended. The DJ announced that he'd been playing a tune called *Boogie Oogie Oogie,* by a brand-new rhythm and blues/disco group called A Taste of Honey. *Boogie Oogie Oogie* was the group's debut single, and it was Number 42 on the Hit Parade "with a bullet," which meant it was rising fast.

I was groggy from sleep and didn't take this in for a minute. Then it hit me. This was the band Perry Kibble had been talking about at Guitar Center some three weeks earlier, the band he'd wanted me to sign up with. And they really did have a hit single, *Boogie Oogie Oogie*, which was storming the charts! The offer had been for real.

It seemed like my inner voice was powerfully guiding me.

I got dressed and rummaged around the apartment for Perry's number. After almost two hours I found it, tucked away neatly in the top pocket of a shirt I hadn't worn for awhile. I telephoned. Perry Kibble answered the phone.

I told him who I was and said I'd just heard the song on the radio. "Man," he exclaimed, "am I glad you called! Our song is a hit, and we're going out to do a major tour with the Commodores in a few weeks, and we still need a musical director who can not only play but also arrange and conduct." He'd been looking all over for my number, because he knew I was the guy they needed, but he hadn't been able to find it.

I went over to Perry's place and sat in with A Taste of Honey. The group consisted solely of two beautiful black chicks, Hazel Payne, who played the guitar, and Janice-Marie Johnson, a bassist. Both could sing and write Rhythm & Blues and Disco as well as play them. At the time, it was very cutting-edge for two black divas to be doing all this. Perry signed me up with the group, and the next thing I knew I was heading off on tour.

Boogie Oogie Oogie was a pleasurable, mindless, fun tune that you could dance to in your sleep. Within two months, it was the Number One R&B bestseller in the country. It would eventually sell nine million records and become the Number One R&B/Disco best-selling tune in the world! The song garnered A Taste of Honey a "Best New Artist of the Year" Grammy Award for 1978. In 1980, Hazel and Janice-Marie had another chart topping hit, this time the non-dance tune *Sukiyaki*. In 1982, they would put out another popular tune, *We've Got the Groove*. After that they would drop out of sight.

That period when A Taste of Honey was topping the global charts was an amazing one for me. We flew from gig to gig in chartered jets, playing in halls that seated at least 20,000 and, at one point, drawing 90,000 howling fans at Soldier Field in Chicago. I made quite a bit of money and acquired quite a few contacts. The only downside was that I didn't really like R&B Disco music, and was always dreaming of starting my own band and playing and composing the rock fusion jazz that had so caught my interest at Berklee.

As things turned out, I left A Taste of Honey after three years. But I have to say that, right from the start, the greatest thing about my touring the world with this R&B Disco group was that I was no longer a nobody and even, perhaps, on the road to becoming a somebody. And that gave me the courage to call up Gloria Rusch.

For, once I was on the road with the band and had put some distance between L.A. and myself, I realized that my relationship with

Carol was definitely not working. And so on my first return from the A Taste of Honey tour I called up Chris, the guitarist I'd met at the Manor Hotel, and asked him for Gloria's telephone number. On my second return, I made use of my newfound status as jazz artist on tour to call up Gloria and invite her to sit in on a A Taste of Honey rehearsal in Los Angeles.

Of course, I had already fallen in love with her from looking at her picture. Now, seeing her in the luminously-beautiful flesh, hearing her voice which was at once so warm and smooth and vulnerable and inviting and unique that you could pick it out in a crowd of a thousand voices, my heart was totally stolen away from me. Gloria felt the same. She told me, not long after we'd met, that one day she had written down a list of everything she was looking for in a man and put it away in a drawer. And now, when she looked at the list again, she saw that she'd described me to a tee.

Chapter Five

Gloria's Odyssey

Now, what had Gloria been up to before I met her? In many ways, her background and mine could hardly have been more different. I was white, of Italian descent, a Catholic, and brought up in an upper-middle class suburb of Erie, Pennsylvania; Gloria was black, with one-sixteenth Cherokee blood, a Protestant, and reared in a lower-middle class district of Los Angeles, a continent's-length away from where I was born and raised.

Her father, Neal Charles Bowie, designed custom signs for businesses and was very much in demand. Marguerite, Gloria's older sister by three years, says:

"Dad was a sign painter by trade. But what he really wanted to be was an artist. He completed 21 months at Frank Wiggins' Trade School and used to say that if he hadn't married Mom, had so many kids, and been black, he might have done as well as Walt Disney or Norman Rockwell. We grew up believing they had been classmates of his at Frank Wiggins' Trade School and he had known them personally.

"On Saturday nights, when Dad came home from work, he brought Gloria and me pads of paper and new crayons. On the first page of each tablet he'd draw something to give us an idea of what we were expected to do. He told me—and I'm sure he told Gloria—about the Wyeth family of American artists and believed that he could encourage us to follow in their footsteps.

"Mom took classes to make lampshades and ceramic doodads; our early lives were immersed in artistic pursuit by someone at every turn.

Mom said if she hadn't married Dad she would have been a Katherine Dunham dancer."

It seems as if, in that household, there was every encouragement for Gloria to become an artist. It wasn't only that both her parents were profoundly interested in the arts, and talented; it was also that in the house there was a slightly self-mocking air of failed aspirations, and Gloria's parents were generous enough to want their children to succeed where they had failed—or thought they had. The Bowie children, looking back at it all much later, wouldn't think their parents had failed at all.

Gloria's father had something of the artist's disregard for money. (In this respect, I am like him, because I despise "having" to make money, especially as an artist. It's such a distraction to the creative process, which is probably why, in classical and baroque times, artists competed with one another to win patrons to support their creative habits.) Gloria's mother liked to tell the children that their father had been "irresponsible" when he was younger. None of them had ever really seen that. They know now that the family had to careful with every penny; but when they were young, they actually thought that they were rich. Partially it was because, like all genuinely creative people, Gloria's father had the knack of casting a sort of spell about him, of giving the impression that he could create something from nothing, and that added to the impression of abundance. And Gloria's mother, like her father, was quite capable of sacrifice, so that on birthdays and at Easters and Christmases, the children felt like they were living inside a cornucopia of plenty.

Marguerite says:

"Our Easter baskets were half as big as we were, and came from the store....Year after year, on Christmas mornings, we awoke to find the biggest and best available dolls, Betsy-Wetsy, Dick Tracy's Baby...teddy bears, table and chair sets, doll cribs and buggies, trains, bikes, fire trucks—all our biggest gifts were unwrapped and arranged around the tree in giant department store-like displays. Beneath the tree itself were dozens of gaily wrapped boxes containing miniature china, metal pots and pans, skates, clothing, doll blankets, books, boxed games, doll clothing. We thought we were rich."

There was an element of illusion in this reality. Gloria's Aunt Lavada and Uncle Frank lived next door with their children who were older, and the two families created the lavish celebrations between them, though not forever. Many years afterward, says Marguerite, "Cousin Glessie revolted, refusing to 'go into debt until June every year to give [us] spoiled kids everything [we] asked for.'" The magic of those times became a part of Gloria. Aunt Lavada would tell the kids that she was not only their aunt, but also "really and truly their fairy godmother." And when, says Marguerite, she had left home herself and was living in New York, she was surprised to find out one day that "Gloria still thought of our Aunt Lavada as our fairy godmother; she actually thought we had a fairy godmother!"

There was tragedy in Gloria's family. High blood pressure ran through the Bowies like an inherited curse. Gloria's father died of a stroke when she was still young; not long afterward, a sister and a brother also died of strokes. By the time she was 25 Gloria had developed high blood pressure herself, which was what made us decide, when she became pregnant, not to have the child. In fact, the threat of a stroke loomed so large in Gloria's life that she became very obsessive about working out, eating healthy, not smoking and drinking, detoxification programs—the whole works. And yet in the end she developed cancer. So, go figure!

Gloria's vivacity was somewhat hidden in those early years. Marguerite says she was a "somber child." Her flamboyant and generous personality wouldn't really begin to show itself until her late teens. I guess it was forged in the fires of those difficult years. When she was 16, Gloria flew to the Fort Rucker, Alabama, Air Force Training Base to marry James Rausch, her high school sweetheart (many years later, for practical reasons, she would change the spelling of her married name to Rusch). This was in the late 60's, and Gloria was in the South; for the first time, she experienced racial segregation at its harshest. She had her first daughter, Rachel, while living in officers' housing, and then her second daughter, Ileane. Jim flew off to Vietnam between births to take up his duties as a helicopter pilot.

They saw less of him than ever. Gloria couldn't accept this. She moved with the girls to Singapore to be closer to her husband!

There was building up in her in those years an extraordinary capability, which would bring into itself and give sustenance to everything else she did. If in later years I brought to our relationship a psychic gift and an inner voice that told me what to do in times of need, then Gloria brought to it something that was also almost paranormal: a gift for bringing people together in such a way as to strike sparks of creativity among them! Perhaps these sparks could not have been set off in any other way. Gloria could communicate to you soul-to-soul, even in the first instant—even if she had hardly known you before.

I think this gift must have really begun to open out in Gloria after her arrival in Singapore. The adventurous life of the artist she lived there says about as much, and those same events in her life must have served to hone the gift. Gloria didn't see much more of Jim in Singapore than she had in Alabama. She became a model and then a singer. The daughters, very young then, can't remember the details. But Gloria soon took them to Manila, where she continued her career both as a model and singer. Recounting those early years, she would tell people that "I started at the Bottom." She meant the Bottom Club, which was the first night spot she played at in the Philippines.

Gloria was helped in those early years not only by her outward-reaching, generous and charismatic spirit, but also by her good looks. At five feet seven inches she wasn't short, but at 125 pounds she was light for her height. She was always slender, with very long legs and thighs, a narrow waist, broad shoulders (which she may have gotten from her Cherokee ancestors), a small perfect ski-slope nose, small ears, perfect white teeth, and thick gleaming jet-black hair. Her features were stunning, ravishing even, in the mold of a Vanessa Williams, as I've mentioned. I'm sure Gloria was working out even then: In our last years in Los Angeles she worked out three or four times a week—aerobics and weight training—and her muscle tone was as if sculpted in ebony.

I remember one night when we went out to dinner at an Italian bistro on Hollywood's Melrose Strip. The waiters acted like fanatical fans the whole time they were serving us. Gloria couldn't figure out what all the fuss was about. She was really very shy and naïve about the effect her beauty had on others. I wasn't, however, and I knew instantly that they probably thought she was someone famous—like Vanessa Williams. I mentioned this to Gloria and she didn't believe me. But, sure enough, one of those grinning male waiters approached and asked for an autograph.

Gloria looked at me as if to ask: "What should I do?"

"Just sign your own name and see what happens," I said.

Gloria signed "Gloria Rusch." The waiters laughed; they didn't believe her. Smiling her vulnerable smile, Gloria insisted she was nobody but Gloria Rusch. They still gleefully refused to believe her, instead calling her Vanessa. The manager finally came over, apologized to "Vanessa" for his staff's intrusive behavior, and, thanking her profusely for her patronage, handed her a bouquet of flowers. We had a whole lot of fun with this incident—especially as, even while we were leaving, the staff all still "knew" that Gloria was really Vanessa Williams! Of course, I knew she was Gloria Rusch; and, trust me, if Vanessa is a ten, Gloria was a twelve.

But all that was for far in the future. Meanwhile, back in Manila in the late 1960's, Gloria was beginning to have real problems with her marriage.

Marguerite says:

"At a point, Jim wrote to Gloria to obtain her agreement that, while they were apart—when he was on mission [from time to time he was in Cambodia or Thailand as well as in Vietnam]—he would have a 'Thai Wife.' He wanted her to agree, but I didn't have the impression she willingly did so or had any choice in the matter. In fact, she seemed very upset by it."

By now, Gloria was in a band and touring parts of Southeast Asia (including even Kabul in Afghanistan), and it shouldn't be surprising that she had taken up with one Mau Nanas, whom she had met in Manila, who was a musician—a keyboardist/bandleader just like me!— and who would later became her manager. Gloria, Mau Nanas and the girls soon headed off for London, England. They set up shop in a London suburb called Twickenham. Gloria began to play in clubs in and around the city, including some well-known places like Ronnie Scotts, a favorite nightspot of celebrities such as Tom Jones and John Hendricks.

Gloria loved the English, and might have stayed there forever. Events, however, were about to bring her travels full circle.

Chapter Six

Gloria Back Home

At 3:30 one morning in Twickenham, when she had been in England for about a year-and-a-half, Gloria received word that, after seven years as a helicopter pilot in Southeast Asia, her husband Jim had been killed.

Despite all, Gloria was grief-stricken. She headed home to California within the week. With her came the girls, and Mau, who was still her manager and would become her second husband. In L.A., Gloria didn't pause. She formed a band called The Hollywood Swingers, in which she was both lead singer and percussionist. Soon the band was playing to packed houses up and down the coast.

But now, after the succession of deaths strung through her early life—those of her father, her sister, her brother, her husband—tragedy struck again. During a church counseling session, Gloria learned almost by accident that Mau was sexually abusing her two daughters.

Says Rachel, the eldest:

"She said that had she had a gun she would've shot him right there. She threw him out that day. And we were a threesome for awhile. She felt terrible about that for a long, long time."

Gloria had much to keep her mind off this disaster. Her career was moving forward on several fronts. There was the singing. She loved Nat King Cole, Billie Holiday, Luther Vandross and Ella Fitzgerald; when I first heard her perform, I was amazed at how effortlessly she duplicated the styles of Ella Fitzgerald and Sarah Vaughan. Somewhat later, *Music Connection Magazine* wrote: "Gloria Rusch is en route to solo stardom. She has a virtuoso voice with a 3-1/2 octave range that will knock your socks off, and she's got looks to spare." Gloria was also becoming an actress. Periodically over the next several years, she would pop up in roles in TV shows like *Twilight Zone*, *The Bold & The Beautiful*, *General Hospital*, and *What's Happening Now*. From time to time, she appeared in movies; her film credits would eventually include films like *Rocky III*, *48 Hours* and *Dreamers*.

She liked live theatre most of all. It brought out all the best things in her. Playing a role on stage, she excelled. Of her performance as Leatrice in *On the Line*, at L.A.'s Group Repertoire Theatre, *The Los Angeles Calendar* raved: "Actress Gloria Rusch physically and vocally is wonderful in the role, all sass and mouth. She steals the show." When Gloria starred in *Amphitryon 38*, also with the Group Repertoire Theatre, that same *Calendar* gushed, "Alcmena is cast black, with a bedazzling and exuberant Gloria Rusch." The role that she felt the most pride and joy in playing, however, was that of Coretta Scott King in the musical *King,* when it was performed at the Barnsdall Art Park Theatre in L.A. "Gloria Rusch delights," proclaimed the *Los Angeles Times Calendar*. "Earthy, funny and fine," effervesced the equally bewitched *Dramalogue*.

As might be expected from someone who loved playing Coretta Scott King, Gloria was active in African-American affairs. She was president of Ebony Awakening, a group that disseminated L.R.H. to the African-American community. And not only the African-American community; she met with community and civic leaders of all persuasions to ally them with the activities of the World Literacy Crusade. She would eventually be involved with many other, similar, associations.

In hindsight, looking back at the marvelous things Gloria did, I can see even more clearly now the extent to which communication played an overarching role in her life. She was forever in training as a communicator: as a singer, as an actress, as a networker who reached out and out—and out again. She was, for example, responsible for hooking me up with Billy Sheehan, which led to the successful musical group collaboration called Niacin (of which, more later). And maybe most important of all, she was a communicator as teacher and as author. I'm not sure teaching was anything she ever expected to be doing. She came upon it almost by chance—though, looking back at it now, I wonder if it was chance at all, but really purpose.

At a certain point—fairly early on in her singing career in L.A.— Gloria's voice had become what they call in the business "burned out." She had, after all, crossed whole continents singing! She soon found a way to refresh her voice: by undergoing training in the singing techniques of the "Old Italian School," with David Kaufman as her teacher. Gloria became extremely interested in these techniques, and eventually she and David co-founded the School of the Natural Voice. When David retired to Europe, Gloria took over the school.

The singing methods of the Old Italian School were perfected in the sixteenth and seventeenth and eighteenth centuries. For a while, they were lost from sight; then, in the early part of the twentieth century, they resurfaced due to the efforts of one E. Herbert Cesari, who refurbished and restructured these techniques as a comprehensive vocal method that he re-christened the Cesari Old Italian School Vocal Method.

The Cesari Method focuses on breath control exercises, since 80 percent of the act of singing consists of breath control. And it focuses on exercises that develop and strengthen the muscles controlling the vocal cords—of which there are approximately 60! Of central importance is performing these exercises naturally, in such a way that the singing is carried out within the ordinary parameters of breathing and the vocal cords. Gloria would write in her book, *The Professional Singer's Handbook* (Hal Leonard, 1998), that "when you know how all the parts of the voice work together, then you are able to control your voice more easily. When you have control of your voice, then you can pretty much sing whatever you want with much more ease and no strain."

Gloria loved the Cesari Method and loved teaching it. Pupils came to her from all over the world, rank beginners to platinum-level artists. They would eventually include Stevie Wonder, Paula Abdul, Mia Peeples, Rebe Jackson, Maxine Nightingale, Lisa Presley, Kevon Edmonds, Tracy Spencer, Mint Condition, the multi-platinum rock group Mr. Big and many more. Stevie came to Gloria to learn how to sing more naturally in the upper register; after all his years of "belting" (that is, forcing) his voice—the opposite of what the Cesari Method teaches—his upper voice had become damaged. Gloria worked on helping him to restore this upper voice, getting him to use the Cesari Method exercises to not force his voice but use its natural sound. I can well remember Stevie's joyful presence at these sessions. One day, Gloria called me in from my back studio because Stevie had a present to give me. It turned out to be a brand-new portable synthesizer, for use on my upcoming Niacin tour. "Let's play some jazz!" exclaimed Stevie. "Sure!" I replied. Stevie started playing, at a breakneck tempo, John Coltrane's famous and difficult song *Giant Steps*. Although I knew this tune it seemed like Stevie was playing it in a different key, and I was struggling. Then he stopped playing and started laughing: he had transposed the synthesizer to another key as a practical joke!

Toward the middle of the last century, the Cesari Old Italian School Vocal Method was practiced by great singers like the Italian tenors Enrico Caruso and Beniamino Gigli. Gigli taught it to Mario Lanza, who used the method to great effect in his portrayal of Enrico Caruso in the hit movie *The Great Caruso*. Not many singers know this technique and use it systematically today; offhand, I can only think of Eric Martin of Mr. Big, Kevon Edmonds and, of course, Stevie Wonder—but, gradually, it is re-emerging into prominence. It's difficult to master, due to all the breathing exercises; but, once mastered, the technique permits the human voice to do just about anything it wants, effortlessly and without damage.

Around the time Gloria was first running the School of the Natural Voice, and enjoying it immensely, she and I became a team—"an item," as they still like to say in Los Angeles. Often, of course, we were obliged to continue our careers on separate tracks, going off on this tour or that for extended periods. It was while I was on one of those tours that something very synchronistic happened to me.

Chapter Seven

Meeting Donna Summer

When Gloria and I got together, I was still touring with A Taste of Honey. This gig lasted for three years. Then I went on a world tour with Donna Summer, who had heard me playing and had subsequently asked me to perform with her. But before this happened I had gotten to know Donna personally, in a way that illustrated that my inner voice was still chugging along to give me the proper guidance.

This particular piece of interdimensional communication happened when I was on tour with A Taste of Honey in Japan. We were playing the Tokyo Music Festival along with Al Jarreau, Donna Summer, Rita Coolidge and several other acts I can't remember. We had all met at rehearsals and we all had a day off in Tokyo before the actual festival at the Buddha Khan. I decided to take a subway ride down to the old Tokyo Wharfs, where I'd heard I could get some great local Japanese food. The Japanese food in the hotel was good, but not as good as that of the small restaurants in the old Japanese neighborhoods.

I got off the subway and literally got lost in an ancient Japanese neighborhood near Tokyo Bay. I was getting hungry and I saw a small restaurant on the corner. I went in and sat down at the counter, but nobody spoke a word of English. This is usually a good sign, as it means that you'll most likely be eating authentic Japanese cuisine. I had to point to the dishes I wanted, which worked out well. I had an incredible meal.

Since I was the only foreigner in the restaurant, all eyes were upon me. Two Suma wrestlers were sitting at the end of the counter, gazing at me with particular interest. During the meal, the waitress came over to me and handed me a mug of beer. She was smiling. I tried to tell her with sign language that this must be a mistake, that I hadn't ordered beer, but she insisted and pointed to one of the Suma wrestlers at the end of the counter. I looked over. He was grinning in anticipation. Then I realized he wanted me to drink his 'gift' and that this must be some sort of a 'welcoming' custom. When I thought about his size, and also thought, Christ, we bombed these people—when I considered these two things—I accepted his gift, and he immediately brightened up and thumped his partner as if to say, "See, I told you he'd accept!"

You'll never guess what happened five minutes later. Another beer came my way, and this time it was from his partner. I of course had figured out the politics of it by now, and I immediately took a sip. Mind you, I don't drink much at all, but during my meal I had managed, in deference to local customs and out of respect for the neighborhood I had invaded, to finish off both the beers. Everyone was happy—but I must confess that, when it was time to leave, I was more than a little tipsy.

Now, when I walked outside, I was not only a little tipsy, but it had gotten dark, and I suddenly remembered that I was lost. Being lost in Tokyo proper would have been no problem. Wave down a taxi and tell the taxi driver what hotel, and away you go. But I was in a residential neighborhood. There were no taxis and no one spoke any English. Luckily, I didn't have a concert that night, so although I didn't know how I was going to get back to the hotel, I wasn't too concerned. I consulted my inner voice, or, as I was coming more and more to think of it, my higher spiritual self.

At first I got no response. So I said, "Hello-o-o! This is no time to desert me. It's pretty dark and devoid of traffic. All I need is for a taxi to come by in this obscure neighborhood. Is that too much to ask?"

Then I got a funny answer: "How about I send a limo?"

I laughed, because that seemed pretty unrealistic. I kept on walking for a couple of blocks, hoping to see some signs of the city where I knew I could find a cab.

All of a sudden, I heard from behind me: "Hey, white boy, do you need a ride?"

I turned around and, sure enough, there was a limo. "Who could this be?" I wondered. The back window rolled down and who should stick her head out but Donna Summer. I had met her and her body-guards earlier in the day at rehearsals, and when they spotted me walking down the street they remembered me.

Donna wondered what the hell I was doing all the way down here by myself at night. I told her and she laughed, because she had gone shopping and then come down here for the very same reason: to get some great down-home local Japanese food. I jumped in and got my limo ride back to the Tokyo Prince Hotel. We had a good time talking and we became friends. The following year, she asked me to play keyboards in her band.

Figure that out with normal logic!

Is this luck at work here? I don't see how that could be. These events that were happening to me seemed somehow orchestrated. I say "somehow," because I do believe that we have free will and that I could have made many other decisions, or just not been observant, or not paid attention to my inner voice. But I listened to it and, whether it was my heart or my inner higher self or my spirit guide, or God or the force—whatever you want to call it—things just worked out. In fact, when it came to my inner voice things sometimes worked out even when they seemed not to initially. How could I have known that a limo would be happening by in ten minutes? And what were the chances that in the gigantic city of Tokyo—population 12 million in 2002—Donna Summer would drive by in her limo? Besides, I could still have been in the restaurant eating and could have missed her just as well.

On a more practical if different note: As I've said, it was Donna Summer's getting to know me in Tokyo that led to her later hiring me. And this is often how we get jobs in the business of being a musician. I always tell other musicians, those who work with me and those whom I teach, to give more than is expected on every gig, even on a wedding or a lounge gig, because you never know who might be listening.

Chapter Eight

The Contemporary Keyboardist

Gloria and I are both published authors. In the mid-80's and early 90's, she produced and self-published three volumes of the recorded vocal exercises of the Cesari Old Italian School Vocal Method. In 1998, her *The Professional Singer's Handbook* was published by Hal Leonard, and it continues to be very popular.

I never expected to be an author myself. It happened as the result of a great deal of urging on the part of my inner voice. After touring with Donna Summer for a couple of years and greatly enjoying seeing the world and playing with a number of accomplished artists, I realized there was just one thing I wanted to change: instead of playing other artists' music, I wanted to compose and perform my own (I must admit that at the same time I had pretty much had it with Disco music, which was never a great love of mine in the first place).

I felt sure that eventually I would compose and perform for myself, and I was happy with my progress. But my inner voice added to my impatience by chiming in one day with:

"You're done, John! Quit! New game! It's time to change horses in the middle of the stream."

"I know," I said, "but what am I going to do for survival money?"

The voice had an answer for that. As usual, the answer was unequivocal: I should quit touring and write a definitive book on contemporary keyboard playing.

This communication came to me while I was in the middle of teaching a student. "What?" I exclaimed mentally. "Have you flipped your spirit-guide or inner-voice wig!"

When I was off the road and in town, I would teach to supplement my income and because I loved sharing my hard-earned musical knowledge with others. I had kept meticulous notes of all my musical studies. I haven't come easily by my musical talents—at least, not in this lifetime. I didn't fall out of the womb a Mozart or a Chick Corea. I've had to study hard and practice hard to get where I've gotten. Yes, I had raw talent, that's for sure; but it took a lot of doing for me to develop and hone it. And so, when I got this inner voice advice to just quit touring and write a book on contemporary keyboard playing, I thought: This can't be right! Maybe Keith Jarrett or Chick Corea should write this book, not me.

But then the voice said something that made perfect sense: "They can't write this book because they don't really know exactly what they're doing. They just do it. Though at times you feel cursed that you've had to figure things out the hard way, because of this you are in a position to organize and map out the path for others. So, get busy!"

I did just that. I turned down so many road offers that it scared me. How was I going to pay the bills? My inner voice gave me the answer the moment I asked the question: "Why don't you teach full-time, maybe 30 hours a week? That will not only pay the bills but will also give you many hours of hands-on teaching while you write the book."

Then, almost magically, with very little promotion, more students than I could ever have asked for began to ask me for lessons. From small children to older adults, from beginners to top professionals, they came from all directions. So, beginning in 1981, I immersed myself in teaching and in writing the book. It wasn't until 1985 that I finished it.

(While on the subject of teaching: People ask me about the relative importance of hard training in the fundamentals of musicianship, on one hand, and just having soul and feeling it and letting the music rip like you feel it should, on the other. My answer is that the fundamentals of musicianship, which I teach—ear training, technique, harmony, rhythm, improvisation, and repertoire—are important, certainly, but that without focused, honest, in-the-zone playing, you will never amount to much as a musician. How do you get into the zone? By learning who you are, by tapping into your highest self, and by making that melody or that piece of music your own. When you play that piece, it's got to be your piece now. You must own it. You've got to play honestly what you feel and what you hear. You mustn't be thinking, "Oh, God, here's this tune again. I've played it on every tour, and now I'm sick of it." It doesn't matter if you've played it 30 times in a row on 30 dates, whether you're playing it at Cobo Hall in Detroit or Carnegie Hall in Manhattan or at your local Holiday Inn lounge: you should be playing that tune like it's the first time you've ever played it and it's going to be the last time.)

As I was saying, in 1985 I finished my book, which I called *The Contemporary Keyboardist*. I took it to all the major music publishers, but they all turned it down. They told me my book was too big (it was 551 pages), too highbrow, too philosophical—too everything. A friend of mine, a publicist named Kaye Champagne, suggested we send a copy to the music trade magazines. I did so and forgot all about it. After all the work I had put into the manuscript, I was more than a little bummed out that I hadn't gotten a big publishing deal immediately. I felt I'd done a great job, and I just couldn't figure out why these publishers couldn't see that this book was needed and that it could sell well.

About three months later, my subscription copy of *Keyboard Magazine*, one of the top music trade magazines, arrived in the mail. I made some lunch and started scanning the book while I ate. I turned to a page and all of a sudden it said at the top, "Book Reviews." I thought to myself how nice it would be if I could get a good book review in one of these trade magazines. I scanned down the page and just about choked on my mouthful of food, because, lo and behold, there was a review of John Novello's *The Contemporary Keyboardist*!

I immediately became terrified and closed the trade magazine. I called my publicist friend Kaye and told her that *Keyboard Magazine* had done a review of my book. She said that was odd, because usually when she sent books to the trades, someone called back and either said the magazine had declined to review the book or that it would review the book in such-and-such an issue. She hadn't received any call about my book. She asked me, "Well, is it a good review or what?"

I said, "I don't know. I'm too terrified to read it. What if it's bad? That's four years of my life possibly gone up in smoke."

Kaye laughed and scolded me and ordered me to read her the review. I finally confronted it and read it to her—and, to my surprise, it was a fantastic four-star review. I was elated. This was one of the biggest wins of my life!

When you carry out with no thought or concern whatsoever for making money a project that is a labor of love, and then get validation for it from the industry in which you work, that is quite a wonderful feeling. Within a few weeks I was receiving checks from people all over the world who wanted to purchase my book. I didn't even have any printed up yet, because I didn't have a publishing deal. Kaye told me: "This is a *good* problem!"

So I hired some people to put the book together and print it up, and I self-published it. After two years of further stellar reviews and great sales, it was then easy to get signed to a major publishing deal. Chalk up another win for intuition!

Chapter Nine

Novello/Rusch

Gloria and I lived in a spacious one-story white stucco house in Valley Village in the San Fernando Valley area north of Los Angeles. In the center of our large living room stood a Yamaha grand concert piano. One side of the living room was all glass, with French doors that opened out onto a large slate patio. The patio gave onto a large lush backyard that was a sea of colors because of the 150 plants that Gloria kept there.

Gloria's powers of communication extended even to the plant world. I loved to sit at my grand piano and practice and watch her tend her 150 plants. I loved to play in the yard with our German shepherd Bronco while she fed and watered and pruned them and had a grand old time. The plants were her special friends. She took care of every one of them as if they were her children. Gloria could sense when any of them was not doing well and nurse it back to health, whereas I was good mainly at killing them, not intentionally of course, but because of my ignorance and neglect.

On Sundays Gloria would bring certain special plants in, certain privileged members of her plant family, and add to the inner environment of our house their color, their shape, their scent, their life-energy. She made everything wait until she had handled those plants, in the backyard or in the house—and I mean everything, including lunch, dinner, and the satisfaction of any and all appetites! Always, when I seemed to be too caught up in the fast lane of our many businesses, she would simply say, "John, come here," and lead me outside and point out a certain rose and tell me to totally look at it until I saw its incredible beauty. And this always made me feel great.

I had a studio in the remodeled garage out back and Gloria had hers in the house. Between those two studios we carried on the activities of our business, Novello/Rusch. Novello/Rusch included under its umbrella Gloria's School of the Natural Voice, our contemporary adult jazz act Novello/Rusch (voted by *Black Entertainment* the West Coast's top up-and-coming contemporary jazz group in 1995) and eventually the progressive jazz rock fusion group Niacin. The principal focus of our daily activities, however, was the music we taught during the day and created during the night. Gloria and I both liked to create music that was uplifting to others, and we both loved to teach people the arts, especially the vocal and music arts.

This was a happy time for us, and each day dawned full of hope. Gloria got up earlier than I did because she went to the gym every morning. Usually, I was up by the time she arrived back, and our teaching day generally began at 11 A.M. Students came and went all through the day. Usually we taught until 5:00 P.M., seeing each other during breaks or when a student cancelled, when we would snack together or hang out talking or just jam on the piano. And, yes, sometimes we fought, over some stupid thing, but the whole time we were fighting we both knew it was just an act, a sort of game we'd invented to inject randomness and the unexpected into our daily routine.

After the last student left we ate dinner, and then usually we had the evening to ourselves. There would be a brief business meeting during which we would discuss the latest Novello/Rusch musical project—a record, a gig, the contents thereof, promotional materials, reviews, agents, managers, attorneys and so forth—whatever might help put Novello/Rusch on the map. Then we wrote music together. I would play a new composition and Gloria would supply the lyrics and the scatting.

The scatting? Everybody knows what scatting is—but not everybody knows that it's called scatting! I'm referring to the singing in which the singer substitutes improvised nonsense syllables for the words of a song, trying to phrase and sound like a musical instrument. Jazz instrumentalists improvise with their instruments; vocalists do by scatting, taking off on vocal improvisations where they use, not words, but syllables like "*du-be-do-ah*" or "*scoo-bee-doo*."

Scatting is a fine art, and vocalists who practice it are rare because they must be capable of great articulation and control as well as have a musician's ear. Scatting mistress Ella Fitzgerald was Gloria's mentor in this art; other virtuoso scatters are Sarah Vaughan, Carmen McCrae, John Hendricks, George Benson, Bobby McFerrin and Al Jarreau.

So, as I say, Gloria scatted the melodies to my compositions, using her voice as a musical instrument. She was so great at this that one day she succeeded in altering the entire nature of the Novello/Rusch band. Our guitar player had gotten sick and wasn't present, so we asked Gloria to try to scat his lines. She did, with such success that our guitar player became history, since Gloria's scatting with me and the sax player unintentionally created a whole new sound. I called the new sound "scat funk." Normally, scatting is done over swing jazz, but I had been writing a whole lot of jazz funk grooves, so I would have to say that Gloria's scatting over these groves ended up producing—scat funk!

Sometimes we worked together at our music until the wee hours of the morning, say 2:00 P.M. Other times we went on until only 9:00 or 10:00 P.M. Sometimes we went our separate ways for the rest of the evening; other times we went out together. We were so comfortable with each other's company that I could decide at the last minute to go out and catch the last set at The Baked Potato, a local favorite jazz hangout, for example, and Gloria would say, fine, see you tomorrow if I'm in bed when you get back.

Sometimes Gloria would be the one to do the solo going-out-late. It would happen when a party came up where it seemed like it might be a good idea for us to do some networking. I've already said that I hated networking, and at times like this I was just as inclined to sit at the piano and practice for hours. Gloria, being incomparably the better networker of us two, was sent out on these PR missions. You can imagine that her good looks were an asset on these occasions. But just as important was her ability to smile at someone and make that person feel as if they'd suddenly come alive. She communicated with you just by being there; she made you communicate with yourself!

Sometimes she would come bubbling back to the house at 2:00 A.M., all excited that she had met a certain person and set up an appointment for that person to come to one of our shows—and, sure enough, whenever she told me this sort of thing was going to happen, then it really did happen. One time she came home and told me she had met John Dykstra, special effects wizard for the *Star Wars* movies, and had wrangled an invitation from him for us to go see his special effects studio in L. A. "Really?" I said, not entirely believing her and so not taking much interest. But, sure enough, a week later when Gloria called up Dykstra he kept his word, and we ended up going out to his studio where, at the time, the effects were being created for the Clint Eastwood movie *Firefox.* Dykstra took us on a complete private tour of the studio during which he showed us all the behind-the-scene tricks that were going into the making of *Foxfire.* Gloria made this sort of happening come about all the time. Whenever I wanted any doors opened, I sent her out on a networking mission.

I haven't mentioned Gloria's clothes. They, too, were a part of her life mission of communication. She knew how to choose the right ones that would make her optimally appealing. Her mother—the same who used to tell the kids she would have been a Katherine Dunham dancer had she not married Gloria's father!—was an elegant lady, a great shopper and a keen-eyed searcher after unusual shoes, fancy furniture and fancy clothes. This talent, this inclination, this gene, Gloria had inherited in spades. She had the patience and the aesthetic eagle eye to go to innumerable of the finest boutiques and find the foxiest clothes—and the ones most suitable to the special qualities of her beauty—that there were then in existence. I could never go shopping with her because although I had an eye for the beautiful, I did not have Gloria's patience for finding the right aesthetic object. I would just as soon stay home and, again, practice the piano or write a song.

Adding it all together, I can see now that this networking gift of Gloria's had taken her about as far as communication in this world can go. After she passed away, she didn't stop communicating, though this time from a higher reality, and—because of our love which became greater and greater as the days of her life marched toward their final day—that communication came to focus directly upon me.

Chapter 10

The Primordial Beast

What I'm about to describe is really just an example of being true to one's own inner communications.

As a musician, I had grown up playing the organ. It was also true that I played the piano, the electric piano, the accordion and the synthesizer; if it had a keyboard, I played it. But, for some reason, when I jumped behind the organ my musical abilities expressed themselves even more dramatically. I was good at playing all keyboards, but the organ and I were one.

I mentioned earlier that while I was in Erie I was the leader of a contemporary blues trio called C.J. Bri. The instrumentation for that group consisted of Hammond B3 organ, bass and drums. The Hammond B3 was a particularly popular organ model that could be found in groups of the time like Emerson, Lake & Palmer, Yes, Jimmy Smith, Led Zeppelin, Steppenwolfe, Traffic—the list went on and on. There were other organs, such as the Farfisa (Doors) and Vox Continental (Paul Revere & The Raiders), but the Hammond B3—B3 for short—was considered the king. When I moved from Boston to Los Angeles in 1978, however, the Hammond B3 was falling out of favor. The new technologies of electric piano and synthesizer were fast becoming the fad of the day. Nobody wanted the big, heavy and cumbersome Hammond B3 organ any more. And so I thought about jettisoning mine.

But my inner voice told me better. "Don't sell it," it said. "It's part of your soul. It will come back into favor, and you'll be one of the main cats!" I tried to query my voice further, but could get no answer other than, "Trust me."

So I carted my Hammond B3 out to Los Angeles with me. When I arrived and began promoting myself to get work, I always told people that I not only played piano and synthesizer but also the Hammond B3. Most of these people either didn't acknowledge the Hammond B3 part of my communication or commented that the B3 sound was out-of-date nowadays.

Every now and then, though, I would convince the band I was playing with to let me bring my B3 to the gig along with my synthesizers. I would pay the extra cartage. And the funny thing was that, every time I did so, all the musicians would come up to me afterward and say, "Man, what a sound! You really make that thing talk!" or words to that effect. That would make me feel really good, because playing the Hammond B3 was such a totally authentic act for me, the expression of my deepest, realest self. There were many many piano and synth players but not many organ players. I figured the old maxim applied here: To be successful, you had to be the first, or one of the best, or the only one. I'd already blown being the first, at least in this lifetime, but I knew that when it came to the Hammond B3 I still had a chance of being one of the best or one of the only ones. And, considering what my inner voice had told me, I wanted to be prepared. Destiny is a nice concept, but I firmly believe that we make our own destiny. I wanted the Hammond B3 to be my destiny.

So, after years of work in the Los Angeles area, I had a name as one of the few B3 players around. Unfortunately, there was not much work for the instrument, but at least I was a known commodity. (Incidentally, I did convince A Taste Of Honey to let me play the Hammond B3 on their tours. That was a good move, as with all the publicity we received I was promoting myself—and my truest self at that.)

But, though the follow-up would take ten years, one day something happened that ensured that the time would come when I would be wailing away at my Hammond B3 as the centerpiece of a compact, three-man, far-out rock fusion band. That event was my meeting the world-class bassist Billy Sheehan one day when he and his band, Mr. Big, came to our house to take vocal lessons from Gloria. I happened to be there and Gloria introduced us (this meeting was also, of course, another wonderful example of her ability to bring people together in a fateful manner). I told Billy I played the Hammond B3, and he lit up. He told me he'd always loved that "retro-type sound" and that he'd always wanted to be in a band with the B3 sound.

"Well," I said, "Call me some time, and we'll jam."

That meeting was very exciting for me, as I regarded Billy as an outstanding musician, in fact the Jimi Hendrix of the bass. There is no doubt that he has changed the way the bass guitar is played. Billy's credits are innumerable. He recorded two platinum-selling albums with David Lee Roth before he formed Mr. Big in 1989. This latter group achieved a *Billboard* Number One single in the U.S. and 14 other countries with its *To Be With You*. Billy was voted "Best Rock Bass Player" five times in *Guitar Player* magazine's Readers' Poll, an honor that landed him in that periodical's Gallery of Greats. On January 27, 1999, his handprints and signature were preserved in cement on the Hollywood Rockwalk at Guitar Center, which is an outstanding honor.

These latter accomplishments of Billy Sheehan would not take place until some time in the future, but I certainly had no trouble recalling my meeting with him when, late in 1994, he phoned me up and asked me to write and play a tune with him for the *Guitar Magazine* compilation CD *Smell the Fuzz*. Billy told me that many famous guitarists and other players would be contributing tunes to this CD, and I realized that being included would mean great exposure for me. The cool thing was that Billy had called me specifically because he wanted me to do my thing—play the hell out of the Hammond B3.

We had such a good time working together for *Smell the Fuzz* that we decided to continue working together. By the end of six months, we had gotten together enough material for a CD. But we realized we couldn't produce it without a drummer. A single name came into our two minds at the same time. I said to Billy, "Hey, Dennis Chambers is one of the baddest cats around. We don't know him, but let's see if we can get hold of him." Billy couldn't have agreed more.

Dennis Chambers is one of the great natural geniuses of the progressive jazz world. He started playing drums at the age of four, and by the time he was six he was playing in nightclubs. All of his musical training came from playing in nightclubs. At the age of 18 he went from high school to playing with a band called Parliment Funkadelic (a.k.a. "P-Funk"). Since then, he had been with all manner of excellent and interesting bands, such as Special EFX and the Mike Stern/Bob Berg Band, and bandleaders such as Bill Evans, Mike Urbaniak and Steve Kahn. Dennis lived in Baltimore, so I put together a demo of our tunes in my recording studio and we sent it off to him. Almost before we knew it, he was padding into Chick Corea's Madhatter Studios, which we were then using, and with no rehearsal whatsoever we were making our first recording. The minute we started to play, we all knew the chemistry was there. Then and ever afterward, when we got together things caught on fire.

We called our band Niacin, which was actually the name of the song that Billy and I had done for the *Guitar Magazine* compilation. The name is sort of an inside joke with us. Niacin is vitamin B3, and since all of our music was expressly written around the retro sound of my Hammond B3, this seemed like a fitting name for the band. I must confess, though, that Niacin is sometimes used to help people improve their circulation, and that it helps you to sweat out toxins—including the toxins in drugs. But, truly, we named our band Niacin only for the correlation of vitamin B3 and the Hammond B3—though, again, I must admit that our wild fusion music is so in-your-face, so non-elevator, that it can create a rush in the listener analogous to the histamine release that Niacin can cut loose in your cells!

We combined old progressive rock and old progressive fusion riffs in our band, despite the fact that everybody told us, "That music is dead and there's no market for it." We didn't care. Our band was a labor of love from the start. The Niacin musical philosophy is as follows: We play with no stylistic boundaries, with no compromises. Every note is totally honest. We don't care about success or failure, or sales or radio, or what anybody thinks. We just write what we want and play what we want. If it succeeds, then that's great. If not, we'll do it anyway.

I wish here to express my depth of gratitude to Billy, who wanted to pool his resources with the way I played the Hammond B3 organ, and with my skills as a composer, enough that he very generously financed our first record himself and helped launch it with his excellent reputation. We did not even think about whether we would get a record deal. We finished it, we loved it, and all three of us had no problem saying, "Let's not kid ourselves. This is pretty much a self-indulgent project. It's not rock, it ain't contemporary jazz, it ain't easy listening music, it ain't real jazz—it's retro-progressive instrumental self-indulgent music that we want to play. Is anybody going to arrest us for this?"

We decided that nobody was. Billy was big in Japan, where he had been named best bass player a total of 19 times by Japan's two leading music magazines, and where, on January 1, 2000, he had started off the new millennium by performing with Mr. Big before 40,000 fans at the Osaka Dome in Osaka. We decided that if we had a market anywhere, then it must definitely be in Japan. We pitched this first recording, which was titled *Niacin* after ourselves, to two Japanese labels, Video Arts and Pony Canyon. To our astonishment, both companies loved it and both offered us a deal. Video Arts made the better offer and we took it. This first recording sold very well in Japan. We didn't even have a deal for any other part of the world. We looked at each other dumbfoundedly and said, "My God, this is strange!" The strangeness continues: Niacin has released four CDs as of 2002, and all of them are selling well in Japan.

I was very pleased with all this, because here I was, some 25 years after the C.J. Bri band in Erie, playing in an organ blues trio again—and this time with a famous bassist and a famous drummer and with my favorite instrument. We became known both in the U.S. and Japan as one of the new contemporary rock super-trios that was bringing back the famous B3 sound. The reviews have been stellar. It's a dream come true, and it has turned out just like my inner voice had predicted. Who would have thought it? Again I wonder: Do free will and destiny operate side by side? When I look back, I see that there were many forks in the road; had I taken a single wrong turning, none of this would have happened.

I have to tell you that I passionately enjoy playing the hell out of the Hammond B3 organ. I love to take command of that instrument and unleash a stream of furiously felt notes that are full of burn and absent of compromise. For me, the Hammond B3 is a primordial beast that I have to struggle to keep under control at all times. For some reason, when I get behind that monster, I come to life. When I think of the piano, I don't think of it in that way at all. I love the piano, and I love the synthesizer, and I play them well—but when I play the organ, it's just (semi-pun unintended) more of an organic experience. Somehow, the beast allows my soul to speak! It is such a beast to tame, with its double manuals and draw bars and all, and the settings and Leslie speakers behind you that spin and morph the sound while you slip and slide on the keys, that it's like a bear or a mountain lion that dares you to tame it. That is how I think of it. If my B3 could think, or say anything at all, I think it would look up at me and say something like, "Oh, it's you again. I guess I'm going to have to really put out now!"

I'm really fussy about my B3. I have a very proprietary, very souped-up B3, and I try to take it with me at all times. But sometimes in the U.S., shipping-wise, it becomes financially detrimental to do this. When that situation arises, I call on a good friend of mine in Buffalo, Sal Azzerrelli, who's an absolutely incredible B3 tech and player, to make the necessary modifications to one of his own already great-sounding B3s. What I'm trying to say is that I expect the B3 to talk and do what I feel and hear inside my head. And there are certain modifications that I've made on my B3 that are necessary for duplicating what I hear in my head. A real B3 gets about 90 percent of that, but if I don't have some of the little frostings on the cake that I've tweaked over the years, then I don't get that last 10 percent and I can't do what I want to do, and that definitely bums me out.

It's the same way with any musician. Dennis is very fussy about his drum kit: He's got to have this one Pearl set, and it's got to be set up a certain way. Billy's got to have certain speaker enclosures and his Yamaha bass has to be a certain way. All musicians want their tools to be ready to carry out the task for which they intend them.

While on the subject of contemporary music: Some of you may be wondering why the music of Niacin, and of other beyond-the-leading-edge, they-threw-away-the-mold, avant-avant-garde groups like ours, is more popular in Japan than it is in the U.S. My answer is that, in Japan, and in Europe as well, art music and progressive music are still growing strongly. It's a question not only of the classical backgrounds of those countries but of the way in which the contemporary cultures have come out of these backgrounds.

Popular music has been destroyed in the U.S. This is because the technological revolution, which has come to define the nature of the quick-fix culture of the U.S., has both a good side and a bad side. The good side is that incredible related hi-tech tools now exist to enable musicians to realize their dreams quickly, to carve out and edit music in a jiffy. The bad side is that this encourages laziness; people who are lazy and don't want to learn their craft can pick up these software plug-ins and programs and computers and make very mayonnaise-type music in a hurry because they've got the computer playing in time for them, and they cut and paste it and then release it and call it music. To me, that isn't music at all. It has no soul.

The ultimate culprits are the record companies, who, some 15 years ago, went very corporate. They lost their A&R departments, and instead of looking for talented artists whose careers they could develop further, they started looking for quick bucks and the latest fads. Now, those of us who are authentic musicians, who have paid our dues by sweating out a real apprenticeship to our craft, go over to Asia and Europe to make a living—unless we get lucky in the States with something or another.

Asia and Europe genuinely do appreciate music with depth and character, and they provide it with every kind of support. They ask far higher ticket prices than we do here in the States. When we play the Blue Note in Tokyo, the tickets are $100 a show. And not only do the fans pay it, but many of them come to several shows! Here in the States, everybody bitches about paying ten bucks for a ticket and extra for a two-drink cover charge. That, in my opinion, is pathetic.

In the U.S., the production of music is totally money-motivated. You've got radio stations with programmers who don't know the difference between smooth "jazz" (elevator music, in my opinion) and real jazz, let alone the difference between good music and bad. And even if they did, what with their general lack of integrity they would only do and say what their sponsors dictated with their big bucks. Sadly, things are getting worse every day. Nowadays, radio stations only play "music" that fits into pre-established musical categories— and sometimes they can't even get that right. Niacin is not rock enough to be rock and not jazz enough to be jazz, and so forth, so radio pro- grammers—I call them radio robots, as robots are programmed and can't think—don't know what to do with us.

But at least now there are a lot of progressive college and Internet stations and new jam stations popping up, and so progressive music— music from the heart and soul of the musician—is getting its day in court and thus getting to be more and more in demand.

How can you play from your heart and soul and still make a living in this industry? By being very stubborn. By maintaining personal integrity and doing what you love, for in the end that is what produces true happiness. I notice all the time that when I'm around someone who loves what he or she is doing, then that person is always a better person, whether you're talking about an automobile dealer or a chef or a bank teller. If you're only doing your job for the money, then even the job will suffer. And that is resoundingly not the case with Niacin, nor with me and the primordial beast.

Chapter 11

Riga: A Prelude

I got my first premonition of what life would be like without Gloria when I went to Riga, the capital of the tiny Baltic state of Latvia, for three months in the summer of 1992 to work on the movie *Red Hot* with director/writer/producer Paul Haggis. Paul Haggis is responsible for the TV series *Due South* and *Family Law*, among others; *Red Hot* starred Donald Sutherland, Balthasar Getty and Armin Mueller-Stahl.

Paul was a good friend of Gloria and mine. In May 1988, we were married on the spacious grounds of his home in Hancock Park, an opulent suburb of L. A. Over 400 family and close friends were in attendance. Geoffrey Lewis's Celestial Navigations group was playing as the ceremony began. Standing at the altar, I—a skinny, scrawny, Italian white boy from Erie, Pennsylvania who'd never been able to get the good-looking girls in high school—almost passed out when I turned and saw the ravishing beauty in a gleaming white wedding dress who was Gloria, and about to become my wife, walking toward me up the path alongside the glittering creek that wound its way through the Haggis's estate...

Anyway, as I was saying, Paul, an old friend, had hired me to make sure the actors who had scenes where they played the piano (none were musicians except for Armin Mueller-Stahl) looked authentic when they were doing so. *Red Hot* was based on a true story from the 1950's when rock and jazz and the blues were trying to break into Eastern Europe and Russia but were still forbidden (you could end up in Siberia for selling such decadent wares). In the movie, Alexei, a teenager with great musical talent, receives a bunch of rock records from his uncle who travels a lot. Alexei has a friend who decides to copy the records and sell them on the black market. Then Alexei falls in love with the daughter of an important Russian official played by Donald Sutherland. The records become a national threat. Then the KBG moves in, and more mayhem ensues...

My three-month stay in Riga began with an incident that paralleled the somber tone of this movie. I got mugged by two Russian civilians on my first night there (though Latvia had just won its independence from Russia, Riga was still occupied by Russian troops who hadn't yet been given the order to return to Russia). It happened at 11:00 P.M.—though it wasn't dark, as, like St. Petersburg, Riga has its "white nights" when the sky isn't really dark but is pinkish in a very surrealistic way. I was walking back to my hotel through the center of downtown when suddenly a man strode rapidly and menacingly up to me and started yelling at me in Russian. Luckily, I was able to subdue him with the little martial arts I know. Then his sidekick leapt up at me out of some bushes and I had to light out of there as fast as my legs could carry me (there were people standing around, but they acted as if nothing were happening). I didn't want to end up in a Riga police station with a lot of explaining to do.

Film security had told us not to get involved in any incidents, as foreigners like myself were considered rich, and who knew what could happen—especially in this city still crawling with KBG and the Russian Mafia and where there were disaffected individuals and groups on just about every street corner. In fact, nothing of so serious a nature happened to me again during my stay in Riga. But I got increasingly bummed out by this city which was dilapidated and gray and featureless in the unimaginative communist mode, and which had been so badly maintained since the Russians took over in World War Two that hardly anything worked at all.

This hit me most of all when I tried to telephone Gloria. The phone system was terrible and I could rarely get a line out, and even to try I had to go to the top floor of the horrible hotel I was staying at and wait in line to be connected to the U. S. When I did get connected, the line was so noisy I could barely hear Gloria. I would try and tell her how bad it was here and how much I missed her, but she just reiterated that this job was good for me and my career. It wasn't until I got home that I finally got it across to her how lousy the situation had been. Maybe I'm somewhat of a spoiled American, but for me it was Gulag Riga. As those three months crawled by, I actually got very lonely, which was something I had never experienced before. I longed to go home almost every day.

Now, don't get me wrong. Overall, the trip was amazing. I got to work with Donald Sutherland and a lot of other wonderful actors. During one of my brief periods off from working on the film, I took a train trip up to historic St. Petersburg in Russia, where I got to see the six magnificent buildings of the State Hermitage Museum laid out along the embankment of the Neva River. And there was one saving grace in particular: Since I was a bit of a celebrity and working on an American movie there, I was given permission to go and practice the piano at the Riga Conservatory anytime I wanted to, even though that famous old conservatory is closed during the summer.

Still, as wonderful as that privilege was, in part it merely made me feel more lonely: Picture me, in the middle of the night, playing all alone with my choice of 40 empty practice rooms and two empty concert halls, in this huge, deserted (albeit historic) conservatory, with that weird pinkness playing through the night sky outside and a million gloomy denizens of this former socialist state prowling around just outside the walls. Picture this—and picture me having the blues and seriously missing Gloria.

One night, after a 12-hour movie shoot, I hightailed it to the conservatory at 3 A.M. and began wailing away on my choice of the concert grand pianos. I was at just about my lowest ebb. But then something happened to me that often happens to artists. Out of my anguished mood, I was suddenly able to create some of the best music I've ever written in my life. This continued for a number of nights— and then I wrote the best song of all, a song for Gloria called simply *For You.* This was a soulful gospel bluesy expression of my missing her, and I was humbled once again to see how effortless it is to write and perform a song that comes straight from your heart.

I couldn't wait to fly home, hug Gloria, and play her my new song.

Little did I know that, some eight years later, our song was going to be suddenly and harshly interrupted.

1. Gloria Rusch as Coretta Scott King in *King*, performed at the Barnsdall Art Park Theatre, Hollywood, January 7-28, 1985

2. Gloria Rusch, aged 14,
in Los Angeles

3. In her early 20's

4. In Asia

5. With Isaac Hayes, 1995

6. The author sings with Stevie Wonder at the
life tribute concert for Gloria Rusch-Novello, April 27, 2000

7. The author tames the primordial beast

8. Gloria Rusch-Novello in the 1990's

PART II

THE INTERRUPTED SONG

Chapter 12

Misdiagnosis

It was late in the evening of October 22, 1998, when the curve ball from hell was hurled in our direction.

Gloria was unbuttoning her blouse. We hadn't gone to bed yet and were standing in the middle of the living room, so I thought it must be the beginning of a moment of unscheduled intimacy.

But she didn't take her blouse off. Instead, she took my hand, put it on her breast, and said, "John, feel that lump." Her voice was scared.

I could feel the lump all right. It was hard and as big as a quarter. I got a very bad feeling. How, I asked her sternly, could it have gotten so big without her noticing anything?

She said she didn't know, that she examined her breasts every month and that last month everything had seemed all right.

And, right then and there, I bawled her out for being negligent. Which was a really stupid thing to do and an indication of how scared I was, for I was soon to learn that tumors can grow like a shot, seeming to come right out of nowhere.

The next day we went to our family doctor. He referred Gloria to a breast clinic. I took her over and then went and did some errands. I was nervous as all hell. When I got back to the clinic, Gloria came out to the waiting room in her gown, smiled her glorious million-dollar smile, and told me the mammogram/sonograms had been negative, showing only three liquid-filled cysts that were benign.

I was relieved. But I still had that bad feeling. I went in and talked to the doctor myself. She assured me the tumors were benign and added that if the cysts continued to grow and bothered Gloria, then she should come back for a "fine needle aspiration"—a procedure in which a needle is inserted into the cyst to draw off the fluid. The doctor told me this procedure would shrink the cysts, although it wouldn't guarantee that they would not grow back. She saw no reason for removing the cysts. "Why do invasive surgery at this point when the mammogram and sonogram confirm no malignancies?" she asked me.

This was all that Gloria needed to hear. A physically beautiful woman, a performing artist into the bargain, she didn't want to run the risk of unnecessary surgeries that might cause complications and/or disfigure her. Instead, she wanted to try to shrink the cysts with diet and homeopathy. This was something she'd done 15 years before, when the doctors had diagnosed her with fibroid tumors. To the amazement of these traditionally minded doctors, she'd been able to shrink the tumors down to a negligible size. She wanted to do this again for the cysts in her breast.

I hesitated to say anything. Who was I to coerce Gloria into having invasive surgery? Especially when a doctor in a breast clinic, a specialist in diagnosing cancer and other women's illnesses, had told us for certain that her breast tumors were benign?

But my extrasensory faculties had begun to kick in. I did not feel good about any of this. I know now that we made a crucial mistake, that I should never have doubted my intuitions. We should have gotten a second, then a third, opinion; and we should have gotten them right away. With any aggressive cancer, time is the enemy; in our case, it would prove a deadly enemy.

But we did not know then that Gloria had cancer.

She set about trying to shrink the cysts in the same way she had shrunk her tumors 15 years before, through diet and homeopathy. She tried this for seven weeks. During those seven weeks, the tumors got bigger and bigger. Watching those three cysts swell up drove me crazy. Gloria insisted this was what had happened to the fibroid tumors: First they'd gotten bigger and bigger, then they'd begun to shrink, and finally they'd shrunk back to almost their normal size.

At the end of seven weeks I couldn't contain myself any longer. I persuaded Gloria to go back to the clinic and at least try the fine needle aspiration. We made an appointment. It was then that she noticed that she had a swollen lymph node under her arm. This was hardly a good sign; it could mean that there was cancer in her body, probably in her breast, which had spread to the lymph node. It could mean this—or not. I was extremely apprehensive.

We went back to the same clinic, though this time to a different doctor, the one who would perform the fine needle aspiration.

He examined Gloria's previous mammogram and sonogram carefully. Then he said, "I wouldn't have been so quick to tell you these are benign cysts filled with fluid. To me they're suspect, and I don't know if the aspiration will be successful, because it looks like there might not be any fluid in them."

I expostulated, "You mean, two different doctors can look at the same film and come up with two opposite evaluations?" He replied that he could only tell us what he personally saw and thought. Then he went ahead with the aspiration. It would be useful, he told us, if only because any fluid or tissue extracted could be sent to the lab for a proper pathology report.

I wondered why we hadn't been advised at the first examination that we should have a biopsy performed.

The aspiration was not successful; no fluid emerged. The doctor extracted some tissue and sent it off to the lab for a report.

This procedure took place December 23. At 11:00 P.M. on December 28, Gloria and I were sitting in front of the fire at home basking in the afterglow of Christmas. We were feeling pleased about everything except one thing: The growths in Gloria's breast had almost doubled in size during the nearly eight weeks she'd been doing the diet and homeopathy cure. This was a bad sign; benign tumors do not usually grow this fast.

The phone rang. It was the doctor who'd done the aspiration. He was working late and had just gotten Gloria's report. She told me this in frightened tones, holding her hand over the mouthpiece. I jumped up, grabbed the phone and asked for the results.

The doctor told me the report showed malignant cells. He had wanted to tell us as soon as possible, so we could immediately schedule a meeting with a surgeon and oncologist.

Our worst fears—anyone's worst fears—had been confirmed.

It was then that our nightmare truly began. We were still only in the opening stages. "Can this really be happening?" Gloria and I asked each other. "What the hell is going on here?" We both had so many confused and painful emotions that we were overwhelmed. We went from being mad at God, to being mad at the doctors, to being mad at each other for God knows what. It was as serious as hell, this thing that was happening to us. But it was the sort of thing that only happened to other people. It *couldn't* be happening to *us*! Not *now*!

But it certainly was.

Chapter 13

Tijuana

It was the Christmas holidays and so we couldn't get an appointment with a surgeon until January 5. In the meantime I set about ransacking the library and the Internet to find out everything I could about cancer.

I was amazed at the conflicting views of the disease. Traditional medicine scoffed at alternative medicine and advocated surgery, chemotherapy, radiation, and a few experimental drugs administered in trial studies. Alternative medicine dismissed these traditional approaches, called them profit-oriented and archaic, and recommended a crazy quilt of non-toxic, non-invasive, holistic approaches. The traditional doctors warned against the over 200 alternative therapies that were not approved by the U.S. Food and Drug Administration, while the alternative practitioners insisted that the big drug cartels were in bed with the FDA, which was why that government body approved only chemotherapy and other patented, drug-based therapies.

I was blown away by the fact that, even though there was a longstanding "war on cancer," statistics for the disease were on the rise; it was even becoming an epidemic. The FDA and traditional medicine were not only failing to prevent new cases of cancer—which was easier than curing it—but they were using techniques that didn't work all that well, and sometimes even hastened the death of the patient due to toxic side effects, or even caused new cancers.

As bewildering as I found all this, I had to keep a clear head. Gloria was depending on me to help her make the right choices. Already, we'd made a wrong choice; we'd been referred by a reputable doctor to a reputable breast clinic, and the results had been a misdiagnosis and the loss of two valuable months. Those vanished two months had reduced Gloria's chances of survival from 75 percent to fifteen percent. Her cancer was now a "Stage Three," which meant it had gotten bigger and metastasized to other parts of her body, the lymph nodes as far as we knew, but God knew what else.

By now we were mistrustful of conventional medicine. We were very inclined to believe what the alternative practitioners told us. If Gloria had only a 15 percent chance of survival, we had little to lose in pursuing the safer of the many alternative methods. Not only did they offer better odds for success, but they also did not degrade the quality of life as did the toxic treatments of traditional medicine.

Yikes! What did you do in such a situation? Find a good traditional oncologist and place yourself, robot-like, in his or her hands? Pick a few of the many alternative therapies that seemed to have a good track record? Combine the two? Our insurance covered only traditional therapies; we would have to pay for the others ourselves (which is one reason most people never try alternative approaches: these therapies can be cost-prohibitive).

We were hardly multimillionaires. But we made a good living and we had plenty of friends, and so I was not about to let money be an obstacle. Whatever it took, I would do it and worry about paying for it later. I loved Gloria beyond words, and nothing was going to get in the way of my helping her beat this—nothing!

We quickly settled upon an alternative approach. Just days before our appointment with the surgeon, a friend had called to tell us about a treatment in Tijuana, Mexico, that had worked for him and his wife. She had lymphoma and he had skin cancer; both cancers had gone into remission apparently due to the intravenous immune-system boosting therapy of the Tijuana-based Jim Keller Clinic (which is now associated with Bajanor Hospital). Although Tijuana was only 15 miles over the border into Mexico, it was a good 300 miles, round trip, from the northern Los Angeles suburb where we lived. Still, we decided we would try this clinic. We figured that we had nothing to lose.

Our emotional state at the time was, to put it mildly, turbulent. We were horrified and we were incredulous. One minute we'd been working on our careers, remodeling our house, recording in our new studio, working on projects and enjoying life, and the next minute we were plunged into the daily hell of having to combat cancer. It was as if life were pushing us as hard as it could to find out what we were made of, as if we were caught in an episode of *Twilight Zone* from which we hoped we would very soon awaken. A hundred times a day we looked into each other's eyes and wondered what had happened, and then wept, and then got angry.

Right in the middle of that awful time, something wonderful happened.

A Novello/Rusch concert had been scheduled for Saturday night, January 2. So far, we had only told a few friends about Gloria's illness, so we decided to go ahead with the concert. We both experienced something that night that we had never experienced before. All through the concert, Gloria and I were so much in communication, performing at such new levels of inspiration, that we could hardly believe it. We had always enjoyed performing together; it was our dream and our life. But, tonight, under these circumstances, the moment was many times more special than usual, and we both felt this. We discovered how a life-threatening situation can put everything into perspective. Although we didn't realize it fully at the time, a new journey of love was beginning for us both.

On January 4, the day before Gloria's appointment with the cancer surgeon, we made the trip for the first time to the Bajanor Hospital clinic in Tijuana. Located in an other-side-of-the-tracks section of the dusty, noisy Mexican city of two million, the clinic was housed in a large one-room building attached to the main hospital. Gloria's intravenous immune-system treatment would consist of laetrile, hydrogen peroxide, shark cartilage, Hoxsey, polypeptides and germanium, along with special vitamin C and B complex shots and other supplements and immune system-building substances. The founder of the clinic, Jim Keller, was thrown in jail in 1991 for practicing medicine without a license, even though his polypeptide IV formulae had given a great many people a new lease on life.

Gloria underwent the treatment five times a week for almost three weeks. The change in life style necessitated by our commute was wrenching. Usually we could cover the distance from our San Fernando Valley home to Tijuana in two hours, me driving at 75 miles per hour while Gloria tried to sleep. Sometimes we came and went in a single day. Other times, we stayed at a hotel or motel in Mexico or on the American border. Dozens of patients streamed through the clinic on a daily basis, often arriving in shuttle buses from one or another of the hotels. The patients came from all over the world, many of them from Europe, others from as far away as Mongolia. We liked the ones we met very much. They were friendly and often they were very willing to share their terrible dilemmas with us. Gloria and I were ready to sing the praises of this clinic to the world, if only the treatment worked for us.

But it did not. Though the I.V. immunotherapy made Gloria feel better and seemed to boost her energy level and immune system, it did nothing to halt the cancer. Her blood parameters—LDH and liver functions—worsened steadily, as did her red blood count. Toward the end of the third week we were told that Gloria's cancer was spreading to her liver.

This was extremely unpromising, especially given that her cancer was a highly aggressive one. In fact, it sounded like a death sentence. "I can't believe all this," Gloria sobbed as I held her in my arms. "I don't smoke or drink! I work out three times a week. I eat wholesome organic foods. But I still got this tumor! Then it was misdiagnosed! Then I'm told it's one of the worst types of cancers and is now inoperable and has spread to my lymph system. Now I'm being told it's probably in my liver, and I'm a goner!"

Understandably, she was beside herself. I listened with total attention. I gave to my beloved wife total affirmation of the rightness of her feelings. The best we could do was admit to the full horror of the situation.

I came away from the Bajanor clinic experience in a grimly thoughtful mood. Beating cancer by boosting your immune system sounds great if cancer is a disease that is eating up your body because your immune system has been weakened. But why do some bodies, and not others, permit pre-cancerous cells to hang around long enough to grow into deadly tumors? Only when we've understood all the subtle and complex components that make up cancer—and I'm referring to the spiritual as well as the physical components—then, and only then, will we be on the way to curing the disease.

Chapter 14

Is This Really Happening?

We had, of course, consulted with the cancer surgeon in Los Angeles on January 5. We had wanted a second opinion; we had wanted to know if the tumors could still be removed. Perhaps surgery could give Gloria some relief before she started on whatever therapy the doctors recommended.

Our new oncologist studied the mammogram and sonogram and agreed that the films were definitely suspect and we should have had a biopsy done right away and been advised to have the lump taken out immediately. We would have known then and there that it was cancer, and we would have been in a position to have the main tumor removed right away, thus preventing the spread of the disease. According to all the statistics, treating cancer in its early stages gives you a much better chance of survival.

Gloria and I stared at each other in horror. How could the doctor at the breast clinic have so fatally misread the X-rays? It seemed like everything that could go wrong was going wrong! But accidents, mishaps, missteps—even illnesses—just didn't happen to Gloria Rusch and John Novello! That wasn't because we lived a charmed life. It was because we worked very hard to keep bad things away. Gloria never smoked or drank, and she kept in such top physical condition that at 52 she looked 35. To me as a musician, her predicament seemed especially unfair, since, aside from the fact that I loved her so much, I knew she was a talented artist and a wonderful person who still had so much to give to the world through her singing, her vocal instruction, her acting and her writing.

The surgeon told us that Gloria's tumors had grown to an inoperable size. He recommended we start chemotherapy and radiation soon to try to shrink them down to a size that would enable him to remove them. If in fact the tumors could be reduced in size, he said—and that was a big "if," since some tumors were unresponsive to therapy—he would recommend a modified mastectomy and then follow-up plastic surgery.

The surgeon told us that the high dosages of chemotherapy and radiation involved were so toxic that Gloria might have to have a bone marrow transplant. To top it all off, he told us that even a bone marrow transplant might not be successful.

Faced with this evaluation—invasive, possibly deforming surgery with all of its potential complications, plus chemotherapy, radiation, and a bone marrow transplant with a poor prognosis—Gloria elected not to undergo these procedures at this time. I respected her wishes.

Our goal was not just to beat the cancer, but to do it in such a way that Gloria's body wasn't destroyed in the process. She wanted to be able to continue being a performer with the same quality of life she'd had prior to the disease. Being mutilated and incapacitated, however free of cancer, was not a goal either of us could embrace, especially given the lousy prognosis for such a treatment. We wanted a total cure. We would seek a total cure. Such, at the time, was our game plan, rightly or wrongly, and with that plan we moved forward.

A new horror was added to our predicament. Soon after we talked to the oncologist, I found out that, once again, a physician had misled us. I was told that, even at the time of the January 5 appointment with the surgeon, Gloria's tumor, big as it was then, was nonetheless still operable. I was told that there were expert surgeons who would have taken it out right away, and that such an operation would have lessened the tumor burden and Gloria's eventual horrific suffering. It had *not* been true that she would have to undergo three to six months of chemotherapy and radiation in order to shrink the tumors down (provided they responded) so that she could have the operation.

It seemed that these physicians had their own agendas, separate from those of the patient. Was there no one who operated for the greatest good of the patient? Three to six months of chemotherapy and radiation would have made a lot of money for certain people, I later thought bitterly. I was furious. I wondered how these people could live with themselves.

You must be wondering by now why my inner voice, which had been so helpful to me in the past, hadn't warned us in advance about Gloria's cancer, while that cancer was still developing. And you must be curious about whether my higher self made any suggestions as to the choice of therapies.

My inner voice had not been silent. From the beginning, it had conveyed to me the message that Gloria's illness was somehow meant to be, that she would not survive this cancer. It had intimated that Gloria and I could choose to make the most of this illness by accepting it as a spiritual test that, on some higher level of reality, we had chosen to experience in this lifetime in order to learn an important spiritual lesson.

Of course, I didn't tell Gloria this. Nor did I dwell on it myself; it wasn't anything I really wanted to believe. I'm not sure I was meant to believe it. To do so wholeheartedly might have weakened my resolve and courage to wage the battle alongside Gloria.

I'm sure that the powers that guided me, these expressions of my deepest instincts and intuitions, were just as fully engaged in this battle as I was. I'm sure they were prompting me at every turn to try this therapy or that, and that they were prompting me to have courage and to trust in the will of God in this terrible struggle.

The lesson that I believe all of this had to teach us will become clear to you in the course of this book, just as it became clear to us in the course of our battle and in its stunning aftermath.

Chapter 15

At the Klinik Benediktusquelle

It was only the third month of Gloria's illness and we were already balked: The alternative treatment at the Bajanor Hospital's clinic in Tijuana had not worked, not for Gloria at least, and the traditional treatment of the oncologist—as horrifically tardy as it was—showed little promise of working either.

I did yet more research, got yet more referrals, and found out that there was a clinic in Germany that offered traditional and alternative therapies under the same roof. In Germany, there are no FDA-type controls; if a therapy seems promising, and reasonably safe, its practice is allowed. The facility I discovered was the Klinik Benediktusquelle, founded in 1998 by Dr. Alexander Herzog, and located on the Main River in Ortenberg, some 25 miles from Frankfort. Reading about this clinic piqued our interest. We decided to give it a try. Near the end of January 1999, Gloria and I boarded a plane and flew to Frankfort. The airport limousine taking us to Ortenberg barreled along the *autobahn* at 100 miles an hour; we welcomed the speed, so great was our sense of urgency.

The Klinik Benediktusquelle is housed in a spacious and modern building that boasts a hot springs in the central court (hence the name of the clinic, as it is associated with the Order of the Benedictine Brothers and *quelle* means "spring"). It is a residential hospital, and Gloria and I had roomy quarters on the premises. The clinic emphasizes local and whole-body hyperthermia. Local hyperthermia consists of the heating of a specific part of the body to 109 degrees Fahrenheit by ultrasound or infrared rays. Since cancer cells, being tightly packed together, can't easily recover from such temperatures, two hours a day of this treatment can slow their growth or even kill them without creating too much toxicity.

Whole-body hyperthermia, as the name implies, is more intensive. The entire body, except for the head, is placed in a chamber. The patient's body temperature is gradually raised to 105 degrees, with all vital signs being carefully monitored. While this is happening, low dosages of chemotherapeutic drugs are gradually released into the bloodstream. The low dosages, in conjunction with the heat, can be effective in killing cancer. The patient is sedated during the process; even so, the intensive nature of the therapy, which lasts for eight hours, can wipe the patient out for 24 hours afterward.

Gloria underwent the usual testing. Then her treatment began. The program called for two sessions of whole-body hyperthermia separated by one week and daily sessions of local hyperthermia of the left breast, the lymph nodes under her arm, and the liver.

I was especially concerned about Gloria's undergoing the first whole-body hyperthermia session, as I couldn't be there at the time. I had arranged to fly back to L. A. three days after our arrival to perform at the annual convention of the National Association of Music Manufacturers—the industry's trade show. I would be gone for ten days. Leaving Gloria that morning was one of the hardest things I've ever done. After all, the next day she was going to be baked in an oven at 105 degrees and given toxic chemotherapy! We were both scared out of our wits. How had our lives come to this? On one hand, our love and our friendship had risen to new heights. On the other, a vicious disease called cancer was trying to take my wife's life away.

I packed and brought my luggage downstairs. The driver wasn't there yet, so I ran back up to Gloria's room and cried my eyes out. I absolutely did not want to leave her. We hugged and I told her I loved her like I'd never loved her before. The bond that united us was amazing. We felt as if we were one. Then I went back downstairs and loaded my luggage into the car. When the driver had to leave for a moment, I ran up to our room again and repeated the whole thing.

Gloria was crying tears of joy at our newfound expression of love and appreciation for each other. Something incredible and magical was happening between us. She hugged me and said, "John, I really,

really love you!" I looked into her eyes and caressed her hair and forehead in a way I never had before, then told her, feeling more certainty than ever, "I love you too, baby, I really do!" I gave her an eternal kiss of love. We were so high on each other's love that it was heavenly! I wanted the moment to never end.

The entire time I was flying back to L.A., I wondered if I would ever see my wife again.

I telephoned Germany the moment I got home. Gloria's doctor told me all was proceeding well and that they were prepping her for the hyperthermia chamber. I slept five hours of agitated sleep. The doctor called back. All had gone well; Gloria was back in her room recovering and I could talk to her in a couple of hours. I was extremely relieved. When I finally got to speak to her, she said, "Boy, John, was that an intense experience!"

Gloria's daughter Ileane had arrived in Ortenberg to be with her when I left for L.A. When I arrived back in Germany, Ileane flew back to L.A. At least, Gloria had not been alone for those ten days.

During the three weeks at the Klinik-Benediktusquelle, Gloria didn't only undergo the whole-body and local hyperthermia treatments. She also underwent a number of other, more conventional therapies, such as low-dosage chemotherapy without hyperthermia, mistletoe injections, and others. All these treatments occupied eight hours of her day. It was a nightmarish way to spend the day. However, by the end of the third week we could rack up our first success: The tumors in her breast and lymph nodes had shrunk by 22 percent. It looked as if we finally had the cancer on the run. Gloria was feeling much less pain. Even during the second week, she'd felt improved enough to book us into a jazz festival in Frankfort! She was amazing. In the midst of all this intensive and horrendous therapy, Gloria had found the spirit and energy to network and to book us for a gig.

Our Frankfort jazz festival performance took place at the end of that third week. I rehearsed the musicians and Gloria, and we performed three original songs. We got a standing ovation. Gloria's doctor and some of the clinic staff were there and they couldn't believe their eyes and ears. Three weeks earlier, Gloria had come to them in great pain—and now she was on stage and tearing down the house. All I can say is: That was my baby and I was so proud of her. Gloria was a fighter, and she was making her comeback.

Though the cancer was reversing, our doctor warned us that unless we were extremely lucky it would likely start spreading again in a few weeks once the effects of the chemotherapy wore off. He urged us to continue with some form of treatment.

Naturally, we didn't want to hear this. We decided we were going to be lucky and beat this disease without any further serious medical intervention. We felt absolutely sure of this. Against the doctor's advice, we decided that Gloria's body was strong enough now that it could fight off the cancer by itself, though she would continue to take supplements and receive intravenous immune treatments.

On Valentine's Day, 1999, we flew home in a triumphant mood.

That triumphant mood was short-lived. We hadn't been home for very long before Gloria's blood tests showed signs that the cancer was probably returning. Our oncologist urged us to go back to Germany for another two-week treatment. He suggested that as an alternative Gloria undergo a similar chemotherapy program in Los Angeles; in this way, the cancer might be prevented from mutating and becoming resistant.

But we decided we were done with the hyperthermia for awhile, that we would try something else. Not only was it cost-prohibitive for us to go to back to the Klinik-Benediktusquelle therapy—the first session, lasting three weeks, had cost $20,000—but Gloria was extremely reluctant to travel all the way back to Germany and undergo the grueling whole-body hyperthermia treatments (not to mention the various other treatments) for a second time.

Chapter 16

Relapse

In hindsight, I would have to say that our decision not to return to Germany was probably a mistake, though there is no way of knowing finally. I know of other people who have achieved excellent, lasting results at the Ortenberg clinic. Certainly, we achieved some positive results ourselves. But Gloria didn't like what the Klinik-Benediktusquelle therapies had done to her "bottom line"—her body. She didn't like the way the chemotherapy had made her feel overall. I agreed to research other alternative therapies.

It's well-nigh impossible for the non-cancer sufferer to imagine what it's like to have this disease. We're used to being sick for short periods of time only. Whether it's a sore throat or a broken bone or the flu—or even pneumonia or bronchitis, or whatever—we can almost always be certain that we'll get over it, if not quickly, then in time. Like everyone else, Gloria and I had been conditioned to think of illness in this short-term way, and we still tended to think that way, even in the case of cancer. We would examine Gloria's breast and feel sure that the disease would eventually run its course and just go away.

But it did not. In fact the cancer was metastasizing, spreading rapidly to other parts of Gloria's body. Metastasis is a maddening and frightening process. Most of the time we felt totally helpless before its onward march. This feeling made us all the more susceptible to each new offer of hope held out by each new alternative therapy.

Three weeks after our return from Germany, it was obvious that Gloria's tumors were growing again. It was around this time that we heard about a new kind of anti-cancer therapy that claimed to kill cancer cells with an electromagnetic wave. The clinic offering this treatment was also located in Tijuana, Mexico.

The basic premise behind this treatment is that cancer cells are immature, embryo-type cells with metabolic processes of only five or six steps, as compared to normal adult cells whose metabolic processes comprise at least 35 steps. A modified type of magnetic resonance imaging (MRI) machine locates the "immature," cancerous cells, then emits a type of electromagnetic wave that is supposed to render these cells harmless. Its proponents claim a success rate of 80 percent.

Gloria wanted to try this approach which was apparently both non-invasive and effective. We raised another $15,000 and were off to Tijuana once again. Gloria's treatment would last six weeks this time. There would be five sessions a week, as at Bajanor Hospital's Jim Keller Clinic.

I was scared out of my wits. The tumors in Gloria's breast and under her arm had not only grown back but they were as big, or bigger, than they'd been before we'd gone to Germany. In three-and-a-half weeks, we'd lost all the ground we'd gained and then some more. We had begun to understand what people meant when they said someone had "lost the battle" against cancer; not only is it a 24-hour-a-day fight, but it is as if something in your body is literally trying to do you in. "How can this be?" we asked ourselves over and over again, a million times. But there was no time to think about it. We had to focus on the fight. We never thought about losing. Losing was not an option.

We began the electromagnetic wave treatments on March 15. Each session lasted an hour-and-a-half, certainly an improvement over the eight-hour-long Ortenberg regimen. The clinic manager told us that they could usually tell within two weeks whether a patient was responding or not. It occurred to me that that was two weeks lost if the treatment didn't work, which was a serious matter when it came to a highly aggressive cancer growing at warp speed. Moreover, the arduous commute to Tijuana wasn't doing Gloria's condition any good.

Over the two weeks Gloria's tumors just got bigger and bigger. All her blood counts worsened. I watched in growing horror, then told her that I personally didn't think she was responding to the therapy well. She didn't want to hear this; she wanted to continue. And so we did, though we tacked on another alternative treatment, live cell therapy, which aims to "jump-start" the immune system with a series of injections. But, ignoring both these therapies, the tumors continued to grow.

We tried homeopathy again, this time with a L.A. homeopath reputed to have an excellent cancer cure rate; but this, too, was a failure. I told Gloria I thought that, barring a miracle, she needed more chemotherapy because we needed to buy more time. I located an oncologist, in Reno, Nevada, who treated aggressive cancers both traditionally and with alternative methods. We stopped the Tijuana-based electromagnetic wave treatments in the fifth week and flew to Nevada to see this new oncologist.

The new doctor did exhaustive testing, then told us Gloria's cancer was so aggressive that he thought we shouldn't waste any more time with alternative therapies, which were mostly only effective against the slower-moving cancers. He added a hopeful note: If the oncogene (gene that can cause cancer) underlying Gloria's disease was Her+, then she would be a candidate for Herceptin, a "wonder drug" that was covered by insurance. Herceptin had shown considerable success in combating aggressive cancers.

The doctor did a core biopsy and determined that the oncogene Her+ was indeed present in Gloria's system. He advised her to start right away on Herceptin, which would be taken in conjunction with Taxol, a chemotherapeutic drug. The two drugs together, he said, sometimes constituted a veritable magic bullet.

Reluctantly, Gloria agreed. She had little choice; nothing else was working and her tumors were growing quickly and threatening to ulcerate. She took painkillers every six hours now, even though she hated drugs and that "drugged out" feeling that came with them; apart from her blood pressure medicine, she had never taken drugs before. But now the pain was awful.

The struggle was intensifying.

Chapter 17

Complications

For the next three weeks we flew to Reno on a weekly basis so that Gloria could take the five-hour Taxol/Herceptin chemotherapy treatment. To our dismay, at best the treatment only slowed the cancer down a little. Gloria was coming down with edema of the right arm, legs and feet; the lymph system was not draining properly and her limbs were swelling up. She could hardly walk. Her blood count was dropping. On the third visit, the doctor gave her a blood transfusion. This helped, but traveling to Reno had become too much of a strain and now was out of the question. We found another oncologist, one in L.A., who was willing to provide the Taxol/Herceptin treatment.

There was no end to our difficulties. One afternoon Gloria began having trouble breathing. I called 911. The paramedics came out, stabilized her with oxygen, then rushed her to the hospital. In the emergency room, her blood pressure plummeted and her heart began to race. Her situation seemed genuinely life threatening. Holding her hand, standing over her, I was terrified she wasn't going to make it.

The doctors found that she was suffering from a pleural effusion of the right lung. The sac surrounding the lung had become irritated, and fluid was building up in the space between the sac and the lung—the pleural cavity—thus making it difficult for Gloria's lung to expand. The doctors performed a thoracentesis, or lung tap, carefully inserting a needle into her back and draining off the excess fluid, of which there was a quart-and-a-half. Gloria immediately began to breathe more easily. Her blood pressure stabilized. She was out of danger.

Throughout all of this, she had exhibited the most wonderful grace. It wasn't just that her body remained strong through it all. It was also that she had been completely uncomplaining. I am quite capable of complaining about a backache or the flu; now, standing watchfully over Gloria, I was humbled.

So was she. She was humbled by thinking about all the things we'd taken for granted—unbelievably simple things, like being pain-free, or breathing, or eating, or sleeping, or working out, or taking a walk or carefully planning the future. I shared this newfound humility with her. We had both discovered a new appreciation for those simple things and for each other. It was a feeling beyond words. Our suffering was forcing us to grow in love and spirit. We realized that if we could make it through this ordeal we would have evolved onto a higher spiritual plane, attained to a newfound, greater love for one another.

Gloria took two weeks off from the chemotherapy treatments in L.A. to recuperate from the pleural effusion. This was scary, since every day that we weren't treating the cancer was one more day when it could grow and spread. But we had no choice. Gloria had to rest.

And then, the morning we were driving to Beverly Hills to begin her new treatment, something extremely scary happened.

Gloria suddenly became violently nauseated. I pulled over and she got out of the car and vomited. This was followed by an attack of not being able to breathe. I had a canister of portable oxygen in the car and I hooked Gloria up to it. She panicked and ripped off the facemask. "Gloria, talk to me!" I pleaded. "What's wrong? What do you want me to do?"

"I don't know! I don't know!" she gasped, terrified.

I pulled her back into the car and stepped on the gas and drove like hell the remaining half-mile to the hospital where the oncologist had his office. I pulled up at Emergency, hustled Gloria out of the car, and without paperwork—by bullying my way past the staff—got her into the Emergency Unit and onto a bed. The doctors gave her oxygen. Our new oncologist hurried down and took over, conducting a battery of tests. He could find nothing wrong—except, of course, for the cancer. Finally, Gloria's condition stabilized. After a short while, she was released. We headed home.

In the car, Gloria turned to me and said, "John, I'm sorry. I don't know what's happening. I'm scared!"

I reached over and grasped her by the hand and said, "You don't ever have to be sorry around me, not ever! I'm here for you no matter what happens, and don't you ever forget that."

That night, Gloria and I cried and kissed and held each other. We were even closer now than we'd been in Germany. Neither of us could believe this awful thing that was happening to us; but at the same time we could not believe this new expansion of love blossoming between us. It was miraculous. We both knew that we could never have experienced this love had we not been thrown into this terrible situation. It seemed so ironic to us. What the hell was going on? What was this strange, pain-filled—and love-filled!—destiny that was being thrust upon us? Were there, somehow, here, some important lessons for us to learn? If, so, then we would do our best to learn them.

The next day, we were scheduled to resume the Taxol/Herceptin program we'd begun in Reno. But Gloria was reluctant to go. She told me that the new program was much harder on her body than the low-dose chemotherapy/hyperthermia at the Klinik-Benediktusquelle. I asked her, did she want to go back to Germany? Her answer was an emphatic: "No!" Germany was too far; she hated the salty German food; we couldn't afford another $20,000.

So it was that, on June 13, we reluctantly resumed the chemotherapy program. At least we only had 12 miles to travel, to Beverly Hills this time; it wasn't like we were flying off to Reno again.

Neither Gloria nor I were happy with this new doctor. He had a good reputation, but he seemed to us to be uncaring and hard to talk to. By the end of four weeks the program had produced almost no results. Gloria's tumors had ulcerated and were bleeding and draining. Her daughters and I had to be trained in wound care so we could change her dressings every day. Her pain was worse than ever, and she had to switch to a stronger medication. Gloria hated all this. Her blood parameters were worsening; her protein and albumin levels were crashing, and so were her hemoglobin and RBC, her white blood count, her liver proteins and her LDH.

The new oncologist wanted to start her on a much higher dosage of chemotherapy, which he was sure would work, but which had potential complications and greater side effects. He thought that, in Gloria's situation, the benefits probably outweighed the risks. But now we were having trouble with the chemotherapy process itself. Gloria had undergone so much of it that the veins in her good arm had all but collapsed. The doctor told us that we should have had a valve inserted in her chest long before, so that the chemicals could be more easily delivered to her body. In fact, this "central line" had been recommended to us while we were in Mexico—but who wanted to do it then? To enter a hospital and be anesthetized and have a valve inserted in your chest—who would do this unless there were absolutely no choice? But, back then, we couldn't have imagined things would get as bad as they did. If only there had been someone there at the time who could have communicated these horrors to me! I believe I could have gotten Gloria to act immediately.

I convinced her that the operation would have to be done now. I didn't know what else to do. Gloria's cancer was spreading; it was eating her up alive. The chemotherapy was suppressing her hemoglobin and red blood count and she needed another blood transfusion. Why not kill two birds with one stone? The insertion of the central port would mean it would be easier for her to receive any fluid intravenously. Perhaps the new chemotherapy program would work—and how wonderful that would be! We needed something to work, that was for sure.

So it was that, on July 13, Gloria went into the hospital for a blood transfusion and what was supposed to be a simple, standard procedure: the insertion of a central port into her chest.

When they brought Gloria back up to her room after surgery, I asked the doctor how it had gone. He told me they'd had to abort the operation, as they hadn't been able to get the cathode implant in. They'd tried many angles, but something was always blocking the entrance to the vein.

I was shocked, and pissed as all hell. Gloria had stitches and scars in four different places on her neck and chest; she looked like Frankenstein's monster. The doctor left, and I stayed with my wife.

She soon started to come to; and as she did so she complained that her good lung, the left one, was hurting. I had the nurse call the doctor. He came, but only to give Gloria more pain medication.

The pain in her left lung just kept getting worse. At 11:00 P.M., I insisted the doctor come around and have another look at her. He did so, and then took me aside and informed me that Gloria's good lung had been accidentally punctured during the aborted central port operation. Chances of this complication's occurring were a-thousand-to-one, but in this case it had occurred.

"In other words," I exclaimed furiously, "you fucked up!" I asked him why he hadn't done an ultra sound-guided operation so he could see exactly where he was going, instead of doing it blind. He replied that they never did things that way. Then he told me Gloria's lung was partially deflated and that he had to act fast. I acquiesced, having no choice. He explained that Gloria's chest had to be anesthetized while she was awake, that an incision had to be made, and that a chest tube, connected to a pump, had to be inserted into her lung. This procedure would re-inflate the lung, if it were successful. Then—if things went normally—after a few days on the pump the lung puncture would be healed and Gloria would be able to leave the hospital.

I was still furious. I wanted to have it out with this doctor for his incompetence, but there was no time. "Okay," I said, "I'll deal with you later." He wanted me to stay outside Gloria's room during the procedure. I said, "Hey, Doc, you work for me. I'm coming in and I'm going to hold my wife's hand and help her through your incompetence, so you'd better do a good job."

Doctors don't like to be talked to in this way. They're used to being the M.D., which stands for Minor Deity. They think you work for them, not them for you. Most people don't ask questions; they just let the doctors run the show. Doctors aren't used to the kind of response I gave; this one certainly wasn't.

The upshot of our confrontation was that over the doctor's protests I went back to Gloria's room and told her why her good lung was in pain. Boy, was she freaked out! Did it piss her off! She couldn't believe it, and she shook her head not only in disgust but also in utter shock at our unending stream of bad luck.

"How can this be?" she asked me imploringly. "Why us? Why now?"

"I don't know, baby," I replied grimly. "I really don't. But we have to be strong. We can do this!"

I grasped her hand to give her reassurance. Holding her hand was another reason I needed to be at Gloria's side throughout this operation. The attendants prepped her while we gazed into each other's eyes. We kissed, we wept, we hugged. Once again, it was impossible to believe that all this was really happening. We had yet another trial to endure. How much longer would we be able to run this gauntlet? We had to be incredibly strong, and our strength was being sapped.

The doctor reappeared. He administered a local anesthesia, then started making the chest incision. Gloria grabbed my other hand and squeezed it hard. Even with the local anesthesia, the procedure really hurt. I comforted her as best I could.

After ten minutes of cutting, which seemed like an eternity, the doctor had made a hole he thought was big enough for the insertion. He began to work the tube in, but he was having a difficult time: he had to go through the chest muscle, then in-between Gloria's ribs, then into the chest cavity. It turned out he had to cut the opening a little larger to do this. Gloria was screaming now. I hollered at the doctor to get it together. He yelled back at me that this was why he hadn't wanted me in the room in the first place. "Tough, Doc," I retorted. "Just do the right thing. Make it go right!" Finally, he did. The tube broke through and I heard a pop, and Gloria's lung reinflated. The doctor dressed the wound and made sure the tubing was hooked up correctly to the pump, which was quite an elaborate device designed to help the lung breathe until it could heal itself and work independently, as well as pump out any blood and fluid that had accumulated.

The first part of the procedure had been successfully completed. Gloria could go to sleep now, and try to recuperate from a botched operation that had been more of an immediate threat to her life than the breast cancer.

All these events were weakening her condition in general. Two days later, when the doctors tried to get her lung to work on its own, they found they could not; it hadn't healed enough. Gloria had to endure another 24 hours on the pump. To say we were scared would be an understatement. All along, our assumption had been that Gloria was going to both beat this disease and do it with her body intact, so that she could continue her singing and acting career. At this point at least, she wasn't the type of person who wanted to play the game of life with a crippled body. Lung problems were a serious threat to her goals.

Finally, Gloria's lung healed and she was released from the hospital to recover at home. A week-and-a-half later she resumed the chemotherapy program, though without the central port. We would have to make do with the collapsed veins.

Chapter 18

Pride and Preparation

But Gloria's edema had gotten worse, to the extent that it interrupted the chemotherapy program. Her right arm and legs were so swollen she had trouble walking. We brought a hospital bed into the living room and a nurse began coming in twice a week. Gloria's breast tumors had gotten bigger and had spread to the lymph nodes in her neck; they were continuing to ulcerate, as were the underarm nodes. The tumors were as big as lemons; Gloria couldn't raise her arm over her head or let it hang loosely at her side.

She had lost so much weight in her rear from being in bed that the friction between the mattress and her tailbone had created a nasty bedsore on her tailbone. Any pressure at all created so much pain that it was impossible for her to relax, let alone sleep. She hated this, not only because of the pain, but also because it is a point of pride among "sisters," that is, black women, to have a shapely behind, and Gloria's had been something to be proud of. White chicks are generally flat in the behind, whereas sisters are jacked up (sorry to be so "street," but I want to convey exactly what we were going through). Gloria and I would joke about this when we saw a white girl in a pair of jeans: from the front the girl was beautiful, but when she turned sideways there was no booty. Now Gloria would sometimes joke that perhaps I was getting rid of her because she was losing her behind. This made me laugh, which I commended her for, but I assured her that, as much as I loved her body, I loved *her* more.

For situations such as these, there is an air mattress that can be hooked up to a pump. I had medical home care exchange the bed we had for a bed with this special mattress. The difference between the two beds was the difference between day and night, for now Gloria was sleeping on an air cushion she could make as hard or soft as she wished. The nurses also began treating her bedsore with special bandages and medicine.

In the meantime, Gloria's daughters and I were changing her dressings every day, giving her pain medication, and trying our best to make her as comfortable as possible. But, to my deep dismay, she appeared to be going downhill fast. It had only been eight months, and here we were apparently on death's doorstep.

I had a serious talk with Gloria. This talk was the hardest thing I've ever done, and I cried during most of it. I felt we needed to get all our affairs in order in case she didn't make it. Gloria agreed, and made a very thorough will, dictating onto a cassette tape her last wishes and communications to her loved ones. This was extremely hard, but a critically important thing for her to do. She told me that after she had done it she felt better, knowing that her communications and wishes would be carried out.

In a situation like ours, it's tricky knowing just how and when to put your affairs in order. How do you prepare for death without feeling you're giving up? Gloria and I were in no way close to giving up, though things did not look good. In hindsight, I'd say the best time to put your affairs in order is when you're healthy, not when you're fighting a life-threatening disease like Gloria's cancer.

After Gloria's affairs had been put in order, it was time to focus on her condition again. The edema made her extremely uncomfortable, but dealing with the cancer had to be our first priority. I'd read that local radiation could sometimes put a tumor on the run, especially if it's done in conjunction with chemotherapy. Although early on we'd been dead set against such invasive, toxic measures, it did seem as if this could buy us some time, whereas the alternative therapies we'd tried so far hadn't proved at all effective in fighting the cancer.

We met with a radiation oncologist on July 27. He privately told me that Gloria's prognosis was not good but that he felt he could drastically reduce her pain and make her overall condition less severe, if only temporarily. I discussed this with Gloria and she agreed to try the treatment; her will and body were as steely-strong as ever. The chemotherapy oncologist changed a couple of drugs in her program to make it more compatible with the radiation treatments.

We started the treatments on August 2. Gloria was to have radiation treatment every day for four to six weeks, depending on her response and the side effects, the latter varying greatly depending on the individual. This regime meant we had to get up at 6:30 A.M. to be at the clinic by 8:00. The radiation therapy began at 11:00 A.M.; from 8:00 to11:00, Gloria received treatment at the center's lymph edema therapy clinic. By now she was in a wheelchair, which helped a lot.

I have never seen such heroic behavior as my wife displayed at this time. Other than mention the pain, she rarely complained about her condition. She fought to live with every ounce of her being. She walked to the car every morning with my help, taking one step at a time. Her right arm was so swollen she couldn't lift it; we had to hold it for her as she walked.

But her valor did not improve her physical condition. By the third week of radiation treatment, her red and white blood counts were dropping fast. She had to go into the hospital for another transfusion. Though the tumors had begun to shrink again and the ulcerations had begun to heal, Gloria seemed to be losing the battle.

We needed a miracle.

Chapter 19

Miracles

At about the same time we started Gloria's radiation treatments, a friend of ours sent us the leaves and stem of a plant called the Dragonfly plant which grows wild in the rain forests of Puerto Rico. This plant had a reputation for being able to put some cancers in remission in three to four weeks if four glasses of tea were made from its leaves and stems and ingested daily. Nobody knew how or why this worked, but my friend had given the plant to three other friends of hers and they were all doing much better. What the hell. I boiled twelve leaves and some stems and let them steep overnight. This made a burgundy-colored tea. One concoction lasted about a week.

Using non-toxic remedies that had good word of mouth was a welcome change after all we'd been through. The tea was delicious. Gloria and I started taking it daily. I had a mildly swollen prostrate condition for which I'd been taking the herb *saw palmetto*; when I started taking the Dragonfly plant tea, the condition totally cleared up in a little less than two weeks.

But Gloria was still suffering from the severe lymph edema that had made her limbs swell up painfully. None of the doctors seemed to know what to do, so I set about learning as much as I could about the condition.

I found that lymph edema is caused by an obstruction in the lymph system resulting in an abnormal fluid build-up in the affected area. The excess fluid collects in the space between the blood cells. Normally, there is a continual osmotic exchange of fluids through the membrane that separates these interstitial spaces from the blood cells; in the development of edema, this exchange system becomes unbalanced. One factor that can cause this imbalance is a decrease in osmotic pressure due to a decrease in plasma protein concentration. This latter decrease can result from the liver's producing less albumin and globulin protein than usual; one of the functions of these proteins is to give the blood osmotic force.

I knew Gloria's liver had been going through hell. Her liver enzymes were up and down all the time. I looked at her charts and saw that her albumin and total protein production levels had dropped to dangerous lows. It occurred to me that this wasn't surprising since, for the past two months, Gloria had been on an anticancer diet that included fruit, vegetables, raw foods and juices—and very little meat, since protein supposedly "feeds" cancer. I suggested she get off this stupid "have-not" diet and eat anything she wanted. She did so with alacrity, and had some meat—and immediately brightened up, since her body had in fact been craving protein.

Two days later, a miracle occurred. Gloria woke me up—I was sleeping beside her in the hospital bed—by calling out my name as if it were a crisis. "John," she cried, "look at my legs!"

I freaked out. Her legs, that had been so swollen, were almost normal. We hugged each other and cried tears of joy. The fluid imbalance in Gloria's body was righting itself. Her body was reabsorbing the excess fluid and eliminating it; she had been to the bathroom eight times that night.

In four to five days, she lost almost thirty pounds of fluid. She could walk again. When she walked into the radiation clinic unaided one morning, people cheered. They had never seen anybody with such a poor prognosis recover so quickly. And, sure enough, the next time her blood tests came back, they showed Gloria's albumin and protein levels going back up; they were now at the low end of normal.

The radiation was also working as well as could be expected. Over five weeks, it had substantially reduced the size of the lymph node tumors under her arm and around her neck, and it had reduced the tumors in her breast by almost 40 percent.

(Who knows what role the Dragonfly tea played in all this? We'd been told that, if it worked, it usually took about three or four weeks to put the cancer in remission. That was roughly the time line Gloria was on—and now she was much better.)

We completed the radiation sessions. The oncologist was pleased, but didn't dare do any more radiation for awhile. He strongly suggested we return to our chemotherapy oncologist; radiation treatment was localized, whereas chemotherapy, in that the chemicals it introduced into the blood stream circulated throughout the entire body, might put still more of Gloria's cancer on the run.

All Gloria could think of was that she had come back from the brink of death. She wanted a break from therapy. She wanted to enjoy herself in whatever way she could.

We walked to the local grocery store and she talked to all her friends who had been worried about her. We went out to dinner. Friends and relatives came over to visit. We drove to the ocean and just kicked back and renewed our newfound love for each other. Bill Sharp, Novello/Rusch's bassist, invited us to a jazz concert called *Women in Jazz* featuring Chaka Khan. I convinced Gloria to go and we had a wonderful time.

When we got home from the concert, she looked at me and began to cry. "Wow," she said, "that was so much fun, John, to be able to go out with you and hang and see a concert instead of traveling to some God-awful therapy." I hugged her so hard we became one. I thought, "Please, God. Please help my baby. Please!" Though she still had cancerous tumors and was still on pain medication, she was a far cry from what she'd been just a few weeks before. She was making a comeback! Go, Gloria, go!

The battle against cancer still had to be waged. But now Gloria was loath to resume the chemotherapy. I learned that there was a clinic not far from us that practiced local hyperthermia and low-dose radiation together and claimed a good success rate. You'll recall that a similar combination therapy, provided by the Klinik-Benediktusquelle in Germany, had put Gloria's cancer on the run for several weeks. So, after a two-week vacation—which Gloria enjoyed immensely—in mid-September we found ourselves in the office of a new oncologist and ready to begin a new, daily round of treatments that were scheduled to last six weeks.

Radiation treatment is administered for a grueling five days a week; chemotherapy only once a week, sometimes only once every three weeks. Gloria's new radiation sessions lasted fifteen minutes each. Then she went on to an hour-and-a-half of local hyperthermia, the doctors alternating the areas that they treated.

We'd been worried that, though her breast cancer was shrinking, all Gloria's affected areas still showed signs of cancer and new areas were appearing in her neck and her left arm; all this was why the previous oncologist had wanted her to resume chemotherapy. But after three weeks of this new radiation treatment all the visible cancerous areas were diminishing in size and the primary tumor in the right breast was still shrinking. And she had a lot more energy.

Another complication arose. One day, turning over in bed, Gloria felt a sharp pain in the mediastinum area (where the heart, esophagus and some important nerves are located). X-rays hinted at another area of metastasis in this center-chest area; whatever the cause, the pain was so intense that Gloria could barely move in some directions. The doctors, feeling a tumor mass must be impinging on a nerve, concentrated the radiation and hyperthermia in the mediastinum area.

But now Gloria started to lose the low end of her voice. She began to talk like a chipmunk. This was devastating for her as she was a singer with an extraordinary vocal range, who wanted not only to beat this cancer but to beat it with her body intact so that she could continue with her singing career.

The oncologist said he'd seen this condition before: The tumor mass was likely impinging on a nerve connected to the vocal chords. Once the swelling of the mass went down, the voice usually returned to normal—but sometimes it did not, and remained drastically changed.

We cried and cried and cried, and prayed for strength. How many more complications could Gloria's body take? How much more could I stand to see my baby go through? Although she never once said to me, "John, please, please help me," I knew she was hoping that somehow I could find a way to cure her. I consider myself a strong and resilient human being, but all this was starting to get to me. When I was by myself, I would very regularly lose it now. But I knew that, when I was around Gloria, I had to be strong.

She had no real voice for over three weeks. The doctors put her on steroids for the chest pain. Even though she didn't want the steroids, she'd been on pain medication for so long that she didn't care anymore; she would do anything to get rid of the pain. As it turned out, in addition to helping with the pain the steroids gave her new energy, which helped her to confront her daily treatments.

One day I went out to do an errand, and when I got back she had rearranged the whole house, including her office, and had watered the plants. It felt like my wife was back. She said she felt so good because she had no pain and lots of energy, so she had to get productive. I cried right there on the spot as I remembered how vibrant and productive and classy a lady she really was. We embraced for a long time and made another firm commitment that we were going to beat this.

Yet another new complication arose: Gloria's temperature was shooting up to 103 and 104 degrees at night. This was due to the radiation, and not necessarily dangerous, since a high temperature can hinder cancer metastasis and is the body's way of handling infection. But it was extremely uncomfortable, and we had to use Motrin and other drugs to keep Gloria comfortable when she couldn't tolerate the fever any more.

In the meantime, I had found a new therapy, called transfer factor, that was administered by injection. The doctor providing it had an experimental license from the FDA to do so. To qualify, the cancer patient had to have tried chemotherapy and radiation already, which was Gloria's case. So, one weekend when she felt better (though she still had her chipmunk voice), we drove up to San Francisco to visit the doctor.

We needed to get away and had been looking forward to this trip. We had a blast driving up the coast and even got lost a couple of times while taking the scenic route. Who cared! We were together and enjoying the hell out of each other. Once we had gotten into the city and checked into our hotel, we walked to the corner, found a great French restaurant, and had a gorgeous meal. We needed this. It almost made us feel like a normal couple. But the feeling was short-lived, as Gloria's pain returned, as it always did after four to six hours. Dammit!

Our appointment with the doctor was the next morning. He examined Gloria and gave her the first shot of transfer factor. The crux of this treatment is that numerous factors of immune agents are extracted from blood taken from blood banks and injected into the cancer patient in the hope that these positive factors will "jump-start" the patient's immune system. Once we had seen the doctor one time, we could order the shots and administer them ourselves.

Gloria had a good time on the trip, and it was good for both of us to get out of town. We went shopping and ate out at a couple more restaurants and even visited Gloria's niece who lived in the area. On the way back, we stopped at a mountain lake and watched the sunset together. We were so much more in love now than before this horrific disease had invaded our lives. It wasn't fair that we could experience this much of heaven and hell on earth at the same time. Yet we both knew that, ironically, the hell was the cause of the heaven.

We wanted to keep this newfound level of love *and* be back in our normal lives. We really had transcended to another plane of relationship. It was real love—something we both admitted we had never experienced before, not on this level. It was an unselfish love, a love without ego involvement—a love that demanded nothing. It was an unconditional acknowledgment of the pure being of each other. For both of us, it was a spiritual high. We perceived only love, expressed only love, *were* only love. We felt as if we were one. I read once that the sages of ancient China believed that until we experience a major or terminal illness, our spiritual evolution is not complete. Could our newfound unity be an expression of this principle?

Chapter 20

A Primal Diet

Once back in Los Angeles, we felt turbocharged. We had the new immune system-enhancing injections that we knew wouldn't hurt—and, just maybe, might help. We had our new love for each other, which made us feel invincible, for it transcended that illusion of the physical universe which says we all must die. Unfortunately, I had to go to Japan for five days to promote Niacin's latest release. Gloria insisted I go; her daughters would take care of her while I was away, I needed a break—and I needed to make some money for us!

The promotional tour went well, and I was soon back home with my love and my best friend. It was early November 1999. Gloria's voice was coming back. This was good news indeed.

We now embarked on an alternative therapy called Nambudripad's Allergy Elimination Technique (NAET). NAET operates on the principle that if the immune system is too busy coping with allergic responses to minor items, it will be hindered in coping with real threats like cancer. Through computer analysis and Muscle Response Testing (MRT), various allergies are located; these may be allergies to food, vitamins, minerals, chemicals, perfumes, air conditioning, plastics, pollen—almost anything. Then—to greatly oversimplify—NAET "reprograms" the brain to believe that these allergies are actually harmless and even beneficial. Thus the immune system is freed up to effectively tackle the biggest "allergy" of them all—the cancer.

For us, this treatment did not seem to help. The cancer was too aggressive, and it was spreading again. By mid-November Gloria had developed blister-like bumps on her right breast a second time.

This meant that the original breast cancer, which had been under control, was active once again and threatening to ulcerate. The radiation oncologist, busy treating the other areas of metastasis, had let the primary breast cancer go untended. Cancer sites seemed to be springing up all over Gloria's upper torso now; I counted nine different spots. We were losing ground again; moreover, Gloria was very close to the maximum safe dosage of radiation to her breast area.

But she was adamantly against undergoing any more of this toxic treatment that had made her deathly ill. She had just about had it with damaging toxic treatments. She knew that she was close to, even beyond, the point where she could expect to be totally cured. She knew that even if she could arrest the cancer her body was now very damaged, not only on account of the cancer and its complications, but also because of the toxicity of the treatments she had been receiving. Her blood parameters, too, were getting worse again. She was becoming very frustrated, and it was my job to keep researching and keep her hopes up in this deadly fight. Boy, was it a challenge! The stakes were nothing less than life and death.

I had learned of the "primal diet," a holistic approach to fighting disease pioneered by iridologist/nutritionist Aajonus Vonderplanitz. The primal diet is based on the belief that food is best eaten in its live, raw condition, when it is still rich in enzymes and other nutrients. The diet consists primarily of raw animal meats (beef, fish, poultry, organic eggs); raw dairy products (unsalted raw butter, raw milk, raw cream, unsalted raw cheeses, raw kefir); raw whole fruits and vegetables (especially vegetable juices); and unheated honey. Vonderplanitz asserts that the biochemistry of raw fat and raw meat is so different from that of cooked fats and meats that the former really constitute a whole other category of food. He maintains that eating raw fat and raw meat can be hugely beneficial.

Despite our disillusionment with dieting—we had found the literature to be contradictory, and none of Gloria's many diets had worked for her—we decided to try Vonderplanitz's primal diet. Within two weeks, all of Gloria's blood parameters had rebounded. She had more energy. Her appetite picked up. She was gaining weight. She felt this must be the right approach, and wanted to go for it 100 percent.

Looking back on it now, it seems to me that we started this diet too late. By this time, Gloria's body was too damaged to be able to expel the cancer and rebuild tissue. The primal diet gave her energy and built up her blood, but the cancer was still visibly spreading in her right arm and breast, under her arm, and in seven places on the chest wall. New skin eruptions on her back made it impossible for her to sleep well, and fluid was building up once more around her lung. Periodically, Gloria and I panicked and ran back to the radiation/hyperthermia treatments, which we knew did in fact kill the cancer cells or slow them down. But we couldn't help wondering, as we watched more and more sites of metastasis appearing on her body, if the radiation were helping her or hurting her.

What with all that we had been through that year, it seemed to us that it probably would have been better if we'd just gone off to live in the mountains, far from the world's thoroughfares, with no stress other than the disease itself, and simply breathed in the pristine air, relaxed, and done Vonderplanitz's primal diet. We believed finally that we would have done no worse than we had done to date, and maybe better, and that for sure we would have avoided all the damage done to Gloria's body by allopathic medicine and doctors and stress, not to mention avoided the huge financial burden of it all. We surmised all of this without even knowing at the time that, according to statistics, untreated cancers have about a 76 percent chance of being cured.

We were at a crossroads again. Though the primal diet finally seemed to be giving Gloria's body what it needed—real nutrition—the cancer had spread too far and it did not look as if her body had the necessary time to pull off the miracle of healing itself solely through the right nutrition.

Still, we were not giving up. What a battle of spirit, mind and body! Gloria's spirit and will to win were amazing, even when her body appeared to be losing. We met with the radiation oncologist. He examined her and said he'd seen worse cases turn around. There were no guarantees, but he wanted to try treating two to four sites a day and increasing the radiation dosage. So Gloria and I said, Let's rock and roll! For almost two weeks she underwent this treatment every day. But it soon became apparent that her body could not handle any more radiation. She was coming down with symptoms of radiation poisoning—high fevers, lack of appetite, nausea, vomiting. On December 22, she and I agreed that that would have to be it for this kind of treatment.

We were still fighting fiercely. But Gloria wanted to enjoy the holiday season with her family as much as it was possible. The radiation treatments had brought about a slight remission of the cancer and a lessening of her pain. We decided to celebrate Christmas, bring in the New Year, and pray, and pray, and pray.

On New Year's Eve, Gloria met with her near family, thanked us for our unselfish support, and told us she still hadn't given up, even though she knew things didn't look so good. She told Ileane, who was pregnant, that she wanted to be around to see her grandchild arrive in June. She told Rachel she wanted to be here for her marriage in August. It was a very emotional speech, as Gloria really meant it. I broke down. I had had to be so strong for so long that I couldn't hold back my emotions any more. This time, Gloria had to comfort me.

We all watched the New Year's celebrations on TV and brought in the New Year of 2000. We thanked God for helping us get this far, and we prayed for a miracle.

Chapter 21

The Final Stand

A week earlier, Gloria had gone shopping with Rachel to get a wedding dress. That was a miracle in itself. To get out of bed and confront going out shopping with her daughter was amazing. As she was getting ready to go, I asked her what she thought she was doing. She replied, "Maybe if I just do what I want, my body will realize that I have things yet to do in this lifetime, and it will knock off this sick BS and get well!" I loved the concept and agreed wholeheartedly. Go for it, baby!

But, on January 3, I very reluctantly had to call medical home care and reorder the hospital bed. Since this bed was automatic and adjustable, it gave Gloria more control over her resting and sleeping environment and it eased her getting in and out of bed. But she hated seeing the bed again. It was a symbol that she was losing the fight. It was a blow to her pride.

However, the bed was necessary. Her edema was getting very bad. Her cancers had ulcerated and spread to her back and forearm. It was like watching leprosy spreading. We had to change Gloria's dressings two or three times a day. She hated the smell, her appearance, the hassle. One of the most beautiful and classy women in the world, my soul mate and best friend was being eaten alive before my eyes. My emotions ranged from anger at God, if there was one, to pain, to grief, to trying to be strong and comforting for my immensely courageous wife. There were times when I wished someone would try to mug me so I could look at him and say, "Buddy, thank you for making my day. You've just picked the wrong guy to rob!" and then proceed to do a

"Charles Bronson" on him. Luckily for me, these feelings stayed just feelings, and did not find expression in reality.

Gloria was having increasing difficulty breathing. It turned out that her pleural fluid was building up again. She underwent a second successful lung tap. But this did not alleviate her breathing problems, and after a week we went back to the doctor. X-rays showed that her fluid level was okay. Our internist thought that most likely multiple problems were causing her breathing difficulties. He did not feel that Gloria had much time. But he didn't want to put her through the trauma of more tests; he didn't think there was any way to treat her at this stage. He tried to persuade me that it was time to call hospice and make Gloria as comfortable as possible at home, so that she could pass away as peacefully as possible.

My brave wife overheard this conversation. She insisted on leaving the hospital immediately. Neither of us wanted to hear this, and neither of us believed it was true. So, on January 10, we said to hell with the doctors. Gloria did not want to pass away in a hospital with all kinds of tubes coming out of her body; we would go home, and there we would either make a last and triumphant stand against the illness, or Gloria would peacefully depart this lifetime for the next stage of her soul's existence.

My emotions at this time were devastating and jumbled and tossed me about in a way I had never experienced: from anger to grief to an overpowering sense of failure to apathy to fear to unconditional love, and back again to anger, fear and all the rest. I wondered if I could take much more. My whole universe was becoming unglued. The partnership I had with Gloria was multifaceted: She was my soul mate, my best friend, my lover and my artistic business partner. We gave such purpose to each other's lives. We had so much in common. We were John Novello and Gloria Rusch, a.k.a. Novello/Rusch. The idea that Novello/Rusch would not exist any more seemed unthinkable. I felt this couldn't be happening. Every time I had had a personal win in my career, she had been there to share it with me, there to cheer me on and validate my achievement. I had always done the same for her. Talk about the rug being pulled out from under you! I was devastated and I was reeling.

For the first time in my life, I was afraid for the future. I was afraid for Gloria, for her pain and sorrow, for her unfulfilled dreams if she did not make it. I was afraid for myself. How could I deal with this? Talk about the supreme test! I went further with the potential loss: I imagined a time when I would never be able to write and perform with her, never be able to accompany her while she sang oh so sweetly and soulfully all the tunes we had written together. Just the thought of this caused a loneliness and emptiness, a coldness and silence, to suddenly engulf me.

I abruptly pulled myself out of my 'daymare' and went over to Gloria. I hugged her so hard I almost hurt her. She looked into my eyes and knew what I was feeling, for she had been mentally rehearsing this nightmare for some time now. How could she not have been, given that she was fighting for her life day in and day out? Even though I was hugging her closely, I wasn't hugging her close enough. I wanted to crawl inside her spirit. I wanted to *be* her. I thought of the old *Star Trek* episode in which McCoy has contracted a deadly disease. He is dying, but an alien being with incredible powers of empathy becomes him to such an extent that McCoy's disease is actually transferred to the alien's body. Then the alien gets sick, but, since his body is stronger than McCoy's, he eventually heals himself—and at the same time McCoy.

I wanted to enable Gloria to survive in this same way. My love was so unconditional at that moment that if only I could have taken on her illness, I would have done so. I would have done it in a second, even if I were risking my own life in the process. Suddenly, every love song, every movie, every book I had ever experienced that told of these life-and-death scenarios, came to my mind, and I realized that I had never even remotely understood any of these feelings, that not a single one of them had impinged upon me in the least. I remembered saying to myself when I was merely a bystander at such experiences, "What's the big deal? So he lost his mate. It's only a song. It's only a movie. What's the big deal?" Man, had I *not* been there; how completely detached I had been!

But now these emotions were rampaging through me. They were the real thing. I was numb, not only on account of the situation that lay before us, but also at the realization of what a dilettante I had been about life right up until this very moment. What a severe reality adjustment I now had to make! How could I have lived an entire half-century and remained such a complete spectator when it came to this thing called love? And this was only the beginning! If only, I thought, Gloria and I could go to sleep now and wake up and look into each other's eyes and realize that it had all been only a nightmare—or, better still, discover that the cancer had suddenly gone into full remission. I say better still, because then we'd not only have had that miracle, but also the miracle of our newfound love, of our new and total surrender to each other.

So it was that, in early January, 2002, my wife elected to stay home with her family and fight her illness with love and prayer and various alternative approaches such as nutrition, supplements, herbs and so on. She had not given up the fight at all. It is one thing to say, "I'm going to pass away at home with my family." But she had not yet decided that she was going to pass away. Despite the degree of deterioration of her body, she was still planning to beat this disease at the eleventh hour.

As for me, I was now on the horns of a dilemma of my own. Niacin had a major tour scheduled to start on January 31, my birthday. I didn't want to cancel the tour, as we needed the money to help us continue the fight. But I wouldn't be able to live with myself if Gloria passed away when I wasn't at her side. On the other hand, her condition was deteriorating so rapidly that at this rate she'd be gone before the tour began. If that happened, it would probably be good for me to blow town, do the tour, and try to channel my emotions into my playing. I also knew that staying at home without my wife on my birthday, and then on Valentine's Day, would devastate me even further.

I telephoned my manager. "It's your call," he said. "Technically, it's a bit late to cancel a tour. But what with your extenuating circumstances, the legal contractual flaps could probably be handled."

I was totally freaked out about what to do. I talked it over with Gloria. She kept saying, "Do the tour." But I felt that she was just being polite and considerate because she didn't want me to miss this opportunity. Then, to top it all off, I got a call from Andy Summers, guitarist for the rock band *The Police*. He wanted me to play on his next CD, which was going to be a tribute to Charles Mingus, one of my favorite composers. Career-wise, this New Year was starting off excellently for me. And how ironic it was, because, with Gloria fighting for her life, my career did not mean very much to me at all.

The *yin*-and-*yang* dilemma was ripping me apart. Why such agonizing timing? This was the most crucial time of her battle, and Gloria needed me more than ever—and now, just coincidentally, it was the busiest time of my career, first with the Asian tour, and now with a major CD project in the works. Yikes! How much more of this stress could I take?

I decided I would try to do everything. I arranged to have Gloria's friends and daughters take care of her while I rehearsed the CD with Andy. I checked in constantly from rehearsals to see how she was doing. While I was away I managed things from the phone; when I got home I took over.

Then, on January 20, something extraordinary happened.

I was in my studio just back of the house, doing some rehearsing on my own for the CD. At a certain point I came back into the house to see how Gloria was and to be with her.

I went over to her where she lay in her hospital bed and took her hand and held it and asked her how she was doing. There was a serene and beautiful smile on her face. She looked up at me and said that she had finally confronted and dealt with the spiritual unrest that had broken down her own body and allowed her to become so ill.

I should explain that both Gloria and I believed that a disease like cancer comes as the result of multiple stress factors impinging on the spirit, the mind and the body of the individual. We believed that too much constant unhandled stress greatly weakens the body and sets the stage for all kinds of ailments, dependent on the person's nutrition, toxins, carcinogens, exercise or the lack thereof, and similar factors. We believed that personal loss and upsets related to sex are probably the greatest of these stress factors.

By the time she was 18 Gloria had lost her father, a brother and a sister. In her late 20's she had lost her husband in the Vietnam War and been left with two kids to raise on her own. Her second husband had sexually abused her daughters; Gloria blamed herself for this. Later on she had gotten pregnant with me. She had had an abortion because her chronic high blood pressure could have made the pregnancy life-threatening. She had never ceased to feel guilty about this abortion, even though the decision was mutual and indeed medically justifiable. But it had lain heavy on her, and she had taken to noting the birthdays of the child as if it had lived. She would say, for example, "Our child would be about twelve years old right now."

It was almost as if the cancer had come upon her not only because of the stress of all these events, but also in order to push her to a point of egoless perspective where she could see these events for what they meant in themselves, and finally come to deal with them—as if this dealing with them were somehow compulsory, and now that she had dealt with them, she was free to go.

And now, when she looked at me and smiled at me and told me she had finally handled her stress and guilt, I was both happy and devastated at the same time, for it seemed to me that Gloria was also trying to tell me that her work here was done and that she would probably be leaving very soon. I had never seen her so serene and happy, not even when she was healthy, and this was amazing, given the ravaged state of her body. It was obvious to me that Gloria was now operating almost totally on a spiritual plane, and not at all on a physical one. I was happy for her; but I was also scared for both of us.

I knew it would be selfish of me to demand a miracle now, since something bigger than life and death was occurring here. But, nevertheless, I still wanted that miracle.

But it was not to be.

Chapter 22

Hell Week

The next day, Gloria had trouble working the motor controls of her speech mechanism and therefore trouble communicating. This seemed to me to be an involuntary sign that her spirit was getting ready to depart. She would say a few words but most of them would come out as gibberish. We didn't know if this was happening because the cancer had metastasized to her brain or because of the heavier pain medication, or both. At this point, it didn't matter. Gloria seemed very frustrated with her condition; so was I. I began working out a code with her, telling her to squeeze my hand once for yes, twice for no.

The first question I asked was whether she could understand everything I said. She squeezed, "Yes." That was good news, as not having some form of two-way communication with her would have been really rough now, even though we'd been preparing for this moment for almost a year—that is, if this moment had truly arrived.

Gloria was still on oxygen, since the lung tap hadn't really alleviated her breathing difficulties. Even with the oxygen, she was having more trouble breathing. We'd had to more than double her oxygen intake level. But now she was starting to take very labored wheezing breaths that sounded like soft screaming.

My inability to help Gloria in her pain and struggle was tearing me apart. One minute I wanted to trash the house; the next, I was crying; and everything in-between. I asked her again if she wanted to go into the hospital where they could take better care of her medically, but her answer was the emphatic double-squeeze of "No!" Gloria knew, though, I'm now certain, that she was about to make the final transition, and she did not want any unnecessary distractions such as a hospital environment and medical personnel poking around at her body.

I continued to develop the communication code. As closely as was humanly possible, I imagined myself in Gloria's position—on death's doorstep, nervous and scared, and having difficulty communicating. Once I had managed to put myself in her place, I could think of what she might want to communicate or what questions she might have. I could begin wording these questions in such a way that they could elicit a yes or no answer.

What she was saying was still mostly gibberish, and I wanted to know how aware of this condition she was. After a series of yes and no questions, I knew she was not only aware of her condition but also extremely frustrated by it, since, while her thoughts were clear, she could hear them coming out of her mouth in this garbled fashion.

With her permission, as a one-time experiment, I asked her the same question over and over again. She tried to answer it with the same answer each time. Each time, the answer came out in the same gibberish. Obviously, there was a real breakdown in her speech motor controls. I eventually determined that with a lot of concentration Gloria could sometimes actually get her thoughts correctly translated into words, but that this was very difficult for her.

When I had figured out her level of understanding and communication, I explained to everyone how they could communicate with her more easily in order to get answers to questions like, "Are you hungry?" "Do you need any pain medication?" "Do you need to go to the bathroom?" "Is there something you want to say but are having trouble saying?" and so forth. The scariest question of all—it was one that I asked—was, "Will you, if you're able, let me know when it looks like you'll be leaving?"

It was Sunday, January 24. Gloria and I had still not totally given up the fight. When I asked her, I discovered that even she was hoping for a miracle—which we both believed was always possible. But, as things weren't looking very good, I telephoned her mom and her stepfather and her sister and two brothers and told them that they should come and visit, as they might not get another chance to see Gloria if things continued in this way.

So, that Sunday, her near family all came over and visited. Gloria was very happy to see them, especially her mother, with whom she had a great relationship. Her mom stayed by her side holding her hand during the entire visit. It was a special moment for them both. Her mom had already experienced a great deal of loss. She had lost her husband, Gloria's father, over 30 years before, and she had lost two of her children. Gloria's mom was not at all happy about losing another daughter, especially one to whom she had grown so close over the past several years. She reluctantly left late in the afternoon.

The next week I call Hell Week. I was to start rehearsals for Andy Summers's CD project on Monday. I would be gone every day for six to eight hours. This was an agonizing dilemma for me. In hindsight, I realize I should have canceled everything that week. But at the time my thinking was that the project was good for my career and that we needed the money for the fight.

I went to rehearsals on Monday and Tuesday, the actual recording sessions being on Wednesday and Thursday. I was only minutes away from home and I kept in close touch. Each night, I came back and hugged Gloria and talked to her as best I could. On Tuesday, Aajonus Vonderplanitz, her nutritionist—the man who had put Gloria on the primal diet—came over to comfort her and see how she was doing.

Aajonus told us that, as bad as it looked, there was still a possibility of recovery. He had seen this before: a patient's blood parameters suddenly getting better and the cancer being expelled from the patient's system. The question was, would her body be able to hold on? Was it strong enough? Would Gloria, the spirit, hold on and endure this, or would she decide that it was time to leave? Aajonus believed that if she could hang on past the coming weekend, she could recover. It would be what they called a deathbed recovery; but if it were, so what? And if she did recover, it would take a year or more for her to rebuild her diseased tissues and recover fully. I didn't care if it took the rest of our lives—but Gloria was the one who would have to make the decision.

It was Wednesday morning now. My son-in-law Patrick Griffin was with us, and he stayed up with Gloria all night. He woke me up at about 7:30 A.M. There was a look of awe on his face. He told me that while he was watching at her bedside, Gloria had begun to sing a gospel song. She had sung the whole song with all the words. It wasn't a song he was familiar with, except that it had the name "Jesus" in it.

This was very hard to believe! Gloria had not spoken many words for almost a week. Initially, I was furious at Patrick for not waking me up to hear Gloria's inspiring performance, since this was such a significant event for me. Almost as amazing as the love of Gloria and myself was our partnership as singer and accompanist; this was one of the things I treasured most about our relationship.

But Gloria's singing had caught my son-in-law Patrick by surprise, and he knew that I badly needed sleep. Later, I would learn that she had also told him that she knew she was going to die, but did not want me to know this.

Chapter 23

God's Final Cure

It was now 10:30 A.M., Wednesday, January 27. I was about to leave for the recording session. I went over to my wife to hug her and comfort her. She was still struggling to breathe, still on oxygen. She had not been eating very much, and it took everything each of us had to get her to drink the "smoothies" that we made just to keep some nutrition flowing into her body in hopes that a miracle would occur. If her body was still trying to expel the cancer, it needed all the nutrients it could get.

Gloria's eyes were not very focused and they were partially closed. She did not seem to be all that much "there." I sensed she was half on the other side and half on this one. I pulled up one of her eyelids; and, as I did so, her eyes all of a sudden focused on me and she gave me the "evil eye." The vibration I picked up was, "Don't do that, John! You're bothering me!"

I apologized to her. But Gloria's response had actually made me feel good, because it showed that she still had some fight left. I said, "Baby, I'm sorry. I just wanted to see if you were still with me." Then, to check her level of awareness, I asked her, "Gloria, do you know who I am?"

Her eyes opened, and in one of the most touching and at the same time devastating moments I had with her over all these difficult days, she looked right at me and through me and said with no difficulty and no uncertainty whatsoever (remember, speaking words had been difficult for her for the past several days), "John Novello, my husband. I love you!"

I lost it. I pulled her into my arms and I cried and cried and cried. I knew how difficult that must have been for her. But, at this point, she wanted me to know it.

After my grief subsided I got up and got ready to leave. Gloria looked at me again and tried to say something. At first, as she tried to speak, only gibberish came out. Then, after several attempts and a lot of fumbling, she said, "Maybe you shouldn't go, as I might not be here when you get back."

"What?" I stammered. She tried to say the same thing again, but this time it wasn't as clear. I wasn't sure what she meant. Did she mean, shouldn't go now to the rehearsal, or shouldn't go next Monday to Japan? My response was, "Don't worry. If that's the case, I cancel the tour. Don't worry."

She nodded, I think in approval. I told her daughter what Gloria had said, and asked her to keep in close touch with me all day. I would only be minutes away; I'd be able to get home quickly.

Then I left for the recording session. Hospice was due to come that day. Gloria and I had both been fighting this, as hospice was usually called to make comfortable a "terminal" patient who had given up. It provided all the home medical care necessary, including pain medication. Gloria's suffering was becoming very great, but she had refused to go back into the hospital, so we had gotten our insurance to finally approve hospice. The hospice care was due to start that Wednesday afternoon while I was at the studio.

The hospice people came around 6:00 P.M., when I had not yet arrived home. They gave Gloria liquid pain medication, as she had been refusing all pills and solid food since the day before. I'd been able to tell that her pain medication had worn off and that she was in serious pain, so we had to make her comfortable. In the hospital, they would have been giving her shots. Once hospice took over, they would be doing the same thing. But for the moment they gave Gloria a kind of liquid morphine, and it calmed her down immediately.

When I got back, which was about 8:00 P.M., she was much more relaxed and not struggling to breathe as she had been earlier that day. She couldn't speak at all now; there was just moaning and a little gibberish. But she seemed a little more peaceful. Gloria knew immediately that I was home, for she looked right at me with a look I'll never forget.

That look basically said, "It's time, baby. I'm sorry, but I got to move on."

I saw that her clothes needed changing again due to the ulcerations on her breast, so the very first thing I did was help her into new, fresh, clean clothing. This was very tricky, because she did not have much control over her body by this point; but her brother Chaz was there, and between us we managed. It really seemed as if Gloria were outside her body, that she had a line into it, but that was all.

After we were finished, she lay back on her hospital bed and became very serene. Her breathing started to wind down and get slower and slower as she got calmer and calmer. Her eyes were almost completely closed. I held her hand and began talking to her and telling her how much I loved her and how special she was. I told her about all of her accomplishments in this lifetime and about how all of us and this whole planet were better off for her presence. I told her how special a singer she was, and that I would finish her dream of her first solo CD.

We had been working on this CD together in our new studio when Gloria first became ill. The project had been put on hold for all of 1999, but now it hit me that I needed to finish it. So now I promised her that I would finish the CD, and that it would be great. I also promised her that I would do a life tribute for her that would make her proud. We had talked about this the August before, when she had been close to death's door, and she had told me that if I did anything of that sort, to please make it a celebration and not a funeral-type event. Gloria did not want everybody giving long speeches and crying. I told her how great an honor it was to be her friend and husband, and that we would soon be together again. Gloria and I had, and still have, such a deep soul-mate love for each other that I felt that nothing, not even death, could deny us our love.

During all this time, Gloria gave no return verbal communication; in fact, she gave no communication whatsoever, at least none that I could sense in the midst of my grief. Her body was winding down its earthly existence with each breath; Gloria was scarcely occupying it any more. That I knew. Gloria was preparing to leave.

The only ones present were myself, her daughters Rachel and Ileane, their husbands Eric and Patrick, and her brother Chaz Bowie. We had lit candles and we had soft music playing in the background.

At approximately 2:05 A.M., Thursday morning, January 28, something truly amazing happened.

Gloria's body was barely breathing; it was taking breaths only every eight to ten seconds. I knew that this was it, and I was totally devastated. I was immersed in grief and very much aware of my failings. I thought to myself that I had failed Gloria somehow, that on "my watch" she had gotten sick. I thought that, despite all my research and all my promises that I would help her beat this thing, nothing had worked. Gloria had counted on me, and I had failed her miserably. I had promised her we'd grow old together and that I'd help her achieve all her dreams. But the cancer had now ravaged her beautiful bodily temple to such an extent that she had to move on to a new existence. How could this have happened to such a wonderful person? I was sure I was responsible. I was sure I was a bad person. Every kind of thought went through my head. I was in utter confusion and I felt like a total failure. The situation was hopeless. I was a wreck.

Then, very suddenly, it was as if I had awakened into the light. Suddenly, I was pulled up out of the morass of my confused emotions, and instinctively I actually looked up to my left, at a corner of the room near the ceiling.

At first I didn't know what was happening. And then it hit me. Gloria was outside her body. She wasn't in pain anymore. And she was talking to me, clear as a bell! How did I know this wasn't my imagination? Because, as I've said, I had been in the midst of deep shame, blame, regret and a sense of failure. And then, all of a sudden, I telepathically heard the following words:

John, I'm here. It's unbelievable. Everything we ever studied and believed in—that we are immortal spirits and that we survive bodily death and go on—it's all true! We didn't lose! In a few minutes the cancer will not be growing any more and spreading and causing any of us any more pain and suffering. I figured out the final cure: let it have my body. I'll leave. Eventually, I'll get another one. But, for now, I'm free. I'll be waiting for you and be by your side until it's time for you to move on. Continue all of our dreams! You got a lot of work to do, and I'll be helping you, just as before. Novello/Rusch does not have to stop operating as a team just because Gloria Rusch dropped her body. On the contrary, we'll be more powerful than ever!

My crying turned from tears of grief to tears of joy. I tried to explain to Gloria's two daughters what was happening, but I think they thought that Pops was just in shock. But, to me, what I was experiencing was like the scene in *Star Wars* where Obi-Wan Kenobi is fighting Darth Vader and he tells him to go ahead and strike him down; it doesn't matter, as Obi-Wan Kenobi will then become more powerful than ever. That is what it felt like for me: Death would not deny us; our love was too strong. This was just a transition for Gloria—a graduation. She would continue without her body. And what would ten, or 20, or even 30 years matter to a discarnate spirit, a spirit without a body? Gloria and I believed that we have all lived through millions of years and through many, many lifetimes. As long as we were in communication, that was what counted. We could still play the game of life together.

This picked me right up. I had been pretty low. And so, as unbelievable as it may sound, for the next 55 minutes, while Gloria's body lay still, just barely breathing, Gloria and I talked as usual. I talked out loud and she talked in concepts that just formed in my mind. It was incredible.

Then another unexpected thing happened. Gloria's two daughters Ileane and Rachel had always fought with each other. For some reason, they had never really gotten along. But, at 2:55 that morning, Rachel began to cry. Up until this time, she hadn't been showing much emotion; apparently she'd been keeping it all inside. Even during the entire, yearlong fight against the cancer, Rachel had rarely cried.

But it must have hit her all of a sudden, the reality of what was about to happen. And, when Rachel started crying, Ileane went over to her and hugged her. They both seemed to forget about their differences. It was as if their mother had been waiting for this event to occur, because almost on cue, a few minutes later, at 3:00 A.M., while

I was holding her hand, Gloria's body, with a serene smile on its face, took its last earthly breath.

She was free! Free of the pain and no longer trapped in a body that could no longer serve her purposes. My baby was free. And we were all free of the nightmare. The cancer was history; it was cured. It had been cured with God's final cure. True, we would all miss the "human being" called Gloria. But she was not gone. She was an eternal spirit, back now in the place beyond time and space that we all have come from. We are not flesh and bone. Bodies are merely our temples, tools that we use to play our earthly games. And all of us will learn this when the time is right.

We all held hands and comforted each other.

Gloria was free.

In fact, we all were free.

PART III

THE SONG THAT NEVER ENDED

Chapter 24

Gloria's Triumph

On January 28, 2000, at 3:00 in the morning, my beloved wife, Gloria Rusch-Novello, moved on to a new existence. She ceased being a mortal, human, being.

After Gloria passed away, I covered her body with a blanket and called the cremation service I had made pre-arrangements with. I'd had plenty of time to make all of these arrangements and more, and go over them in detail with Gloria. Both she and I believed that cremation was the best approach to bodily death. We felt that it was ludicrous to worship a person's body after the spirit or soul has quit animating it. We also believed that, by cremating the body, the spirit would be freer to move on to its next existence, without the possibility of its attention being stuck on its previous home.

Within two hours, around 5:00 A.M., the cremation society arrived. It took about an hour for all the legal and medical papers to be signed and the body prepared for travel. And then the moment of truth hit me—oh, so hard. They were taking my baby's body, her once-beautiful temple, away for the final time (and, in truth, despite what the cancer had done to her body, she was still beautiful).

I uncovered her and looked at her beautiful face. I gave her a kiss on the lips and said my good-byes, even though I knew she wasn't in her body or animating it anymore. To me, her body, even lifeless, was still a work of art. Gloria had always had the ability to look good under any circumstances, and this was the final proof of that ability. For her to look so good lifeless, with the upper part of her body ravaged by cancer, was amazing and a testament to the finely-honed aesthetic sense with which Gloria always approached the care of her own body and of so much else in life.

Then they took her body away. I realized that, other than in picture form, in movies, videos and memories, this was the last time I would see the human form known as Gloria. And this was terrible to confront. They left, and that was that. Just like that, my baby had been horrifically ripped from me. It seemed like almost yesterday that she had looked at me and said, "John, feel this lump in my breast." And then had come the misdiagnosis, the correct diagnosis, the treatments, the daily life-and-death decisions and fight—and then she was gone. Shock would be a mild word to use for what I felt.

The family was still there. We comforted each other for about an hour and then, at 7:00 A.M., everybody left. I had a recording session to go to around 11:00 A.M. I needed to get some sleep and then decide if I was going to be able to work that day. Nobody wanted to leave me alone, but I assured them that I'd be all right, and if I wasn't I'd call them.

So, after everybody left, I looked at our once-beautiful house anew. There were signs of battle everywhere. The house was strewn with medical equipment—hospital bed, medicines, supplements, oxygen tanks, bed pans, blood pressure devices, inhalers, hyperthermia infrared machine, ozone generator, magnetic pulser, wound dressings of all types—and now, no Gloria!

And then I cried, uncontrollably and at times convulsively.

I realized I was exhausted. I probably hadn't slept a good night's sleep for over eight months. I got ready for bed, but then, as I lay down to go to sleep, something remarkable happened. I closed my eyes and tried to relax my body, but then, just as if she were right in the room with me, my mind filled with Gloria's voice. It was crystal-clear. It began to speak to me as usual.

John, it said, *I'm all right. It's just like you said.*

Let me explain. A couple of weeks earlier we had talked about this scenario—of her leaving her body, of her probably remaining in an out-of-body state in the room, of her viewing everybody, most likely grief-stricken and in tears, and of her not being able to communicate to them very easily, just like in the movie *Ghost*. And now the voice—

Gloria's voice—continued, *I'm right here. There's no more pain. I am free. It's true. We do still exist after bodily death. This is unbelievable. Wow!*

I sat up and started to cry—tears of joy, that is. I said, "Baby, I hear you. I hear you! Keep talking."

I'm right with you. It's all right. I love you. I really do. Thanks for our earthly 21 years together. They were fantastic. But we can still be together. It'll just be a different relationship.

I made a joke and said, "You mean, we used to have an interracial relationship. Now we have an interdimensional one? I don't know if my heart can take it!"

Gloria then started to rattle off so many communications that I could barely keep up with her. When she'd had a body, she was always going at warp speed anyway. And I guess, after more than a year of being sick and not being able to work as usual, she was making up for lost time. She started giving me instructions about how to continue marketing her book, about her vocal exercise tape, about her vocal school, about remodeling the house, about dividing up her possessions, about not being too hard on myself for not being able to help her heal her body, about my career, about her family and friends, about my promise to finish her solo CD, and about the memorial tribute to her life that I was planning.

It was amazing. I knew for sure that it was not my imagination, as I knew her and the way she spoke and operated—and this was unmistakably her!

But, as incredible as this all was, who could expect me to do other than wish that everything would go back to what it was before, with my wife returning to me in her beautiful, vibrant, healthy body and the both of us being able to hug each other and make love and continue on with our careers together. The truth was that I either wanted Gloria back in her body, by my side, or I wanted to be with her in her new state and by her side.

But I have never been suicidal, and since neither of these scenarios was possible I guessed we would both have to get used to operating this way, with the brunt of the problem resting on me. After about an hour of two-way conversation with her from the other side, I was exhausted and I told her that I had to try and get some sleep. Everything, both good and bad, was far too overwhelming, especially without sleep.

Not only had Gloria and I been extremely interested in the paranormal and in spiritual development, but we had actually written two songs about spiritual adventures. Now they were both being all-too-hauntingly played out. My first CD, featuring my wife as lead vocalist and lyricist, was called, believe it or not, *On the Other Side*. The key lyric of this song, written by Gloria, was, *"On the other side, serenity is peace of mind and you regain abilities; you're free!"*

And then, on *Tightrope*, Gloria's tribute CD which I would soon be finishing, there was a song we had written together called *The Firstime*, the key lyric of which was,

Even death cannot deny us; we promised our love.

And now here we were, several hours after Gloria's death, speaking to each other as if her death had not really happened.

In truth, for me, it had not. Yes, her body had died. But the "operator" of that body had not died. Her being, her soul, her spirit, all that was really her—that had not died. She was still alive and kicking up a storm. Although I'd thought I had lost her until we would meet again in a future lifetime just as we had in this lifetime, death did not appear to have interrupted our this-life communication at all. But it was going to take some readjusting on our parts—especially on my part!—to learn how to operate in this mode of being, which I will characterize as "interdimensional." To pursue once more the *Star Trek* analogy: My wife was still my best friend and companion, but now she had a Romulan cloaking device.

Maybe the horrific experience we had both gone through over the past 15 months really was just one door closing and another opening. Our artistic creations and our lives seemed to be so mysteriously intertwined. Had we, years ago, through our lyrics, unwittingly written the love song of our futures?

Both our minds were racing with thoughts and questions. But, being still of this earth, I was the one who needed sleep. Maybe Gloria didn't need sleep, but I most definitely did. So I went to sleep.

Or so I thought.

Chapter 25

Playing the Blues

My eyes were closed for only a few minutes. Then I opened them again, because I had just become aware of heart palpitations. My heart rate was speeding up and my heartbeat was getting louder. I was starting to shiver and shake. "What's going on?" I asked myself. Gloria didn't seem to be around any more, or if she were she was not communicating with me. I realized that for the first time in my life I actually felt all alone. I started to get anxious. Was my body going into shock? Had the reality of everything that had happened to me this past year, culminating in my wife's passing—had all that reality finally caught up with me? Was I outside my own body, having a near-death experience? That was certainly what it felt like. I thought about telephoning someone to come over and stay with me, but I was too proud to do it. I thought: I'm normally the man of steel who has many tricks up his sleeve; I should be able to calm down.

So I got out of bed and started doing deep-breathing exercises. But that didn't really help. My heart continued racing and I continued to shake all over. I took my temperature, and it was 95.8 degrees—a little on the low side. No wonder I was shivering. I wondered if I should be going to the hospital. Maybe this is what body shock is, I thought. But I couldn't even think of visiting a hospital again. Maybe my work was also finished now on this God-forsaken planet and I was meant to join my wife, and I was suffering just a few pre-departure symptoms. That, and a billion other thoughts, swarmed through my mind during this episode.

Then I decided that I was passively allowing events to act on me when I should be acting on them, when I should be taking charge. I ran a bath and made it as hot as I could stand. I got in the tub immediately and let the water fill up gradually. After about 15 minutes, which seemed like all night, at least my body was warm. I then confronted the obvious, as maybe it hadn't sunk in yet: that my wife had been diagnosed with an aggressive cancer a little over a year ago and we had been fighting it nonstop ever since; that it had consumed our whole lives and all our money; and that in the end it had consumed Gloria's beautiful body and ripped her from my arms. I thought I needed to confront that.

Even though there was an interdimensional relationship between the two of us that was becoming more and more real, nevertheless my wife Gloria, in the form I was used to, was gone. I had to confront that head on! I got out of the hot bath and got ready for bed. My heart rate had at least stopped accelerating, and I was much warmer. I prayed for my wife and for myself, and then I went to bed.

It took about 30 minutes for me to calm down, but eventually I went to sleep, around 8:00 A.M. I only slept for about three hours, and then, when I woke up, I decided that it would be good for my head to go to the scheduled recording session. So I went. I didn't tell a soul about my post-life conversation with Gloria. It was my secret. I channeled all my feelings into the recording session. My playing was very inspired, and I realized that I had a gift in my playing that took this form: that when I played, all of my felt life could be channeled through my fingers into the music. Now I had even more inspiration, for I was thinking of my beloved wife. I was thinking of the joy we had given each other and how fortunate I was to have known her and to have shared my life with her.

At this session, I was thinking that this was all somehow the beginning of something very special. Then I stopped thinking and just played from pure love. I had never experienced this before, at least not with such intensity, although I'd had brief tastes of it earlier in my life. I remembered one night, many years before, when I was at Berklee, when somebody I loved had died and I had had a gig to do that night. I was playing a blues, and all of a sudden I had realized what the blues was. I channeled "my" blues into the blues I was playing and into the audience. It had been a magical performance.

Now I had the blues again, only it was of an incomparably greater magnitude. I knew that from now on, when I wrote and played, I would be able to draw upon this blues, this deep lost love, and share it with the audience. What a gift, I thought! Then I got selfish, and I thought: I would give this gift up in a minute if only I could have my soul mate back.

Still, one door had closed and another had opened, and there was no going back. And therein lay one of the hardest things I had to accept. In the past I had always had the ability to make things right, to correct them somehow. But now I had to go on and do it without my partner. The thought of this caused me the greatest pain I had ever experienced.

After the recording session that evening I came home to an empty house. My wife was gone and she was not coming back, at least not as I had known her. In the middle of the living room stood her empty hospital bed that I now had to return to medical home care. The room was littered with the medical debris of Gloria's long fight just as it was when I had left the house. I wanted to sweep it all into a pile and burn it. But what would that prove other than that I was running away? I had to confront this head-on. Everything else was denial.

I made phone calls to various close relatives and friends to tell them what had happened. That was part of confronting the incident, I guess, because telling others was very emotional—but also very therapeutic. I then went to bed and collapsed. I slept for almost fourteen hours. I guess that, after a year, I needed it. It was now Friday, January 29. The tour with Niacin started in Japan on my birthday, January 31. In August 1999, when Gloria had made her miraculous recovery, our goal had been that she would be well by now so that she could accompany me to Japan. Gloria had her own business dealings in Japan; her book and her tapes were selling well there. And here I was about to go on tour. Not only was Gloria not going to be joining me this time, but she was not going to be joining me for anything, at any time, ever again.

For the next two days in Los Angeles, all I did was sleep and pack and talk to a few close friends. Then, the next thing I knew, a limo was picking me up and whisking me off to Los Angeles International

Airport where I was supposed to meet my drummer, Dennis Chambers. Although Dennis knew that Gloria had been ill, he did not know yet that she had passed away.

I stood in the lobby waiting for him and wondered how I would tell him this not-so-good news. Suddenly, Dennis was there; we hugged as usual, and he asked me how I was doing. I said, "Well, I don't really know. Do you know that Gloria passed away a few days ago?"

He almost collapsed. He leaned against the wall and tried to hold back the tears. We hugged and I tried to comfort him as best as I could. It was an intense moment. Dennis is one of the most amazing drummers in the world not only because of his technical facility, but also because of the emotional content he puts into his playing. You could sense this emotion now as he fought to hold back his tears.

We talked a bit. Eventually we boarded the plane. Once I was seated, it all hit me. I really felt alone—no soul mate, and a future that had been totally upset. Although I hadn't realized it before, that future had looked great, not because of all the great opportunities that awaited us—CD sales, book sales, movies, videos, concert tours, kids, etc.— but also because it included sharing our love for each other while we did all these things together. I guess I'd taken this for granted, because without my best friend I now didn't have much interest in the future, no matter how good it looked materially. And I had never, ever felt this way before—never, ever, ever!

And then another amazing interdimensional event took place.

Chapter 26

My Guardian Angel

During this flight to Osaka, Japan, I had my earphones on and was listening to the music to try and take my attention away from the shock of everything. I had the blues, of course, as I've already mentioned. I was in a very serious funk; I was wallowing in the muck and being pretty much of a wimp. The last thing I'd been thinking about was how sorry I was Gloria hadn't been able to make it on the airplane with me to go to this concert, something we'd been planning on since last August. Boy, was I bummed out.

I was right in the middle of suppressing my tears when all of a sudden, just like before, Gloria said to me as clear as could be, *Hey, what are you doing, John? Who said I didn't make it on the plane? Just because my body didn't make it doesn't mean that I didn't. I'm here with you and I am coming on tour with you, so you better play great!*

I started laughing out loud. I didn't realize I was doing this, of course, because I had my headphones on. I guess I had started talking to Gloria out loud, because the lady next to me gave me a funny look. I took my phones off for a moment and she said, "Is everything all right?"

"Well, yes," I answered her. "Why do you ask?"

"Because you were talking pretty loud," she declared.

"Oh, I'm sorry," I said. "I didn't realize that was occurring, because the music was so loud."

"That's okay," she said.

I then kept the headphones off and started communicating with Gloria telepathically. It was awesome! This was the third time this had occurred—once right before she'd passed away, the second time right after everybody had left and before I went to bed on the night that she left her body. And now it was happening again. It was very real. I didn't even doubt it this time. Gloria told me how much she loved me and that she was sorry for all that had happened. She thanked me for all my dedication to her during the fight. This got me out of my funk and I went back to listening to *What Goes Up Must Come Down*, which was one of our favorite songs by Frankie Beverly and Maze. Gloria reminded me of the time we'd seen them live at Universal City. It had been an awesome concert; Patti LaBelle and Luther Vandross had opened up for Maze, and they had been incredible. But then Maze had come out and done a clinic on how to groove. The whole audience was on their feet for over two hours straight.

The rest of the flight, I was high on love. I had never been able to love someone like this before. It appeared that the song we had written together, *The Firstime*, had gotten it right, for it contained the lyrics, "Even death cannot deny us, we promised our love."

I landed in Osaka and after a brief ride to the hotel I checked into my room. I lit some of my favorite incense, had a good meal and a massage, and slept for twelve hours. The next two days were rehearsal days, and I was going to need all my energy.

Rehearsals went fine. The band was sounding great. Our first concert was at the famous Blue Note in Osaka. I was more nervous than normal because of all that had happened. Was I going to rise to the occasion, or was I going to wallow in my loss and play in a mediocre manner or perhaps even badly?

It was February 5, and I was about to go onstage at the Osaka Blue Note with Niacin and our legendary rock bassist Billy Sheehan and our world-class drummer Dennis Chambers and myself on the B3. In a progressive rock fusion super trio such as ours, there is no room for mediocre playing. You had to burn! We were introduced: "Ladies and gentleman, let's give a round of applause to Niacin— Billy Sheehan, John Novello and Dennis Chambers!"

I heard my name and I was terrified that I wouldn't have my edge. But, when the band started the first tune, Gloria was right there with me. I'll never forget her first words.

They say behind every great man there's a great woman. So, what's your excuse, baby?!

That was all I needed. I let it rip! And it was amazing. I was playing at a whole new level of inspiration.

When we got to the fifth tune, something truly remarkable happened. The tune is called *I Miss You.* Boy, did that tune have meaning, not only for me, but even for the rest of the band, as we all missed Gloria. Once in 1998, she had sat in with Niacin at the Blues Alley in Washington, D.C. Dennis had never heard her sing live, and that night he asked her if she wanted to sing a song in our second set. "Sure," she replied. She came up and did a song called *All Blues* by Miles Davis, and she tore the house down.

Before we all went on stage on this present tour, we had agreed that the whole tour and every note in it would be dedicated to Gloria. So we were all playing inspirationally. But this tune had special meaning. And the moment we started it, I knew we were all inspired. We were in the zone. It was awesome. The whole tune was being orchestrated from the heavens. I felt like I was watching the performance from above. Nothing could have been more right.

Every note was perfect. And the audience went wild, they got it! It was a spiritual moment and everybody in the place knew it. Gloria was beaming! And I was humbled. Boy, can God work in mysterious ways. One door closes and another opens. I was crying, but they were tears of joy.

The entire Japanese tour was inspired. Every night we reached new levels. But the real test was going to be in Los Angeles. We would be going home and playing in front of all of Gloria's and my friends. And, of all days, what a day to travel home: Valentine's Day, February 14, 2000! We would be performing at the famous Baked Potato. Gloria's last performance had been at this very same venue, on February 27 of the previous year. We had returned from the Klinik-Benediktusquelle in Germany on Valentine's Day, 1999. We had been very happy then as we had had our first modest success in fighting the cancer. It was Valentine's Day and our love for each other had risen to new heights. Gloria was glad to be back in L. A., and she sang like she had never sung before, straight from the heart and soul. Who could have known that, other than the gospel tune she sang the day she passed away, this would be her final performance?

Now it was Valentine's Day again and I was once more flying back to L.A.—but this time without Gloria. Of course, the minute I started getting upset about this Gloria was right there beside me, reminding me that I most definitely was not alone. I began to laugh. The funk had been diverted once again. This interdimensional relationship was pretty cool!

I remember walking through the door into the club. It was packed with people, most of whom Gloria and I knew very well. So the Niacin concert at The Baked Potato club was very special for me. Our performance was phenomenal, and there wasn't a dry eye in the house during the inspirational performance of the song *I Miss You*. Gloria was at work again from the other side. Although playing had always been very special for me, now it was literally a religious experience.

Now that the tour was over, I had to confront being back in the City of Angels without Gloria. The toughest part would be to live in our house; there were too many memories there. Gloria had warned me that in the event she didn't make it I might have those feelings; now I knew what she meant. She had suggested that I sell the house as soon as possible. But now there was this evolving interdimensional relationship to which we were both getting used; maybe I wouldn't have to sell the house after all. Time would tell, I guessed. Even though I was sure Gloria was getting used to our new game, it was natural for me to feel that it was a whole lot harder on me than on her. She seemed to be having a great time!

Chapter 27

On a *Tightrope*

The next project I felt I needed to work on was the completion of Gloria's solo CD. We'd been working on it together in our new digital recording studio just prior to her illness. It would be a challenge indeed to go into our studio without her and sort through all her songs and tracks and produce the CD. I knew this would be tough; but just before she passed away I had promised her that I would finish it and release it at her life tribute. And I meant to keep my promise. We'd started this together, and "death would not deny us!"

So, for the entire month of March, all I did was go into the studio every day and sort though all her tunes. The ones that were done, I mixed; the ones that weren't, I pieced together from different takes. After three weeks, I was amazed at what I had produced. It was awesome. I was so proud of Gloria, and I know she was very proud too.

I can't tell you how emotional I got during this process. Imagine my being in "our" studio late every night by myself, listening to my wife sing to me. It was spiritually spooky. Any minute I expected her, body and all, to walk through the door and ask me how it was going. But I knew she was there and listening with me. The hardest part of all was to listen to the lyrics of our song, *The Firstime*, which Gloria and I had written with Steve Kipner:

> *The first time I saw you*
> *From a photograph,*
> *You reached out and touched me,*
> *You stole my heart.*

> *I was staring at the future.*
> *The first time I called you on the phone*
> *Your voice was déjà vu, I felt that I'd come home.*
> *O baby baby, we were meant to be,*
> *Me for you and you for me.*
> *In a world full of strangers*
> *Somehow we found our way back to us.*
> *It's more than the here-and-now we've got*
> *'Cause I know it's not*
> *The first time you kissed me:*
> *Every cell in my body remembered*
> *The fire only you can satisfy me,*
> *Even death cannot deny me,*
> *We promised our love.*
> *In a world full of strangers*
> *Somehow we found our way back to us.*
> *It's more than the here-and-now we've got, O*
> *I watch you sleeping*
> *Your breath on my lips,*
> *It makes me remember*
> *Love's eternal kiss.*

God, were these lyrics hitting home! Gloria and I believed we had been together many times before and would be together many times again, and in *The Firstime* we had written

Somehow we found our way back to us./ It's more than the here-and-now we've got

And here I was, communicating with Gloria beyond this life, knowing absolutely that what we had was more than the here-and-now. So, as hard as it was—and it was terribly hard for me emotionally to put together this CD, I cried during the whole process, sometimes tears of joy and sometimes tears of pain and loss—somehow I finished Gloria's CD, and I called it *Tightrope*.

She was at my side during the entire process, helping me make artistic decisions just as she always had. She was especially involved in the artwork choices. I called Gloria's brother Neal, who is a good graphics art designer. We sorted through a sheaf of pictures of Gloria and, with her help, chose the best. I wrote all the copy, including a personal message from me, the husband/ producer, a personal message from Gloria that she had approved in advance, an acknowledgement section, and the legal copy. Neal scanned the pictures into the computer and had his partner Rick put a design together that we used as a starting point.

After Neal and Rick left, Gloria told me the picture they'd chosen for the front of the CD was great but that it shouldn't be on the front. We needed something better for the cover. Gloria directed me to a live video we had of one of her last performances, at The Key Club in Los Angeles. While I watched the video she pointed out a couple of great shots of herself. The next time I saw Neal, I pointed these out to him and he took one off the video—and, sure enough, it was exactly the right picture for the front of the CD. So, here again, Gloria and I were working together as we always had.

We did some research, selected an appropriate CD manufacturer, and turned in the project four weeks before Gloria's memorial tribute celebration, which was scheduled for April 27. I was planning to release *Tightrope* at the tribute, so there was no room for error. When I picked up the CD in its final format, the vendor commented that she had never before done a CD where everything had gone as perfectly as it had for this one: no glitches with the artwork or the duplication process or whatever. She told me it seemed like the project had been "heavenly coordinated!" I laughed, as this was yet another example of Gloria's interdimensional activity.

Chapter 28

Preparations for a Life Tribute

Although the public life tribute to Gloria would be a tough thing for me to do, I could tell there was a reason for it beyond just acknowledging and celebrating Gloria's life. The CD had been difficult enough to do by itself. Listening to Gloria sing to me every night, knowing full well that I would never hear her sing live again, had ripped at my very soul. Now I was about to produce a public tribute/ memorial. I could hear my wife's words from last August: "If you do any kind of event in my honor, it better be a celebration of my life. I don't want everybody crying about my loss."

I wondered if I'd be able to pull it off.

They don't teach you about real life in school. Only life teaches you about life, and I felt like I was a student about to take a test he was wholly unprepared for. It was a test I mustn't fail. Gloria had already graduated, and as far as I was concerned she had done so *summa cum laude*. Now it was my turn, my journey—my supreme test. Truthfully I was very scared, as I wasn't certain I would actually be able to do it. I knew I had to keep moving forward. I was not a quitter and neither was Gloria. We were a power couple that made good things happen, and we were going to continue to do just that. It was up to me to carry on the goals and purposes we had started on "this side." I had to make all of this mean something special. There were new doors opening, and I had to go through them; this I knew for sure.

Gloria was helping. I could feel her giving me strength just as she had done when she was alive. She was not only my soul mate, but now she was acting as my spirit guide and companion. Nothing had really changed. But *I* was sure changing. My heart was opening. I could feel love pouring out of it like never before.

But I wondered why it had had to happen this way. Oh, God, I pleaded, tell me why! I was still bitter. Apparently I had some way to go before I graduated. There was so very much to learn.

Now that the date for the tribute had been set, I began to script it—or rather I should say, *we* began to script it, for, just as she had done with the production of the CD, Gloria was right there with me, making sure her life tribute would be an awesome event. I was getting so used to our new relationship that I talked to her and consulted her almost as if nothing had happened. I say almost, because communicating with her in this manner, without being able to experience her physically by hugging her and kissing her and just plain looking at her beautiful body, was a maddening tease for me, a frustration beyond any that I could ever have imagined. But then again, this was an interface between two worlds, two dimensions, two universes, the physical and the spiritual—and it was unbelievable!

It was a good thing that I was alone during all of this, because anybody watching me would have been concerned for my sanity.

Throughout these preparations, I felt oddly like a spectator at my own life. It was as if my life had a life all its own! Sure, I was making decisions of my own free will. But at the same time as I was doing that it seemed as if I really had no choice in these matters. Not to make the choices I was making would have headed me down the wrong road, sent me through the wrong door; I knew this somehow. My intuitive awareness of what to do was becoming acute, and so I just quit questioning and fighting what was occurring and embraced it. I welcomed this acceptance of the flow of events that was making me stronger than ever. What a journey! If I were going nuts, as some psychiatrists might have said—then I liked "nuts!" If I was hung up on this great loss in my life and "in denial"—then how come I was so productive? Was everything that was occurring just a string of coincidences? I didn't think so. What I did think was that it was too far beyond psychiatry's limited scope to even be evaluated.

I divided Gloria's life tribute into two parts. Part One would consist, believe it or not, of a message directly from Gloria (I'll explain later) and some special performances from our favorite artists. Part Two would feature the main act—Gloria Rusch-Novello. It would consist of a biographical slide show of Gloria's life accomplishments followed by a tribute speech by John Novello—myself, or whatever was left of me (I was nervous as hell about doing this, but it needed to be done and I needed to do it. If I broke down in front of 500 people, then so what? It would be an honest thing to do for sure). Then we would show a video of Gloria's last performance as part of her favorite project, Novello/Rusch.

For our finale, we would begin to play Gloria's version of *Over the Rainbow*, one of the songs on her new CD. I'd envisioned the following: While this version of *Over the Rainbow* was playing, our band—the band that used to back up Gloria live—would sneak up on stage with all the talent and singers that we could muster. When Gloria's version reached the ending vamp and started to fade in volume, then the live band would fade in and take over the song and jam out a tribute to her.

Now that I had a script in hand, the next thing to do was make it happen. The top priority was to contact all of the talent. Once that was done, the next thing was getting people to help—master of ceremonies, sound and stage crew, lighting, video, venue, security, etc. Amazingly, I had no problems with any of this. Gloria was so beloved that everybody volunteered immediately. They were honored that I'd asked. One night, I was so touched by this that I broke down and started crying. If it hadn't been for the spirit intervention of Gloria, I'd probably still be crying—or I'd be with her, as I didn't know how many more emotional tsunamis my body could endure.

On April 26, the night before the event, I was practically in shock. I thought about everything that had happened over the past 15 months. Gloria and I had been moving rapidly toward the fulfillment of all of our dreams and then—meltdown! Aggressive terminal cancer; a more-than-yearlong fight during which Gloria endured horrific pain and suffering; emotional and financial stress for all the family; and then we lost her. Now, here I was on the eve of her life tribute. How in the hell—and why—had all this happened?

I went to bed. I needed my sleep. Tomorrow would be a big day.

Chapter 29

The Concert Made in Heaven (I)

It was 7:00 on the evening of April 27. I stood on the stage of the Garden Pavilion at Celebrity Center International in Los Angeles, anxiously awaiting Stevie Wonder.

I'd been there since one in the afternoon, making sure all the equipment arrived, then making sure it was properly set up in preparation for Gloria's life tribute beginning at 8:00 P.M. I'd nervously conferred with Michael Roberts, the actor and anti-drug advocate who was a close friend of ours and who would be the master of ceremonies. Most of the singers and musicians had arrived and been told when they'd be performing.

Everything was in place except for one. Stevie Wonder, who at one time had himself been a voice student of Gloria, had promised he would be there, but we hadn't heard from him for several days. If Stevie didn't show the tribute would still be awesome—but I had promised Gloria that he and I would perform together, and I very badly wanted to keep that promise.

The doors opened at 7:30 P.M. By 7:45 the room was packed; some 500 people had come streaming in. There was still no Stevie. At 7:55, my line coordinator Joan asked me if we were going to start on time. I was about to say yes when I was suddenly interrupted and told that Stevie was on the phone.

I got on the line with him. Stevie told me he was on the way and would be there in 20 minutes. I asked Joan to hold the doors until 8:30, and of course I told her why. Then Stevie arrived. We met in the Center's Talent Green Room and after a warm hug we discussed how he would participate. It was easy. Stevie would come up after I'd performed with Niacin and say a few words, then play and sing a song of his own choosing. I would bring him back up a little later so he could sit in with the Novello/Rusch band. Since most good musicians know lots of Stevie tunes, we could figure out the song later; now it was time for the event to start. I got Stevie a front table, and then the show began.

Susan Watson, president of Celebrity Center International, welcomed everyone to the Pavilion and read a short biography of Gloria. She introduced Michael Roberts, who had the difficult task of reading a message Gloria had written in July 1999, in the event this life tribute would have to take place.

Gloria had much to say in her message, and her many friends in the audience listened raptly. I will reproduce just a part of the message, that having to do with our growing love and closeness during her horrific ordeal:

"John and I grew very close during this ordeal—closer than we ever could have imagined. So, in many ways, this was a gift from God, as He does work in mysterious ways sometimes, Amen....Boy, did we learn a lot about life in one year, especially love and appreciation of one another and of family and friends, and all the other things that count. Priorities align real quickly when you're fighting a major illness day in day out for over a year, if you can imagine that. Almost every decision was life and death and about drove the both of us crazy at times.

"You should all know that John was awesome during this whole fight....I lost my first husband in Vietnam and so I know how difficult it is losing your mate. So I can imagine how hard he's taking this if I'm gone, as he was taking it pretty hard when I was here fighting the fight. So please keep an eye on him for me. We were sure an item, and he knows how much I really love him.

"Before I moved on, John promised me that he would finish my solo CD entitled <u>Tightrope</u> that I was working on before I got side-lined. I'm very proud of it, as John and I both produced and wrote it, and it's a dream come true. He said he would release it at this event if

it came to this, and so I hope he does, because if he doesn't he will be one haunted Italian white boy!

"So, tonight, please, let's have a great celebration. I told him that if he did any event at all, that I wanted to have a night of celebration and not a night of mourning. A few tears are okay, I guess—but please, just a few.

"I love you all very much. Gloria may be gone, but 'I'll' be back for sure!"

Gloria's message blew everybody away, and, even though there wasn't a dry eye in the house, everybody was inspired and ready to celebrate a great lady's life. And so was I.

The performers came up one by one. They were all favorites of Gloria, and they all performed like they'd never performed before. The evening became magical, just as if it were being orchestrated from above. The first act was the group Celestial Navigations (who, as I've mentioned, played at our wedding) led by veteran character actor Geoffrey Lewis. Geoffrey cast a magical spell over the audience as he narrated two original and mesmerizing stories while accompanied by dual keyboardists Geoff Levin and Betty Ross. Gloria had absolutely adored this group, and they told two stories that were among her favorites. The audience loved it.

Next, the world-class classical pianist Mario Feninger—whose playing was masterful and whom Gloria and I had heard perform many times—came up and played a medley of Chopin pieces. Chopin was one of Gloria's favorite classical composers. Mario was awesome and he was extremely funny (his humor came at a good time for me, because what with Gloria's message and Celestial Navigations's moving performance, I'd gotten a bit on the emotional side). Here's an example of Mario's wit: He was introducing a piece by Chopin, and he announced that it was a very difficult composition. He told us that you had to be a genius to perform it—which was why he was going to do it! His remark made the whole audience burst out laughing, including me; and, believe me, we all needed it.

The next performer was Michael Norris, an actor/comedian from the LaughWorks comic ensemble. Michael performed a brilliant silent skit depicting a spirit entering a body at the beginning of a new life, living out that life, then dying—meaning leaving the body when it had ceased functioning—and then picking up a new, baby body and starting all over again. The skit was awesome, and helped all of us who were immersed in our loss of Gloria to realize that death was merely a transition to a new beginning.

I was next. I'd written a piece for piano and violin called *Wishing You Were Here*. The violinist was Lily Haden, who had her own group on Atlantic Records and had studied voice with Gloria at one time. This was a special song and performance for me. The piano and violin notes seemed to take wing as they left the stage and soar with aesthetic perfection over the audience. I'd been a musician for over 35 years and I'd played over 2,500 gigs, but I had never played a gig as inspired and inspirational as this one. The notes had a unique purpose behind them: they were meant for Gloria, and so they were divine.

After the performance, which had felt effortless, I couldn't believe the reaction of the audience. As I was accepting the applause I thought: Wow! This is what music is really all about. It's about touching people spiritually. It's about reminding them that they are spiritual beings at play in the physical universe. When music has this aim behind it, it goes straight to the spirit and it touches the soul. I knew this already, but the tribute was teaching me about it in a whole new way. This was love! My love, my unconditional love—a love that asked for nothing in return—was the energy flow that was creating this effect.

When I'd played in the past, I'd "loved" playing. I loved what I was doing, of course, and I was competent. But I hadn't been playing fully from the heart. And now I was. I myself was touched. Gloria— who she was, her life, her being, her love—all this had touched me, and I was responding to the touch.

I remembered an incident that had taken place about a month before Gloria passed away. I'd been playing the piano. I hadn't touched it in quite a while, so I was expecting to be a little rusty. Quite the opposite occurred. I played the piano with conviction; I meant every note I played. All the pain and struggle I'd gone through in helping my wife fight cancer somehow acquired meaning and became a part of the music I played. Life was the teacher, and I was the student.

When I was through playing I went into the room where Gloria was resting and told her what had happened. She told me she'd been able to hear the difference, and that she was really happy for me. In hindsight, I realize now she meant that in a very special way. She knew she was going soon, and she was trying to tell me that she was happy for my discovery. She knew our two hearts were one and that the joy and pain we were both experiencing was helping each of us to grow. She knew she had helped, and it made her feel really good.

Next up at the tribute was Niacin. I introduced our bassist Billy Sheehan and Pat Torpey on drums (Dennis Chambers was on the road). We played two of Gloria's favorite Niacin songs, *One Less Worry* and *I Miss You*. *I Miss You* had a special meaning for me, of course, and I dedicated it to Gloria. Our performance was truly inspired. The last song we did was *Things Ain't What They Used To Be* from the third Niacin CD, *Deep*. I brought onto the stage for this song Glenn Hughes, the famed lead singer for the rock band Deep Purple. When Glenn heard Gloria had passed away and that I was doing a tribute for her, he flew from London to Los Angeles, arriving only the day before, just to perform at her tribute. I also brought up Ritchie Kotzen, the guitarist from Mr. Big. The blues ballad that we did tore the house down! The tribute was heating up. There was no stopping it now.

After the applause died down, Niacin left the stage and I went over to the mike and brought up the one and only Stevie Wonder. Most of the audience did not even know he was there, so it was quite a surprise and it got a very enthusiastic reception. Stevie's secretary led him up to the stage, and while he and I hugged each other, Stevie told me the song he wanted to do. I led him over to the acoustic grand piano, and Stevie just took over.

Once he was seated and the audience had calmed down, he took the mike and began to speak. He said that in his lifetime he had had the privilege of meeting many great people who had done great things and then been taken by God, and that for him Gloria was one of these people. He told the audience that he had studied with her for years and he knew Gloria's ability as person, teacher, and singer to help and uplift others was a gift, that the earth was a better place now because of her contributions and her love, and that she would always be in our hearts. It was a moving and wonderful tribute, and it touched everybody—especially me.

I could barely contain myself. Here was Stevie Wonder, a musical mentor of mine and Gloria, on stage paying tribute to my wife and about to dedicate and sing a song to her. The love in the room was truly omnipresent; this was a magical moment. Then Stevie began to play *Overjoyed* in Gloria's honor—and we all knew we were in for an even more magical moment. The audience was mesmerized. In fact, as good as Stevie is, I noticed that even his playing was inspired by the moment. At the end of the song he started to improvise with his voice, and he was having such a good time that he started to laugh, which took the audience even further out the roof. When he was finished the applause was deafening and lasted for at least five minutes.

I walked over to Stevie and led him off the stage, thanking him from the bottom of my heart. Gloria's presence so filled the room now that she seemed more "there" than if her physical body had been present. Everybody sensed this. Gloria was touched by all the love and I could hear her thanking me. But I had to compose myself quickly, as the next act was the Novello/Rusch band. This was the band that had backed Gloria up for more than 15 years. For me to go up on stage without Gloria, knowing that she would never again be up there with me in physical form, was truly a tough scenario to confront.

The band was going to play two of Gloria's favorite songs, *Discovery* and *For You*. *Discovery* had a difficult melody that only she could scat, and *For You* was the song I'd written for her while I was away in Riga, Latvia for three months working on the movie *Red Hot*. I was joined by trumpeter and film composer Mark Isham for the first song. The rest of the band was made up of Melvin Davis on bass, Randy Drake on drums, Eric McKain on percussion and Donald Hayes on sax. Normally, Gloria would scat the melody and then improvise the first solo. But this time she would be scatting from above and inspiring us all. And once again, as had already happened at this tribute, I experienced a level of intensity of performance such as I had never experienced before, not only from myself but also from everybody. I had been in shock every time I'd played since Gloria had left her body. And tonight the intensity was more inspired than ever.

Why did it have to take such a tragedy to bring about this level of focus? I was beginning to wonder if, in the grand scheme of things, this was even a tragedy. I didn't linger on this thought for long, because I was devastated by my loss of Gloria. But it struck me that in the long-term perhaps what was happening was simply a transition for everybody. By everybody, I mean all those who were directly or indirectly involved with Gloria and her passing—myself, her family, her friends and her fans, the performers, the audience, and now, as I write this book, you the reader.

For You was written when I was really really missing Gloria, and I had put all of my longing for her into that song. Every time I played it, I put the same longing into my rendition. It was a soulful ballad, composed in a gospel/jazz style that already lent itself to great emotion. I wondered what amazing energy it might release tonight. In fact I was almost shaking in anticipation of that energy.

The tune began with my playing solo an improvised bluesy/gospel intro. From the first, I knew the notes that were coming out were holy. I was already shedding tears. The intensity was almost too much for me to deal with, but I had no choice in the matter. Everything was just happening and I knew from my past experience as a musician that when this magic happened one did not interrupt the process, one just let it flow. And that was what I did. By the time the band came in, I thought I might be close to joining my wife. I literally felt like I was playing from the "other side." What a journey! Hang in there, I told myself, Gloria is with you and loving every minute of it.

After I took a ripping organ solo, Donald Hayes came in with a heart-wrenching bluesy alto sax solo. The groove that Melvin, Eric and Randy were laying down was also in the "other-side" zone. And it was true, the whole room had been transported to another dimension by the time the song was done. It actually took me a few minutes to arrive back; the thing I remember most vividly is that it was the audience's standing ovation that brought me back. I instinctively looked upward and, as I could feel her spiritual smile, I just told Gloria, "I love you, baby!"

After I had composed myself and after the acknowledgement of the audience, I brought up a gospel singer named Conell Moss to perform a Edgar Winter gospel tune called *You Were My Light*. Edgar Winter and his wife Monique were good friends of ours, and I had asked Edgar to sing the tune at this event. But his tour had gotten moved up at the last minute and he couldn't be here. I had still very much wanted to do his song, since the lyrics expressed so well how I felt about my wife. Then I remembered Conell. Gloria and Conell had performed together in the musical *King* in which Gloria had played Coretta Scott King and Conell had played Martin Luther King. In it, Gloria and Conell had done a duet that brought the house down every night. Conell lived in L.A., and I was able to track him down.

When I'd told him what had happened he was devastated, and immediately asked how he could help. I told him what I needed, and he said, "I'll do it." This brother is from church, and so for him and for this occasion singing a gospel song would be a slam-dunk. Conell came over to my studio to rehearse, and after just one listening he had it nailed. When I brought him up on stage, he looked at me and I knew he had come to wail. I knew we would all be going to church. I also brought up another keyboardist, Larry Hopkins, to play organ so I could play some gospel piano.

Just as I thought he would, Conell preached his sermon and the audience was completely blown away—and so was I. As Conell was leaving the stage, I scanned the audience to see if Stevie was still there. He was, and I took a chance and invited him up on stage again. He came up and everybody started cheering. What further great performances lay in store for us tonight, I wondered?

Stevie came over to me and gave me his great big bear hug. I asked him what he wanted to do. We agreed on *You Are the Sunshine of My Life*. Stevie told me his key and I counted off the tune. Then he did an incredible thing. Just as he was supposed to start singing, he pointed the microphone at the audience and, exactly as if it had been previously rehearsed, the audience became a professional choir and sang the entire first verse. Stevie came in before the second verse and said, "and," and re-pointed the microphone at the audience—and again on cue they sang the entire second verse. It was just amazing!

Stevie looked at me and he was smiling—he may be physically blind but he isn't "blind"—and then he started to sing the chorus. Then he sang the rest of the song. How many times have I played this song? I asked myself, but never with Stevie and never for such an inspired occasion! Another awesome performance! Gloria and I were floating. Our love for each other had not only never stopped, but it was in fact growing, and not only growing, but being shared by all.

At the end of the song I went over to Stevie and we embraced tightly for a few minutes while the audience went utterly wild. During our embrace, Stevie said to me, "John, I mean this. We are now brothers. I mean real brothers. We have to carry on this message of love." I acknowledged his moving message.

That was supposed to be the end of the first part of the tribute, but just as Stevie and I were beginning to walk off stage, he stopped and said to me, "Wait a minute. Let's do something impromptu." Stevie then turned around to Melvin, the bassist, and started humming the bass part of *I Just Called to Say I Love You.* Because I was standing next to Stevie, there was no one to play any chords, so just bass and drums and percussion played and Stevie sang with them, making up new words to his song as he went along. He sang, "Gloria, we all just came to say we loved you!" and on from there. The whole audience then joined in and sang the song to Gloria impromptu. I sang along and could no longer hold back my tears. This was all so incredible— and at the same time the loss was becoming too much for me and I started to break down. But Stevie had his arm around me and held me up, and I continued to sing to Gloria, which revived me. How could the evening get any better? What an ending to Part One of Gloria's tribute!

We all walked off stage and I thanked Stevie for everything. He left—or so I thought. During the intermission there were so many people coming up to me to tell me how incredible the whole event had been so far that I could barely maintain my composure. All were truly touched by the deep love that Gloria and I obviously had for each other and by our willingness to share it with them. Gloria's CD *Tightrope*, which I had released that night, was selling like crazy. The part of me that could be happy was indeed very happy, and also very proud to have been Gloria's husband in this lifetime. But another part of me was devastated by my loss.

Chapter 30

The Concert Made in Heaven (II)

After the intermission Michael Roberts read Gloria's biography, accompanied by a slide show of many great shots of her. In Parts One and Two of this book, I have already told the story of Gloria's life up to and during her illness, so I won't repeat what Michael read that night. Suffice it to say that he dwelt on the unique nature of our relationship, which was not only as husband and wife but as business associates as well, so that what with our both being 100 percent involved in Novello/Rusch, we worked together as well as played together. Michael not only paid tribute to Gloria's voice, which included her "startling, octave-leaping scat singing," but he also paid tribute to her wonderful personality, which enabled her to bring everybody into what she was simply by being present. When I heard Gloria's biography being read, even I, who already knew all the details, was impressed again and very, very proud.

After reading Gloria's biography, Michael asked everyone if they wanted to see a video of her last performance. Of course they did, but no one could believe that they would really be seeing her last performance. For me the description was unreal, and something I still have trouble with, probably because I believed that, long-term, this wouldn't really be her last performance. The body or temple that Gloria's spirit had occupied while she did her good deeds was gone, but that spirit would be back to play for sure. I had found her in this lifetime, and I knew I would find her again in another. Gloria would perform again, but perhaps not for a while. In the meantime, I had work to do. My own journey was beginning.

Next, we showed three songs that had been videotaped at the Novello/Rusch Key Club Concert in February 1999. The songs were *Summertime, Over the Rainbow* and *Discovery.* Watching Gloria work her magic in our ensemble uplifted the audience even further.

Then Michael said a few words of his own about Gloria and how she and I were such an item with each other. He said that whenever you thought of Gloria, you immediately thought of John, and vice versa. Although what he said was true, it wasn't good timing for me to hear this. Michael was about to bring me up to the stage again, but not to play. That would have been easy. I was now going up to speak, hopefully to say some inspired words about my beloved wife.

This was the moment that really made me nervous. I had cried every day since Gloria had passed on, especially when I tried to talk about her to anyone. And I mean real uncontrollable sobbing. I wasn't embarrassed about crying, but I felt that the type of convulsive painful crying I was doing at home would probably prevent me from saying anything tonight. The mystery and uncertainty of what would happen when I spoke was creating real stage fright within me. Somehow, I had to maintain enough composure to get my message about Gloria across to the audience. Well, enough worry! I heard my name being announced, and the next thing I knew I was on stage. I couldn't even remember how I got there. It seemed as if I'd been beamed there.

My whole life flashed before me. Here I was, a guy from Erie, Pennsylvania, now living in the big city, or, as my wife liked to say, in the fast lane. Here I was on stage, in front of over 500 people, about to deliver a tribute to my soul mate who had just passed away from breast cancer. This has to be a nightmare, I thought. Please, can I just wake up and see her sleeping next to me in bed? Please, God? No such luck! "Time to deliver, John," I said to myself. "Get started!"

You, the reader, will already know what I must have said about Gloria in my speech, since it was what I have been saying all along in this book. Sometimes, as I was speaking, I had to stop and frankly tell the audience how difficult this was for me and that I was choking up. "It's difficult to be up here in this situation," I told them several times. I said some things that I hadn't expected to say at all, such as: "And I hate to say this, but I don't think that if we had lived our full time-span together we would ever have achieved what we had in that one 15-month span." I dwelt on how little Gloria had complained during the entire illness, telling the audience that, for example, "It was probably in December 1999, which was about six weeks before she left us to start anew, when she said, 'Boy, do I miss singing and the Novello/Rusch Project.'" I got extremely emotional as I said this and I had to stop, but then I was able to continue, "And only that one time, one time in over a year, did she complain."

I talked about the horrible ups and downs of Gloria's illness, and I told the audience about the time, very close to the end, when she could mostly speak only gibberish and I raised one of her eyelids to see if she was still aware and she cut me sharply with her eyes and then, when I asked her if she knew who I was, she opened her eyes fully and looked at me and said, "John Novello, my husband, I love you." (This story was so personal and moving for me that when I was part-way through I had to break off and ask the audience, "Is it all right if I share this story with you?" and they had responded yes.)

I barely made it through my speech, and at the very end I became emotional indeed, especially since, as called for by the script I'd written, Gloria's voice was now beginning to waft up through the PA system, singing *Over the Rainbow* from her solo CD *Tightrope*.

Here is the story of how Gloria and I began performing *Over the Rainbow* in public together. One day when I was playing it instrumentally on the piano and working on a new arrangement, Gloria heard what I was doing and came in and asked if she could sing along and I said, sure. The next thing I knew, we were weaving some magic. It sounded so good. It seemed as if we were both making the sound ours, so much so that the whole happening gave us goose bumps. I said to Gloria, "Hey, let's do it tomorrow night at our concert at The Baked Potato."

She said, "What about rehearsal with the band?"

"We'll rehearse it at sound check in the afternoon," I said. "I'll write the charts out tonight. Besides, if we don't get time to rehearse, so what? We'll do it as a feature duo. After all, it's our band!"

We didn't get time to rehearse it, so we did do it as a duo and it was the hit of the night. Gloria's voice soared like an angel's over the melody and touched everybody. We got a standing ovation. It's always a striking occasion when as an artist you do something that comes so effortlessly and thoughtlessly and yet gets such a reaction. From that day on, we always did that song, and it always got the same reaction. We recorded it with the band, and it soon became one of our all-time favorites.

To return to Gloria's life tribute: For her CD performance of *Over the Rainbow,* the intro to the song began with me on electric piano and synthesizer strings. Then Gloria and the band, just drums and bass, came in with the first chorus. It was so aesthetically satisfying and yet so soulful that it immediately captured the audience. Everyone was so moved, and at the same time so saddened for obvious reasons. It was a special but a very difficult moment.

What happened next is something that will stay with me all of my life. As the song was playing, the band and all the guest singers were sneaking up on stage and starting to play along with the recording. As the song comes to an end on the CD, the arrangement segues into a very Luther Vandross-type soulful vamp complete with background gospel singers, while Gloria rifts. So, by the time the CD was about to fade out, the live band and performers had completely taken over, and before the audience could figure out what had happened *Over the Rainbow* was now being performed live. Gloria's daughter Ileane had taken Gloria's lead vocal over and a host of other singers were singing the gospel backgrounds. I was on piano, playing like I had never played before, and experiencing so many emotions simultaneously, all so real and amazing, that I almost felt as if I had never lived before until this moment. I felt as if I'd been awakened to a new life.

Earlier, I mentioned my favorite scene in *Star Wars* where Obi-Wan Kenobi looks at Darth Vader and says, "Go ahead and strike me down. I will become more powerful than you can ever imagine!" Then Darth Vader does strike him down, and Obi's body disappears—and he does, of course, become more powerful than ever and from his discarnate state he helps Luke Skywalker fight the Evil Empire. Well, I mention this again because, while I was playing, I felt as if Gloria too had graduated, and that in her transition she had not only grown more powerful but also had given all of us a set of wings. I could feel her newfound and her deserved freedom. Our tribute was lifting all of us up, especially me, to a whole new level of being.

As Gloria passed the performance from her CD recording over to us "earthly performers," the audience was mesmerized and groovin' to the soulful sweet pocket of the ending vamp. And, just when no one thought we could go any higher, Stevie Wonder, who I thought had left after his last number, came up on stage. We passed him the lead vocal mike and away he went and away we all went.

I really felt that the whole place was going to be transported to Gloria's stage—it was ridiculous! Stevie was "blowing" rifts from heaven, the background singers were singing phrases never rehearsed, and the band and I were laying a heavenly carpet of sound for all to float on. The jam lasted almost 20 minutes, and the ovation that followed another 20.

When the applause died down, I grabbed the microphone, looked up to the sky, and said, "That was for you, baby! I love you eternally. Do well!"

Not only had Gloria's journey begun, but my own journey to love had begun as well.

Chapter 31

Talking to Stevie Wonder

I can't tell you the number of people who came up to me afterward to tell me they had been touched in some way; probably it was well over 100. Each of them said unequivocally that it was not only the best concert they had ever attended, but that the deep love that Gloria and I had had and still had, had inspired them to improve their own relationships. No more taking each other for granted! They seemed almost jealous of our love—and I was the one who had just lost his wife horrifically! What a twist!

Then, as if that weren't enough already, on the way out I saw Stevie Wonder sitting in his car in the parking lot. Even though we'd already said our good-byes, he called me over and wanted to talk to me some more. I got in the car, and we all talked for over two hours.

We covered some very remarkable territory. Stevie talked about his main pain—his blindness. That blindness had been the first time that life had ever really bared its teeth and bit him. He talked about how he had used his pain along with his gift to reach out to people and spread the gospel of love. He said that he often got called to memorials and tributes to lend a hand and help out, but that he saw now that God had wanted him to come to Gloria's tribute to be touched himself. He told me that the deep love Gloria and I had for each other had touched everybody in the room and that it was a gift in itself. He said we probably hadn't realized it yet, but not many people ever achieved that level of love during their earthly existence. And not all of those who did had the spiritual awareness and ability to turn it into something special.

Stevie said that he had realized early on that his special talent and his "handicap" were not a coincidence. Such a combination was always a gift, he said, and therefore it should be used to touch people, to wake them up to the message of unconditional love. Stevie told me: "That's why this evening, this tribute you did for your wife, was so inspirational for everybody. You and Gloria experienced the 'joy of pain.' The deep pain of your mutual loss is also the source of your deep joy, and those who also have the gift of talent have a responsibility through that talent to share their joy and pain in order to touch others." He felt that if we didn't, then the world didn't have much of a chance to reverse itself from its present downward-spiraling trend.

While Stevie was sharing his insights, things began to come together in my mind. Why had I felt this need to finish Gloria's CD after she was gone? Why had I felt the need to do this tribute? Why were we both talented in the manner that we were? Why did Gloria have to go so early on, in the prime of life and in such a horrific manner? I was beginning to see what my own journey was all about. I recalled that Gloria had always had the ability to walk into a room and uplift all those with whom she came in contact. I was able to do this, too, but not as easily as Gloria. She had that something special. Through her previous losses she had, of course, already experienced the "joy of pain." That was why she had shared her love so easily, why she was so easy to love. People always told me that when they saw Gloria they immediately felt better and felt they could just go over and talk to her, even though they didn't even know her. Now that life had "bitten" me, my "joy of pain" had also been tapped into.

It seemed to me that it was now my responsibility to use my newfound spiritual awareness to encourage and comfort others, to uplift and enlighten them and to teach them how to use love to break through their own illusions and misconceptions. It would be a sin for me not to try to shine all over the world the light that Gloria and I had found. Perhaps I was now a member of that fraternity of spirits who had the ability and the obligation to do this; that was what Stevie had seemed to be trying to tell me. It was an honor, and I hoped I had the courage to follow through.

I wasn't at all thrilled at the fees I'd had to pay to get into this club.

Chapter 32

Jason

When I was growing up, I never thought I'd be writing books about music, let alone about a terminal disease like cancer. And, for sure, I never thought I'd be writing about love.

And yet, that was most of all what Gloria and I learned from Gloria's cancer. It taught us what love was, and it taught us how to love.

Why is this such a difficult assignment—finding love, that is? In hindsight, I'd say it's like trying to find our car keys when they're right in our hands, or like a thirsty fish looking for water. It's not something that is given to us; it's not something we can buy; on the contrary, it *is* us! We are the source. We create this amazing energy that is common to all and that connects all.

When we operate from the highest part of ourselves, love is what comes naturally. When we operate from the coarsest parts of our physical selves, selfishness and self-importance may replace love and may blind us. It appears that until we surrender our selfish selves, love is not only invisible, but not even sought after. And how could there be a sadder state of affairs?

As a boy growing up in Erie, Pennsylvania, I didn't have the faintest idea that life is love and love is life. How was I to learn this lesson? How could I come to surrender my selfish attachments and operating basis, especially when I didn't even know I had them?

Looking back on it now, I'd have to say the answer was that I was going to have to experience some losses.

As a child, I never experienced the loss of a pet dog, or a cat, or a bird, because we didn't have any pets. True, I lost my grandparents, but somehow I got over that quickly once I'd been told they'd gone to heaven; perhaps I sensed the naturalness of it all. Like any small and selfish boy, by and large I took for granted my "good" life—its relationships, the roof over our heads, my loving parents, my toys, food, money and so forth. I thought everyone had exactly what I had.

The only loss that impinged on me just a little during my days of living at home was when my first serious girlfriend left me. I was very naïve; I had no clue that in a relationship there are two people, and that both of them are supposed to give as well as take. In this relationship, all I did was take. I took sex, which she willingly gave, giving more than I gave her. I called her up when it suited me, rarely thinking about what suited her. She seemed so willing to give—and I was so willing to accept!

One day I got very excited about some turn my career had taken, and out of the blue I called her up to share the excitement with me. I expected her to answer the phone with her usual effervescence and be just as excited as I was about my wonderful news. I suggested that she and I and her dog go to the beach and have a really good time. To tell you the truth, I really liked her and she really liked me. However, when I heard her voice on the phone that day I knew that something was wrong. She told me it was okay to come over; in fact, she had something to tell me, she said. And so, slightly puzzled, I went over.

To make a long story short, she dumped me that afternoon. While we were sitting on her front steps, after she had told me the bad news, her new boyfriend arrived. I was devastated. How could I have been so blind? I hadn't telephoned her in three weeks; I'd expected her to be on standby until the great John Novello called.

I was shocked to see how this affected me mentally and physically. I went into grief and depression. I couldn't eat or sleep. I called her up constantly and I made a fool of myself, because all I did was apologize and ingratiate myself and promise her I'd make it up to her. But, no dice! It didn't work.

This went on for two weeks—this period in which, I now realize in hindsight, I had a great opportunity for personal growth—until I started going out with her best friend. I had originally met with this best friend to see if she could help me get my girlfriend back. But it turned out that this best friend of my former girlfriend had a crush on me herself, but hadn't dared let me know because I was dating her best friend. But now that I knew how she felt, and had also been dumped by that girlfriend, well, one thing led to another, and soon we were going out together.

My ego monster was appeased. I had gotten even with my former girlfriend; when she found out I was dating her best friend, she got angry and wrote me a letter. The lesson I learned was that you can't trust girls. They cheat on you the minute you ignore them. As you can see, I wasn't ready to learn lessons yet—at least, not the right ones. This was a missed opportunity. I had some distance to go.

But, when I was 21, something happened to spur my growth apparently in the only way that could make an impression on me at the time. It occurred after I had moved to Boston and was studying jazz at the Berklee College of Music. Since I was no longer living in my parents' house, I had started to take responsibility for my life. I had to pay rent for my shared apartment. I had to buy groceries and pay for utilities. This was hard for me to face up to, but then one day I had realized, "Hey, this is my place. I can do whatever I want. I can make it messy or I can make it clean or I can write on the walls or I can put posters or anything I want up on the walls." I couldn't put posters up on the walls at home. I used to envy some of my friends' rooms when I went over to their houses, seeing what they were allowed to do in that department. My parents were very tidy and strict and, although such an attitude has its good points, it also has its bad ones.

One day, while living in my own if shared apartment in Boston, I decided to get a dog. I was very excited, not only about making the decision without having to ask anybody for permission, but also about having this new responsibility. I went to the pound, as I didn't have enough money to buy a purebred. I found a wonderful mutt there, part retriever, part shepherd. This was a very spirited mutt, who practically reached out of his cage and said, "Take me!" I took him, and for $15.00 I had myself my very own dog. I named him Jason. And, guess what: I *loved* him.

Boy, did I love Jason! I felt so different. Life was somehow so much better. I couldn't wait to wake up in the morning just to see him and play with him and take care of him and make him happy. Why did doing all this make me feel so good? At the time, I didn't know and I didn't care. I loved him and he loved me, and that was all. There were no conditions either, no "I love you *if* this" or "I love you *if* that." It was my first experience of true unconditional love.

Then, one day, I took Jason to the park where he loved to run and go crazy and play with the other dogs. I had bought him when he was three months old and now he was seven months old, still a pup. But he was chasing a female dog who was in heat when, all of a sudden, she ran out into the street. Jason followed. It was as if it were all planned out, my first heavy lesson in life. There was nothing I could do. Jason chased the dog out into the street. She escaped, but he didn't; a car ran over him.

When I reached my dog I was in shock and so was he. I picked him up off the middle of the street and laid him on the grass. The woman who was driving the car got out and started apologizing. I yelled at her because she was speeding—and how dare she even insinuate that it was Jason's fault! But he was still alive and probably had internal injuries, so I made her drive us to the vet. When I went to put him in the back seat, she was worried about getting blood on her leather upholstery. I gave her the evil eye, and she got the point.

It took 20 minutes for us to get to the animal hospital, and all the while she drove Jason was in my arms, looking up at me as if to say, "What happened, Dad? Help me. I'm sorry. It hurts. Please help me." This was ripping my heart out. We finally arrived at the hospital. The lady ran in and got someone from the emergency room. He came out and they put Jason on a stretcher and brought him in. I actually saw his life force leave him as we went into the room. All attempts at revival were fruitless. The attendants gave me their condolences and asked if I wanted them to take care of his remains, no charge. I was in shock! We had just been playing, and now he was gone! I said, yes, take care of his remains.

I walked outside with Jason's leash, and the woman gave me a ride back home and apologized all the way. I barely heard her, as I was in the middle of my first serious instance of loss. I had just lost the first life that I really and truly loved, and it hurt. And then there was the guilt. My dog was so pure and innocent. I had let him play in a dangerous area. My irresponsibility had cost him his barely begun life! Loss and guilt—these were two feelings that I had never experienced before, at least not on this level.

I opened the door to my apartment and my two roommates asked me where Jason was. I told them what had happened and blew into my room and closed the door. They came in immediately, as they didn't believe me. When I finally got it across that I wasn't joking, and that Jason really had died, they left the room in grief. We were all crying.

That night I had a gig. I had been crying all day. I had never experienced such uncontrollable grief, and just over a damn dog! How could this be? I was feeling so many emotions—grief, apathy, pain, guilt—that I could barely play the organ. My drummer knew what had happened so he did his best to hang in there with me. The next number was a blues. I started playing this twelve-bar blues, and within a couple of seconds I was playing the blues like the blues were meant to be played. "That's why they called it the blues," I thought to myself. When you were feeling kind of "blue," this was a song form that allowed you to express yourself. So I played that tune for Jason, and every note was on fire with my love for him. Our love and now our loss were the driving force of my communication. One door had closed and another had opened. The audience went crazy.

After it was over, my drummer told me he'd never heard me play like that before.

"Like what?" I asked.

He explained: "Every note seemed perfect, so honest and meaningful."

"Well, of course," I said. "Those notes were for Jason."

With hindsight, I see now that those notes were love and love is the spirit. It's what we are. It's our soul. When you love someone "unconditionally"—with true love—you're saying that you love the highest part of yourself. And when you love yourself in that way, your true power and glory and honesty and integrity shine through.

But did my lesson stay with me? Not really. The distractions of the physical universe, the survival obligations we all have—and of course let's not forget my selfish ego—all these soon made that lesson dwindle to a mere memory. Every once in a while, I could tap the feeling in my memory of Jason for some spirit, for some soul, for some love, but I couldn't make that feeling last. The physical universe and its entanglements were still an obstacle in my path. I wasn't yet effort-lessly operating from unconditional love. The lesson was valuable, but it didn't quite stick. My life merely continued.

Chapter 33

Zarathustra

I decided to get another dog, for I still had this need to fill. I loved German shepherds. I knew purebreds were much more expensive but I felt I had to get one. I looked in the paper for dogs for sale. I saw an ad from a breeder about a shepherd that needed a home. I went out to visit the breeder and see the dog.

The breeder warned me that when she brought the dog into the house, I might be shocked because he was so skinny. She assured me that he was healthy, but that he had been abused by his previous owners. He had been tied in a dark hallway and barely played with. She had gotten the dog the week before but this shepherd was very solitary, introverted and mistrustful of humans.

She went out and got the dog. And she was right. When I saw him, I thought, My God, I don't want this baggage! I was about to tell her to forget it, but then something from somewhere, my inner voice, told me that I should get this dog. Looking back on it now, I can see that this was a pretty weird happening.

The dog wouldn't even come over to me. It just went to the far corner of the breeder's living room and lay down. We talked for about an hour, and I decided to take it home with the agreement that I could bring it back if things did not work out. The dog jumped into my van and off we went. Its solitary behavior continued. All the way home and then into my apartment, it just found its own spot and lay down. It wasn't really afraid as much as mistrustful. This went on for three days. It barely ate. My new dog just drank water, nibbled on its food, and went outside on leash to do its business.

Then, on the fourth day, I took this new dog out for his last walk. I had decided that I was going to take him back. I was strangely in love with this animal, though, with this life force. There was something special here; I just knew it. I hadn't given him a name, but then for some reason the theme of Richard Strauss's tone poem *Thus Spake Zarathustra* had gone running through my head. This melody was made famous by Stanley Kubrick's *2001: A Space Odyssey*. I looked at my dog and said, "Zarathustra! What's wrong with you, man?"

He was on my leash and still moping along apathetically. Though he was only 11 months old, he was acting like an old retired dog. But when I said his new name he looked up at me with quite a different attitude. He wanted me to let him off his leash.

I was scared to death to do this. The last time I'd let a dog off his leash, he had run into the street and gotten killed. Yet for some reason, this one was telling me it was okay. I let him off his leash and said, "You're free, buddy. You're free!" He looked at me in a very surprised way, then took off down the sidewalk like a bullet.

I thought, Christ! Here we go again. I fucked up!

He ran about 50 yards and then put on the brakes. Then he turned around and charged me and ran right by me. He turned around again and charged me again. He was playing! He was having fun!

We played for over an hour, and then when it was time to go home he came over to my side and heeled like he had been fully trained. We got home and he ate like a bear. We were finally buds. I had trusted him and that was all he needed. We became best friends. I took him to guard dog school and in no time he became the best in his class. During our five years together in Boston, he saved me from a mugging and twice protected us from a robbery. Zara became an unbelievable friend and bodyguard.

When I moved out to California in 1978, he, of course, came with me. One night, Carol, my girlfriend at the time, took him with her when she went to get her paycheck from the club she worked at. I was on tour at the time. Carol left him in the van. When she came back she got in the van and drove away. Then she noticed that Zara was very uneasy and riled up. She turned on the light, as it was nighttime, and noticed blood all over the seat and shotgun window.

Carol pulled over and saw that Zara had been cut badly on his nose and gums. She immediately rushed him to the emergency room. By the time they got there, Zara was in shock from loss of blood—but he pulled through and was released after 15 stitches.

Carol called me on the road. I flew home the next day, since I had two days off from the tour. I wanted to be with Zara. I loved him so much. There was this incredible feeling again of unconditional love. Wow! What *was* this feeling? It was amazing. There was nothing better than it—nothing!

It was at this time that I met Gloria and it was love at first sight. There was that feeling again. Before we knew it, we were living together. Gloria loved Zara, too. He was an awesome being in the body of a dog. He also knew what unconditional love was, and gave it back to you like a true master.

Now Zara was 11 years old and doing quite well. He had minor hip problems, but other than that this dog was a cool cat for his age. Then one day, during our walk, Zara kept dragging his behind. Apparently he was in pain; I eventually had to carry him home. He wouldn't eat. Gloria and I took him to the vet at 9:00 that night, leaving him in emergency care so the vet could do some diagnostic tests. I did not have a good feeling when I left him there all alone in a cage. He looked at me when I left like he was scared. Then, at 1:00 A.M., the vet called to tell me that Zara had just passed away, suddenly, from respiratory arrest. I drove down to the vet's immediately, in shock. I went into the room where Zara was and petted him and hugged his lifeless body for a half-hour.

I had the vet do an autopsy. He found out that Zara's spleen and liver were loaded with cancer. Zara was bleeding internally, which is why he had been behaving like he had. He had probably had the cancer for a while. Gloria and I went home devastated. It was December 20, just days before Christmas. I thought that the loss of Jason, my first dog, was heavy. That was nothing.

Talk about guilt!

You see, during the last years of Zara's life I had become very busy, and I wasn't taking as many walks to the park with him as I had or playing with him as much. I was taking him for granted. He depended on me for his quality playtime and for our friendship, and I had become too busy. And then I left him, all alone, in a vet's cold cage, to die. What a selfish jerk I'd been!

Those were just some of the regrets and guilt trips that I was experiencing. They lasted for a good three weeks. My Christmas sucked. When was I going to get this lesson right, this lesson of unselfish love? Little did I know that, though I was growing, I still had a long way to go.

Chapter 34

Bronco

Of course, I regressed again. I got an incredible new shepherd named Bronco, and started taking almost everything for granted again. Going after my career goals always seemed to activate selfishness in me. The obsession to be successful, though a valid goal in itself, carried with it this side effect of ego, of self-importance, of taking for granted things not connected to my career. Gloria and I were forging ahead with our careers, and everything was just fine—or so we thought.

It wasn't true. In hindsight, I see that we had gotten so obsessed with "making it" that, however close we were, we were becoming just best friends and roommates and weren't even aware that, ever so slowly, the true love that had brought us together was dwindling.

I see now that this affected Bronco. Eventually, at the age of nine, he contracted cancer. There was that "C" word again. I did everything possible to save him, but it was to no avail. A tumor on his heart was causing fluid buildup around his heart and in his lungs. He was suffocating to death, and I let my vet persuade me that he ought to be put to sleep. Boy, was that my next lesson! I had never put any living thing to sleep. The concept went against every grain of my being— but I couldn't stand to see him suffer any more.

Looking back on it now, I realize that that attitude was a very selfish one. Life is life, and every minute of it is precious. Whether we're in joy or pain, no one should take away from us our chance to grow some more. Every minute enfolds a precious learning experience for every living being.

When we'd gone to the vet that night, Bronco had gotten into the van on his own, which should have been a signal to me that I shouldn't have him put to asleep. While we were on our way, he hung his head outside the window just like he always did, to feel the cool wind on his face. When we got to the vet, we even took a walk down the street and Bronco did his business. True, he was weak and had hardly eaten anything in two weeks, but he was still walking around on his own, even though his breathing had gotten worse and worse.

I met with my vet and he examined him. I told the vet that if he saw any sign at all that Bronco might be able to beat this, then I was not going to have the vet put him to sleep. But after the examination the vet told me that Bronco had no chance at all. The fluid around his heart and in his lungs was steadily building up, and soon—either tonight or over the next few days—his condition would get very bad and he would begin to suffer a lot.

I asked to be alone with Bronco. We hugged and exchanged lots of love. It was awesome, but it was also very upsetting. The vet came in and asked me if I wanted to be in the room. Of course, I said. I hugged Bronco while they gave him the shot.

What was supposed to happen was that within seconds of the shot Bronco would begin to slowly fall asleep in my arms. The vet gave him the shot—but after ten seconds nothing had happened. "What's going on, David?" I asked the vet.

He told me he didn't know; that this was most unusual. At that moment I wanted to cancel the mission, to abort it, since for me this failure of the drug to work was a sign that I had made the wrong decision. But just then Bronco stiffened every muscle in his body. He was a fighter, and he was not about to just lie down and die. He looked up at me as if to say, "John, no. I wasn't ready yet. I had more to do and experience. How could you?" Then, after a fight of about 20 seconds that seemed like an eternity, he went to sleep in my arms.

I cried for 10 minutes. Eventually, I left. I was now into life's next lesson—heavy guilt. I felt like I had betrayed Bronco. I had lured him into the van to take the ride he'd always loved to take, and I had brought him here—and here I had put him to sleep. I felt like a murderer; I sincerely did. It took weeks and longer for me to recover from what

I'd done. The fact that I'd saved Zara some pain seemed to me like no good deed at all. What I had done instead was take from him his last days of growth and experience in the physical universe. I had played God; without his permission, I had forced him to leave his body.

How precious each one of our lives is: That was the lesson in all this, and this time I'd really learned it. Comforting someone in pain near the end and loving them is the correct thing to do. This I learned the hard way. I'll never forget the look on Bronco's face. Even the vet was stunned. I had betrayed my wonderful dog, and for what? Because I, not him, couldn't confront the pain he was in. Mind you that: *I* couldn't confront his pain. How selfish! There he was, confronting it and living out his life to the end with unconditional love. But I—selfishly, because of the pain and stress his life was causing in my own—put him "out of his misery!" In hindsight, I can see that it was more like I put myself "out of my misery!" How revoltingly selfish! Where was the love? Where was the understanding?

I had yet more lessons to learn. Five months transpired before I had the courage to even get another dog. But then, all of a sudden, I started getting the urge, a very strong urge, to have a dog again. So I looked in the paper, and I was drawn to a kennel that had a litter of shepherd pups for sale.

Gloria and I visited the kennel and, though the pups were adorable, none of them bonded with me in the way that would have persuaded me to buy it. However, while the breeder and I were talking Gloria interrupted me, telling me to turn around and look into the dog pen. I looked, and sure enough, one of the pups—the only one I'd even remotely considered, since he was beautifully shaped and his ears stood straight up even though he was only seven weeks old— was pawing at the cage and beaming out at me as if to say, "Hey, I'm the one. Take me the hell out of here!" I went over to the cage. The breeder was a bit surprised, since all the pups were sleeping and for this particular one to wake up and do that was a bit strange. He let the pup out and I played with it, and we immediately bonded very strongly.

Gloria and I felt that we knew exactly what had happened. We were sure the immortal spirit of Bronco, my previous dog, had hung out with us after his death and then had reincarnated as this pup. The more we thought about it, the more we were convinced this was the case. During the five months since he'd passed away Bronco had been giving us signs around the house that he was still with us. I had been considering not getting another dog. But I had changed my mind when, one day, I could have sworn that I got, right out of the blue, a clear message from my late pet, which said, in effect, "Hey, man. I don't want to hang out here in the hereafter any longer. I want a new body to play the game of life with, and I want you to be my master." It was this communication that had made me start looking for a dog again. It was why we were at this kennel.

I bought the dog on the spot and we took him home. Sure enough, within two days he found a bone that he had buried in his previous lifetime as Bronco and began to demonstrate in all sorts of ways that he was indeed the spirit of Bronco reincarnated. One incident in particular erased any doubts in my mind as to whether this was true: this was that our new pup would not, of his own accord, and for any reason, jump into our red jeep. It wasn't that he *couldn't* jump into the jeep; it was that, even when he was nine months old, he *wouldn't* jump into the jeep.

We finally figured it out. The last ride that Bronco had taken in that red jeep had been the ride to the vet's—and there I had betrayed him, had had him put to sleep. For our new pup the red jeep was a reminder, a déjà vu, of that previous-lifetime incident. In his last lifetime, he had experienced being a great guard dog, then getting a cancer that was killing him—then getting put to sleep by a selfish, frightened master. His master had gotten to experience another loss, and then the guilt of taking a life before its scheduled time. Society may have approved of my putting Bronco to sleep—but that hadn't made it right for me to interfere with the karmic progression of a soul, with the spiritual development of that being who was Bronco.

He knew I had regretted putting him to sleep and had learned my lesson, and so he wanted to hang out with me and complete our relationship. This was for me an incredible revelation of the power of the immortality of the spirit and of love. I named my new puppy Odin, and at the time of this writing we are still best buds. During Gloria's fight with cancer, Odin protected her and would not allow any strangers near her who were not sanctioned by me. He did, however, get on Gloria's bad side a few times by digging up the backyard, and he almost ran her over a few 100 times by playing too rough, so he has his own karmic debt to repay her at some time. And, of course, he too misses her now, which is I guess a loss he himself must experience. In other words, he has his own dues to pay.

And so, after all these losses of my pets and the respective lessons that these losses taught me concerning love and selfishness, here I was, a better person. And, in hindsight, I would have to say that these were but prerequisite challenges, to prepare me for an even bigger one—my own wife's fight with cancer.

Chapter 35

Looking for Proof

In *Adventures Beyond the Body*, William Buhlman asserts that "each life is an interactive school, a relentless training ground for developing souls." This is my view. I believe death is simply a movement of awareness from one dimension to another. I have held this belief all my life. And it was brought home to me with tremendous force when, after the passing of Gloria, I found myself still in amazing—this time interdimensional—communication with her.

Still, if I'm a jazz musician who's been steeped in paranormal experiences and study all his life, I'm also someone who majored in math and physics at university and has always had a great respect for the scientific method. And, if I'm a jazz musician who, when he sits down at the Hammond B3 organ, is able to bring emotional power to his playing by letting loose the love in his heart, that doesn't make me a man who has recently lost his mind!

So now, when it came to my amazing post-death experiences with Gloria, I needed more than subjective experience—I needed objective third-party corroboration. I wanted irrefutable evidence that this interdimensional relationship was real, that it wasn't just wishful thinking on my part because I couldn't let her go. I wanted to know that my best friend and lover was indeed okay. We had always said that we would depart this lifetime together. I felt bad that this hadn't occurred, and I wanted to make sure that she was hanging out with me of her own volition and not because I was taking her loss so hard. If she was waiting for me to complete my work and join her, or helping me in whatever way she was able, then that was fine. But I did not want to keep her around babysitting me if she had better things to do. If she and I could have this special new relationship, and it was good for us both, then that was great. Or, if she had already reincarnated, then, so be it; I'd catch up with her again later on.

Whatever was going on, I needed to know for sure.

My intuition told me that everything that was happening was real, and that the scenario I have set forth in the earlier chapters of this section was no less than the truth. But, as strong as my intuitions were about these paranormal happenings, my conditioned "Western" mind could not help but have its doubts. A phrase we often hear is, "If it's too good to be true, then it's probably not." This was certainly too good to be true. My experiences were in the realm of the miraculous. I'm sure you'll agree that what I was experiencing made winning a Grammy or an Oscar, or the Lotto, look trivial by comparison. I mean, your wife gets cancer in the prime of her life and after a horrific struggle of more than a year she dies in your arms. Your best friend, your lover, your artistic partner, is ripped from your life in a most hideous manner by a disease that slowly and painfully eats away her body right before your eyes, despite all of your efforts to stop it.

And then you discover, through actual personal experience, that not only did your wife not really die, but she is still here with you! And along with this wonderful miracle, you no longer have any fear of death. In fact, you're enthusiastically looking forward to completing your life's work because you're certain that, whatever place you go to after death, you will rejoin her there.

It was all too much to take. I needed reassurance that these experiences were for real. Even though I had had and was still having numerous subjective encounters with Gloria's continued existence, I knew that, if I could have some objective confirmation, then I could truly handle all of my remaining doubts. This I needed, and this I wanted.

I'm sure this is true for you, the reader, as well. I'm sure many of you haven't been able to keep yourselves from saying, with the best will in the world: Is he merely obsessed with his wife and the other side? Could he possibly just be in a colossal state of denial? Shouldn't he just be putting all this behind him and getting on with his life?

I know where you're coming from. Though basically I could not deny my powerful intuition that all that was happening was objectively true, still, I too needed third-party corroboration.

Such corroboration began to come to me in March 2000, when I was working on Gloria's life tribute CD.

Chapter 36

Shauvon Senses Gloria

Alan Howarth is my partner in our film company Lunatek (we write music for feature films) and has a studio suite right next to mine. At the time, he was producing a meditation CD for a client who was a medium.

A medium, as is well known, is a person who is allegedly able to receive direct communications from the dead. Alan had mentioned to the medium, whose name was Shauvon Sullivan, that my wife had passed away six weeks before and that I was interested in trying to contact her. She had told Alan that she usually didn't do a reading that early, since it took most disembodied beings some time to adjust to the fact that they were "dead."

Given what was happening to me, I thought that perhaps things might be different for Gloria, that she might have made the adjustment rather quickly. I asked Alan if he would introduce me to Shauvon.

Sure, he said. And, the next time she came to see him, he brought her around to meet me in my studio.

Immediately she took a step backward, exclaiming, "Oh, my God!"

"What's wrong?" I asked, bewildered.

She said, "Well, I don't know if it's all right to talk to you about your wife at this point, because I don't know you, but I'm amazed that your wife is so willing to come through this early." "Come through" meant willing to contact a mortal on this side.

"It's okay," I reassured her. "She's been messing with my mind for the past six weeks. It would be good to get objective data to prove or disprove some of the phenomena that's been going on around me."

Shauvon said, "For now, I can tell you that she's right next to you and has been for a while. I can see you two were soul mates. There's a stronger than usual love bond here for sure. Stronger than I have ever seen, in fact."

I stared at her in amazement. That certainly rang true!

Shauvon went on: "She's really enjoying the fact that you're finishing her CD. She loves how it's turning out and is very proud of it. She's very grateful."

These words brought tears to my eyes. Shauvon had a suggestion. "I'll tell you what. I have about an hour's work I have to do with Alan. Once I'm done, let's actually meet for about an hour and really get into it, since when I came in my mind was not totally ready to do a reading."

Needless to say, I agreed. "Fine!"

I met with Shauvon in Alan's suite about an hour later. I'd never had a reading before. Purportedly, genuine mediums work by simply translating the communications from the departed loved ones who appear to them and know the readee. The medium relays this information to the readee, who can then confirm or deny it. Since the spirits want their loved ones to know it's them for sure and that they are all right, usually they try really hard to give the medium the data that will prove this. Or such is the theory.

No drugs or hypnotism or Tarot cards were used in our reading, or any props at all. Shauvon did not slip into a trance state, which is very often the case with sessions of this sort. She simply began relaying to me various communications she was picking up from Gloria. She gave these to me while she was fully awake.

What I was looking for was information from Gloria that only Gloria and I could know. The generalities that the medium had earlier passed along to me—that Gloria was next to me and loved me a lot—were nice, and perhaps true, but they did not prove anything. That was why I had never been too impressed by the psychics I'd seen on TV; I didn't know if the people in the audiences were plants or not.

The first few messages that Shauvon relayed were pretty general. Then the medium got my undivided attention when she said Gloria was telling her about a favorite romantic spot that we had both loved.

The medium said this place was far away, on a deserted beach. She wasn't getting the name, but she said it was our favorite place on the whole earth. This was true. Moreover, it was one of the last things I'd talked about with Gloria, when she was incoherent and shortly before she passed on. I'd said, "Baby, remember all the good times we had at Larsen's Beach in Kauai?" She had squeezed my arm several times in joyful agreement. So, needless to say, what I was hearing now was pretty amazing.

After ten minutes more of generalities, the medium told me something even more arresting. She said she saw Gloria standing next to me holding hands with a child, a little boy. Shauvon asked me if we had lost a little boy. At first, I said no. Then it dawned on me: Could Gloria be trying to tell her about the abortion she had had because of the danger of her having a child with her high blood pressure? Gloria had never felt good about having that abortion, and neither had I.

In some of the esoteric literature that fascinated both Gloria and myself, I had read that when a being decided to incarnate and the mother had to abort it, that being went back to the afterworld until it decided to reincarnate again. Now, apparently, Gloria was with the spirit form of the being who had been our intended son.

Or maybe Gloria was just making all this up, creating a sort of thought-picture to get this message through to me. It seems to me that, in the afterworld where there is nothing physical, it must be very easy to turn your thoughts into reality, since "reality," whatever it is over there, is not weighed down by the physical. But it didn't really matter whether Gloria was standing beside the spirit of our intended child or just making all this up for my benefit. The point was, how could the medium have known about any of this at all? There was no way!

A few more items like this came up during the reading, and I walked away a believer. I decided I would search out some of the best mediums around and do readings with them, then compare the data and see if it lent credibility to all that was happening to me. My reading with Shauvon had been a success; it had made me feel better and it had validated my own perceptions and moved me closer to being able to accept and carry on this new type of relationship—this interdimensional relationship!—that I was having with Gloria.

Chapter 37

Strolling through Meadows of Joy

The next third-party corroboration I received came about quite by accident. But it was sensational. In June 2000, five months after Gloria had moved on, I was staying with my good friends Dick and Patti Zimmerman in Florida for a couple of weeks. Dick is a well-known fashion photographer who had photographed Gloria and myself a number of times. I told him about the amazing communications that were seemingly coming to me from my wife. Dick shares many of my beliefs, and so he did not doubt that I was really having these experiences. He told me about a couple of strange things that had happened to him just after his father had passed away.

At one point while we were talking about Gloria and about how she seemed to be hanging around and communicating with me, Dick told me that, one night a few weeks before, he had been sitting alone in the entertainment room when he had felt his hair being flicked from behind. He turned around, thinking it must be Michael Fairman, a mutual friend of ours who was staying in the house at the time.

But, to Dick's surprise, nobody was there. He instantly picked up the message that this was Gloria and her way of saying hello to him. He told Michael about what had happened, that it was just too real, and that he was sure his hair had actually been flicked.

My response to Dick was that given all the phenomena I'd already experienced and the fact that we were all close friends, I wouldn't put it past Gloria to have done that. I added that before she had moved on, Gloria and I had made an agreement that, if she could, she would attempt to communicate with me, and that I should be prepared.

Dick and I then retired for the night. His wife Patti was out of town, so we were both alone by ourselves in the house.

At about 6:00 A.M. I was awakened by a loud jolting noise. Since I'm from California I thought at first it must be an earthquake. But I was in Florida, and this type of jolt didn't make any sense. I looked across at the large picture window in my room and saw that the branch of a palm tree was smacking against the top of the window. This explained the noise—a gust of wind had caused the branch to bend— but I thought to myself that this was strange since it wasn't at all windy that night and the branch had struck the window only the one time. Oh, well, I thought, who cares? I got up, went to the bathroom, and then came back to bed. I turned my back to the window and tried to get back to sleep.

I'd been lying there for a few minutes, and was in that subtle state of consciousness between wakefulness and sleep called hypnagogic, when all of a sudden I heard, loud and clear from behind me, "Hey, John! It's Gloria!"

I'm not talking about a telepathic communication or a concept in my mind. I'm saying that I heard a real physical-universe communication, the type that comes out of a person's mouth—in this case, my wife's mouth. I would know her sweet voice anywhere.

I immediately turned around, but I didn't see anything. But my intuition told me Gloria was there. How she had managed to perform this stunt I didn't know, since I would have thought that, without a body with vocal chords, such a feat would not be possible.

But I acknowledged Gloria's presence. Not only was I getting used to these paranormal occurrences, but by now I was intensely caught up in them. After all, this could be my deceased wife, talking to me from the other side! I had read that spirits sometimes try to communicate with us through our dreams because during sleep our conscious minds are inactive, so I decided to go back to sleep and see if perhaps Gloria and I could continue the conversation that way.

And, sure enough, I had the most vivid lucid dream I have ever had, one in which Gloria and I not only caught up on all our news, but also went strolling in an incredible meadow, holding hands and enjoying nature and each other's company just as we always had.

When I woke up, I remembered everything, and I felt thoroughly invigorated and refreshed. I can assure you that this was no dream. In retrospect, I can only theorize that what happened was that, somehow, Gloria actually called my name at 6:00 A.M. I then went back to sleep with the express purpose of getting us both into actual communication. Our love is so strong that, apparently, I slipped out of my own body and visited her in her world, on the other side. Whether I did this on my own or whether Gloria helped me, I don't know, nor, frankly, do I care. I have read about this procedure in Sylvia Browne's *The Other Side and Back,* and now I had discovered that, sure enough, it worked. I use the technique quite frequently now, and, more often than not it is successful.

For those readers who are skeptical and think I was just dreaming, read on, for the story is not over and I have something amazing to add.

I got up three hours later. As I was going into the kitchen to fix breakfast, Dick came out of his bedroom looking pretty wired. I started to tell him about my far-out, paranormal night. He stopped me, saying, "Before you tell me your story, do I have a wild story to tell you!"

He proceeded to tell me that "at approximately 6:00 A.M., give or take a few minutes, I was awakened by a big jolt and some strong gusty wind. I tried to go back to sleep, but before I could I heard my name being called: 'Hey, Dick.'"

He said he'd heard these words out loud, and that he knew it was Gloria's voice. Then, "I turned around and saw a holographic apparition of Gloria, which promptly freaked the hell out of me. I turned back around and tried to go to sleep, but I had a very restless next three hours thinking about what had just happened."

As you can well imagine, I almost couldn't keep my mouth shut while he was telling me this story. When he was done, I told him mine. That actually made both of us feel much better, because our stories corroborated each other. Believe me, when you're dealing with the paranormal and with departed loved ones, you need objective confirmation, as otherwise it's pretty easy to think you're going nuts, even when your background is a reasonably solid one.

This experience led me to the discovery that the best time for Gloria and me to visit is when I am sleeping. At that time my analytical mind is asleep and I am free of many of this physically-dense universe's entanglements. In the same way as when I lucid dream I fly around in my dreams, I also seem able to increase my openness to Gloria far beyond the ordinary when I sleep. I'm even getting better at it when I'm awake, by relaxing my body and focusing my attention on communicating with her. However, this latter is more difficult, as my waking attention usually is already pretty well focused on the goings-on "on this side."

Author/physicist Alan Wolf believes that lucid dreams are visits to parallel universes. He maintains that the experience of lucid dreaming might better be termed "parallel universe awareness." His speculations conform with my own experiences. My lucid dreams don't feel like normal dreams. They feel as real as physical reality itself—sometimes even realer.

Most of us are raised to regard night dreams as the meaningless ramblings of our sleeping inner selves. Can you imagine how many compelling dream visitations and out-of-body explorations we might be going through without our even knowing it? There are new worlds within each and every one of us, if only we will look at them.

Chapter 38

A Hug from the Afterworld

Not only do I communicate with Gloria through dreams, but I also have an experience with her that I call a "spiritual hug" or for short a "SH." This experience is mentioned fairly often in the literature. The first time it happened to me, I wasn't quite sure what was occurring. I've already told you how, shortly after Gloria passed away, I was getting ready to go to bed when I felt a cold but loving sensation pass right through my chest area. That feeling was absolutely incredible, and it immediately made me think of Gloria.

Now I see that, at the time, I unfortunately wasn't ready for this kind of "heavenly" communication. What had occurred then, and what is commonplace for me now, was that Gloria, in spirit-form, had given me a spiritual loving hug. This kind of interdimensional contact can literally overwhelm the mind and body. That was what was happening to me on that first night. If you'll recall, my heart was racing and I had cold chills and extreme shivering. My body temperature dropped to 96 degrees. Between experiencing emotionally the loss of my mate and having this SH contact, I thought I must be going into shock. I had to take a very hot bath in order to get my body temperature back up and calm my racing heart. I prayed to God that my baby was all right. After all, this was the first time that she had gone on a journey when I couldn't go with her and take care of her.

Since that time, I've had many many SH's from Gloria, and although I'm used to them by now and very fond of them, my body still goes through a number of symptoms when they occur, including chills, momentary loss of breath followed by very deep breathing, and tear-duct activity.

The SH's always seem to come immediately after I've begun expressing to Gloria my unconditional love for her, aloud or in my heart. She responds with an awesome SH! Now that I understand the process, I can control my mental and physical reactions to it. Instead of becoming overwhelmed with the feeling of grief because I've lost her, and overwhelmed by the physical sensation of her spiritual contact, now I welcome the contact. I surrender to her spiritual hug, allowing Gloria in spirit form to fill me with her love. Learning to do this took a great deal of time and reflection. But the experience is truly awesome. I become spiritually supercharged.

Here's another example of the kinds of contact I have with Gloria. I had just come out of the shower one day when I noticed that two of the vertical cloth slats covering the sliding-glass doors to my bedroom were draped over my computerized exercise bike instead of hanging down neatly in a row with the rest of the slats.

At first, I thought perhaps the wind had blown the two slats inward with enough force to drape them over the bike. But there was no wind outside—and there was definitely no wind inside, as the sliding glass doors were completely closed! My next thought was that perhaps one of the cats had batted the slats while playing around, as cats love to do this sort of thing. But the cats weren't in the room either and the door was closed.

Being very aware as I was of signs from the other side, I immediately wondered if this could be Gloria communicating with me. If it were indeed Gloria, her learning curve had mounted considerably, as it now appeared she was able to move physical-universe objects. This was getting truly interesting. I tried to recreate logically what might have happened, but I couldn't come up with anything. So I challenged Gloria to perform the feat again, as it wasn't believable to me that she could have done it in the first place. Then I left the bedroom, making sure as I did so that I closed all the doors.

I became very busy and soon forgot about the incident. A few hours later, I had to go back into the bedroom to get something. I went through the door and, as I was walking toward the master bathroom, I noticed that the exact same phenomenon had taken place: the same two vertical gray cloth slats were draped over the exercise bike, which was three feet away from the window where the rest of the vertical slats hung down neatly in a row. I was ecstatic! Wow, Gloria, I thought, that's amazing! Moving physical-universe objects from the other side— and not once, but twice!

I could find no other explanation for this phenomenon. Nobody else lived in the house with me—except, apparently, my non-physical spouse! The door to the bedroom had been closed. But the exact same two slats had once again been draped over the workout bike, and in the exact same position as before.

I filed this communication away in my mind as dramatic and indisputable proof of my interdimensional communications with Gloria. I wondered if there were any particular reason for its coming at this time.

Chapter 39

Expected and Unexpected Mediums

It so happened that around about this time I had made an appointment with a well-known medium, whom I will call Paul—not his real name—for the purposes of this chapter. I had told Paul over the phone that I was writing a book and that I had had many after-death communications and experienced many paranormal phenomena following the death of a loved one. I told him the purpose of the contact session would be to corroborate my contacts with this loved one, and that if such a corroboration were obtained I would publish the results.

I didn't want to give him any more data than this. I felt that if I did so I would be leading him, and that the interview would not then be completely valid and that as a result I would not be able to use it in my book.

Paul was quasi-retired, but after talking to me he told me he would be interested in getting together with me. Two days before our first scheduled meeting, however, he called me to cancel, explaining that his cat was deathly ill and that it appeared he would have to have it put down. He told me that if this happened he wouldn't have enough focus to attempt a contact with my departed loved one, as such contacts took a great deal of focus and energy.

I understood, and we rescheduled for the following week.

Two days before this second appointment Paul called me to confirm. He lived 100 miles away, so I gave him exact directions to my house, along with my cell phone number. Paul gave me his own cell phone number so that we could get in touch on the day of the appointment in the event that either of us had any last-minute schedule changes.

The appointment was scheduled for 1:00 P.M., November 2. One o'clock, 2:00, 3:00 P.M.—all came and went, and still no medium named Paul. I tried calling him on his cell phone and his home phone, but to no avail. I left several messages on his home phone, telling him I was concerned and asking him to call me as soon as he got back.

I thought it odd that this was happening, as Paul had seemed to me like a very responsible person. With my own psychic abilities I picked up that something was definitely wrong.

Paul telephoned me at 7:00 P.M. He had had a very trying day. He'd left the house in plenty of time, but almost halfway to my house he had run into a detour caused by a major car accident. It seemed he took a wrong turn in the middle of this detour, for he ended up totally lost. By the time he was back on course Paul knew he would be late and so he reached for his cell phone to call me. He discovered that his cell phone battery had discharged—which was odd, because he had just charged it. He thought, "No problem. I'll plug it into my car charger." But he could not find his car charger! He had just had his car serviced, and so he reasoned that he'd probably forgotten to put the charger back in.

My psychic's next idea was to stop at a gas station and call me on the pay phone. To his dismay, he couldn't find the piece of paper on which he'd written my address, the directions and my phone numbers. He wondered how he could possibly have left them at home; "I am never this disorganized," he told me. At this point, in light of all that had happened, and since he was so late, he thought it would be best to turn around and go home.

His next words were: "John, considering all that has happened, I need to sleep on this. My gut feeling is that for some reason this attempted contact is not supposed to happen." I agreed with him. He knew that I would be going on the road for a month, and so he suggested I call him when I got back, if I were still interested; we could reevaluate at that time.

Was there a synchronistic connection between Paul's frustrating day and Gloria's interdimensional contact with me three days before? Check this out: Paul had not only done a great deal of work and research on the famed case of the haunted Amityville House, in Connecticut, but he had also done consultation work for the movie *Ghost*. You'll recall that, in *Ghost*, when the character played by Patrick Swayze passes over to the other side, he has a difficult time re-establishing communication with his loved one who's still alive and played by Demi Moore. He also has a hell of a time moving physical-universe objects, though finally, with the help of another discarnate departed human, he figures out how to do so.

Bingo! It had seemed to me that my wife was trying to signal her presence to me when, three days earlier, she had moved the vertical slats, not once, but twice. I had actually gotten the message at the time; I had thought it was a sign. But I had misread the sign. I'd figured it was an indication that Gloria approved of my upcoming meeting with Paul on account of that medium's connection with the movie *Ghost*. But I realized now that Gloria had been saying just the opposite: that, for whatever reason, my contact with this particular medium was not to be.

My next interdimensional contact with my wife was unusual even by the unconventional standards of this kind of communication. It took place through Gloria's granddaughter Naomi, aged 18 months at the time of the occurrence.

I had gone over to Ileane's house to get my regular granddaughter fix. Naomi and I were playing together on the couch. She was at the age where she was oh-so-cleverly repeating everything she heard. We had a game where I said, "Where's Naomi?" and she pointed to herself, and then I said, "Where's Grandpa?" and she pointed to me.

That night, for some reason I was very much aware of the presence of Gloria's spirit in the room. I said to Naomi very matter-of-factly, "Where's Grandma?" She immediately pointed to a point in space just above my head. I turned around, thinking Naomi must be looking at a picture on the wall. But there were no pictures of Gloria on the wall or anywhere else in the room. What could Naomi have been looking at? I decided on a test. I reversed the order of the names, asking Naomi, "Where's Grandpa?" and then, "Where's Grandma?" and then, "Where's Naomi?"

And, although the order of the names was reversed, when I said, "Where's Grandma?" Naomi pointed at the same spot above my head.

This made me feel wonderful, since I was going through this name game in the first place because I was sad that Gloria, who had known that Ileane was pregnant, had never gotten to see her beautiful granddaughter. You'll recall that we had a family meeting at Christmas, 1999, when Gloria thanked everybody for all their help and said she was trying with all her might to heal herself because she wanted to be around for her granddaughter's birth and for the wedding of her other daughter, Rachel. That was why, that night, I'd asked Naomi where her grandma was. And, when she responded in the way that she did— well, that really made my day. For I knew that Gloria was in fact there, seeing her granddaughter and interacting with her. I've read that kids and animals have a keen perception of the paranormal and the supernatural. This was my first experience of that perception.

All of this seeming proof of Gloria's presence coming to me from the afterworld was making me begin to handle my life quite differently. One of our cats, Treka, had been missing for twelve days. This cat used to bug the hell out of me. I'd be writing at the computer or trying to relax and she would come up and rub against me and drool all over me. Normally, I would then yell at her and rudely chase her away. But now I was starting to feel guilty about that. My awareness of the fragile nature of life was hitting home to me, I guess. I had just lost my lovely wife and I was still going through the blame, shame and regret that accompanied that. So now, if Treka—who had actually been one of Gloria's cats—died, or was lost...but I didn't want to think about that. I couldn't take any more guilt. And, in the meantime, I was treating Treka with much more love and respect than ever before.

A new "me" was emerging. On more than one level, I was beginning to handle life differently. Since I knew by now she was listening, I apologized to Gloria for the way I had mistreated her cat and asked her for help in getting it back. I was actually missing Treka! I knew it would take time for me to get used to my new life's *modus operandi*. But I was starting to react differently to life's multi-challenges.

About an hour later, I heard a meow. I opened the front door and there was Treka. Mind you, she'd been gone for almost two weeks. But then I'd asked Gloria for some help and, presto, Treka had come back, just an hour later. Another coincidence? I don't think so.

I picked Treka up and hugged her like I'd never hugged her before. I wasn't only hugging Treka; I was also hugging my beloved wife. I fed our cat and I petted her for more than an hour. She loved it, and so did I. I felt so good inside. I was absolutely certain that this was another sign from Gloria—an acknowledgement that my view of the world was changing. Treka was not only helping me recover, but she was also helping me with my personal growth; she was a sort of a cat-spirit-guide! Treka and I have been best friends ever since. And who was it who changed? Treka? I don't think so!

No, I was the one who had changed. I was doing unto others...! I was now sincerely concerned about Treka's welfare. Just what *is* this thing called love? I thought to myself that whatever it was, it was wonderful. I felt that I was now on the right path, the path for me. What a gift this was! And Gloria, as my twin soul, as my soul mate, was experiencing this joyfulness right along with me.

Chapter 40

Contacting the Beyond: Debbie Webb

A "contact session" is the term I've coined (because the other terms seem to me to be a little misleading) to describe a session where a person with psychic powers tries to contact a departed loved one. The only reason this field interested me was that I felt that accurate readings would constitute independent, third-party corroboration of some of the after-death communications I was directly experiencing myself. As far as I was concerned, I really had authentic extrasensory perception of Gloria, and so I didn't really need the validation. But I had already embarked on this book and I thought the contact sessions would add objectivity and credibility for the reader.

Each of the readings that follow was done completely independently of the others. Each was isolated in time, place and circumstances. The controls for each reading were the following:

1. With one exception, phone readings only, as I didn't want anything that might happen in person to possibly corrupt the reading;

2. The medium never knew my full name until after the reading, just my first name only;

3. The medium was never given any data about my life other than that I was interested in making contact with the beyond;

4. I basically answered most questions with a yes or no, unless I felt comfortable volunteering more data;

5 None of the mediums knew I had done multiple readings;

6. I even made sure that I called from a blocked caller ID phone, so that in case the medium had caller ID, he or she would not be able to get my name in advance to do any research on me.

In my opinion, it would have been possible for these mediums to give me the data I received from them only if they had known in advance the intimate details of my entire life, or if they were indeed receiving that data from deceased loved ones who knew those details. By using the controls I did, I ruled out the first possibility to my satisfaction. Based on these contact sessions, I can come to no other conclusion than that we exist after death, and that the deceased have the ability to communicate with us from the afterworld.

For those of you who think there is one more possibility, namely that an evil demon called the devil responded to my wish for contact and gave me the data I wanted to hear according to some specific agenda, I can only say: hogwash! I know the difference between my loved ones and an evil being. It takes energy to be evil, and this negative energy is detectable by anyone who is normally perceptive. Besides, I sincerely doubt the existence of an all-powerful evil being such as Lucifer or the devil. The propagation of such a belief is simply a way of generating eternal fear to be used as a control mechanism on people. It is an attempt to invalidate our true spiritual essence. Such at any rate is my opinion.

All five readings were recorded at the time and transcribed later. All comments appearing in italics are either my comments after the fact or what I was thinking at the time that I did not want to tell the mediums because I didn't want to prompt or lead them.

The first contact session took place with psychic Debbie Webb, by telephone, on December 28, 2000, some 11 months after Gloria's passing. I was at my parents' home in Erie.

D: Discarnate Spirit Number One: Elderly lady on mother's side is coming through. Says she too had a broken heart and understands what I'm going through. Be strong! No name given. Do you understand this?
J: Yes, for sure.

I understood this spirit to be that of my maternal grandmother Rachel Cacchione. She lost her husband, my grandfather Tom, over 45 years ago, and never remarried as she had loved him deeply and his death broke her heart. She died in April 1999, while Gloria was in the middle of her fight against cancer. I was amazed that my grand-mother came through first, and so quickly, to give me this caring in-formation. She was the one other spirit that I had wanted to come through. The communication was phenomenal, in that Debbie knew nothing about Gloria who had not yet come through, so she could not even understand what the "broken heart" allusion might refer to.

D: Discarnate Spirit Number Two: Younger lady, no name given, comes through.

Debbie now told me it was difficult for her to differentiate between Discarnate Spirit Number One and Discarnate Spirit Number Two, since both were spirits of women and both were coming through and talking at the same time. She said it appeared the elderly lady spirit was riddled with cancer when she passed away. Did I understand this? I told her I didn't, that it wasn't true. After a moment or so, the medium sorted it out that the comment about cancer had come from the younger female spirit. Then my grandmother's energy faded; her communication was apparently done. The session began in earnest, with Gloria taking center stage.

D: You'll have to give me a second, as I'm getting quite emotional. In all my readings I've never had a spirit come through so strong and emotional and clear and with so much intense love! This isn't usual.
J: (*very emotionally*) That's her! I understand this fully!
D: This usually means many, many lifetimes of love and interaction, culminating in soul mates. This is one of my strongest readings to date, and I have done thousands.
J: This is something my wife and I already knew this lifetime, and had even written a song about called *The Firstime*! We are soul mates for sure.
D: She says you two had an incredible bond—still do! She wants you to know that the trouble you're having sleeping around 3 A.M. or so is because she's communicating with you in what she calls "spirit dreams." She's sorry that sometimes it's waking you up, but it's the

easiest way to communicate with you. She knows you're getting some of them, but some you're not, as you're not remembering them when you wake up. It's frustrating for her sometimes. Does this make sense?

J: Yes. I have had many lucid dreams where she and I hung out. They're incredible. I look forward to sleeping because of this.

D: She knows about the two pictures on the end table to the left of the bed. Loves them. (*I had put two of my favorite pictures of Gloria up to comfort me in my loss. Since the pictures had not been there while Gloria was alive, this communication was pretty amazing.*) She at times feels desperate too, as you do, as contact is difficult. Not always easy for her, as it's not been very long and she's not used to how to operate yet. Also, on your end, sometimes you're not aware of the subtleties of this type of interdimensional communication. She knows that you want actual clear voice contact, but it's too early for that now. She too feels cheated by her having to leave this life, but it was meant to be. Does this make sense?

J: Yes. (*I was crying, but the tears were more of joy than grief.*)

D: She says she hugs you a lot from behind, her hands clenched at your chest. When you feel that cool feeling in your heart, it's her hugging you and telling you she loves you. In fact, as an example, if you're feeling a warm tingly feeling in your left arm right now, the one holding the phone, that's her doing that. She's also hugging you now.

J: Wow! I'm definitely aware of my left arm being tingly and warm. I thought it was my circulation. I can't feel her hug, though. But this helps me focus my awareness more finely. Wow!

D: She's pleading with you though, not to call on her too too often, because it gives her a great "heartache" when she can't deliver what you want. She said she needs more time. Do you understand?

J: Yes. I've been coming to her three to five times a day or more, and demanding she give me more signs for my doubting self. I have been desperate at times too. Please tell her I understand and I'm sorry.

D: She said she had a ring and a favorite watch. They're definitely yours first, but pass them on as you see fit when the children grow up. Does this make sense?

J: Well, sort of, yes. There is definitely her engagement ring and her special gold watch that I have. Her children, my stepchildren, are grown up already, however. She probably means our new grand-daughter, Naomi. When she grows up, I may do just that.

D: Also, she's saying something about a necklace and a cross on it. It's very significant. Do you know about this?

J: Not sure. I vaguely remember this jewelry. I'll ask her daughter.

When I asked Ileane later, she confirmed that her mother had a neck-lace with a special cross. I asked Ileane to give it back to me.

D: She says that since you can't leave yet, meaning, death, suicide, etc. is not in your nature, you have no choice even though you have a choice. You must therefore move on with your career. You have to make some big decisions. Do you understand?

J: Yes, unfortunately, I do. Though at times I'd much rather join her, as we made a commitment that we would go from this world together.

D: She knows, but your choice now is you have no choice. She says you also haven't changed the house very much. She wants you to radically change the house around or sell it. Do you understand what she means?

J: Yes, I agree. It's just taking time, tell her, to do this. It also takes money, but I'll get around to it.

I thought this was pretty incredible. Before Gloria had passed away, she had told me to sell the house or at least fully change it around. I hadn't done either—and here she was yelling at me from the other side, no differently than she would have from this side.

D: She's now saying that every step you take, she experiences. She's with you all the way. "We're still a team." She wants you to know too that's she's with "our" child. Does this make sense?

J: Yes and no. Tell me more, as I don't want to give you any data.

D: She's saying something about a miscarriage or a termination. Do you understand?

J: Yes, I do. It was a termination, and we both regret it.

D: Well, she says it's O.K., as she is with your child in spirit.

J: Wow! This makes me happy!

This amazed me as well. I of course hadn't told Debbie about Gloria's abortion. This was the second time a medium had communicated this information to me without knowing anything about me.

D: She wants you to know that you are the bridge for her family. Something about forgiving them or some kind of forgiveness. Do you understand this?

J: Yes, I know that she wants me to help her family get together. They're a wreck. Internal fights, sickness, etc. She wants me to help get them together. I understand this.

D: She is now talking about some double pictures that are "ours." Maybe wedding pictures or something. Do you understand this?

J: Yes, I do. Our wedding pictures, shot by our best friend Dick Zimmerman, are very special. Our wedding was very special.

D: Then, jokingly, she says, "You are hers." But you do have to move on, since you're there in the physical dimension. She knows, however, that you won't do this yet, but she thinks you should when you're ready. Do you understand this?

J: Most definitely! We are soul mates. I am hers and she is mine. But she wants me to have another relationship, if I'm up to it. She's a hard act to follow, though!

D: She's now saying that the flickering lamp or lights are definitely her doing—another sign that's she's around.

J: Wow! Nobody knew about those lights but my stepdaughters and me.

Shortly after Gloria's passing, some living room track lighting had flickered on and off, on and off. It occurred to me one day that this might be Gloria trying to signal me, as I had read about this sort of phenomenon. I asked her do it again, and she did so, on multiple occasions.

D: She is very stubborn, by the way. Won't answer many of my questions that I put to her, like her name. She's only giving me data that she wants to give you. She is admitting that she was very dictatorial. Does this make sense?

J: Yes, that's her!

D: She's saying that you were the strong one though. She admired that. She was weak in comparison. But she was the artistic, simple one. She was different from you. Do you understand this?

J: This is accurate.

D: She is mad about your having no Christmas around you at the house. Something about the tree, and the tree was hers!

J: Yes, she decorated the tree and handled all the Christmas stuff. She was amazing at it. I purposely didn't want to have any Christmas around on the Christmas following her passing, because it hurt too much. I couldn't have decorated the tree and house as well as she could have anyway. That's her job, and she shouldn't have left, damn it! (*This was pretty amazing. I purposely had not wanted any Christmas, and so I hadn't celebrated it.*)

D: I feel like I'm in the middle of an interdimensional quarrel!

J: Yes, we bantered a lot. We even turned the banter into a stage skit. We were both stubborn about our ways. Lots of personal integrity. Our love always remained high, though, always. This is just more proof that it's her! Can I ask her a question?

D: I'll try, but she's stubborn, I feel, about this.

J: Will she describe our special romantic place?

D: She says it was a very scenic visual place. Very visual and aesthetic. Many views and vistas. Does this make sense?

J: Yes, indeed.

Our favorite place was Hawaii. We used to go hiking in places with breathtaking views of the Pacific from the cliffs where the rainforests ended. There was also an incredible secluded beach, called Larsen's Beach, where we would go to for romance. It was heaven on earth.

D: She's saying again that she was riddled with cancer at the end. She was too weak to fight it anymore. She chose to go. Sorry. You were the strong one. "You could have beaten it, but I was the weaker one." Her head wasn't working too well at the end. Sorry she couldn't say goodbye verbally, like she would have wanted to. Her words turned into gibberish. But she said that you and her could say everything with just a look, and she knew you got her communication through her eyes. She's also very happy her name lives on. Do you understand this?

J: Yes, to everything about her head not working and to her name living on.

This was a startlingly accurate description of how Gloria was in the final days of her life, as I have described it earlier. Furthermore, as regards her name living on: I've finished her solo debut CD and her book and tapes will continue to be sold. Her name and works will definitely live on for all to enjoy; that's one reason for this book.

D: She's saying that if you had been the one to pass, she would not have made it, being left behind. She was too weak for that. Do you understand this?

J: Yes. I would have felt very bad leaving her, considering all she had already gone through in this lifetime.

D: She's sorry that now all the pressure is on you. "But you're strong and you can do it. We're still together. I'll always be around and will be waiting for you when it's your time." She wants you to make her song public. Does this make sense to you?

J: Not sure which song she means. It could be this new one I'm writing, called *One Love, Two Hearts*, that I haven't finished yet, or maybe it's *The Firstime*, which is the ballad we both wrote about our past lives together and how we are soul mates. That tune, although it's on her CD that I just finished, is really not that public yet, and it could be a big hit. It's one of these two though, I believe.

D: She says you'll know what to do. She's also saying something about her framed LP. When you make this song public and it becomes gold, then that framed picture of her LP is yours. Does this make sense?

J: (*thoughtfully*) Wow, can she mean her fake gold LP? It's a fake gold record that symbolizes that she will one day have a gold record.

This was an obscure detail that only Gloria and I had known, and that I had practically forgotten myself.

D: Her energy is fading now. I think she's done. If we do any more together, it will only be my opinion, which is not how I work. I suggest we end.

J: OK. Thank you very much. That was awesome!

The session ended.

Chapter 41

Contacting the Beyond: Susan Sanderford

The contact session with Debbie Webb had totally blown me away. Debbie had known nothing whatsoever about me at the start. If she were simply a telepath who was somehow just reading my mind over the telephone—then there was nothing "simply" or "just" about it! Such an act of controlled, creative telepathy would have been astounding in itself. But I was positive Debbie was doing far more than reading my mind. She had provided me with just too many details that were highly specific to my situation. The sheer number of those details seemed to move far beyond coincidence or lucky hits.

It occurred to me that I should have a second contact session, with a different medium this time, to see if what the second medium had to communicate corroborated what Debbie had communicated. So, barely two weeks later, I was on the telephone with a second psychic, this time Susan Sanderford. I used the same controls I had the first time. Susan knew absolutely nothing about me, including why I might want to make use of her psychic abilities. The date of this second, telephoned contact session was January 11, 2001.

S: Wow, I am feeling so much emotion I'm almost choking, and the last time this happened was when a guy's wife had committed suicide. There's not a suicide here, is there?

J: No.

S: Okay. The first thing is that when I did your pre-reading, I was impressed with a sense of a "good friend" energy and spirit around you. Do you resonate with that?

J: Yes.

S: Then I was shown two people dancing together, which always makes me think of a loving relationship. Does that resonate with this person?

J: Extremely.

S: Because it feels like a romantic relationship, but also a really "good friend" energy. And then I got a sense that this person was really, really close to you. The image I get is of two people dancing together, meaning very good friends, etc. Didn't have a clue why I was shown someone exercising. Did either of you guys like to do that?

J: The other person really liked to do that, not me.

S: Well, because I'm seeing this person exercising and exercising. That's just a little validation of telling me about themselves. I saw this hand holding the remote control of the TV. What resonates with you for that?

J: I do that when I watch TV—but, so what? That's pretty common.

S: What about something going on with the TV or channels, etc.?

J: Well, for a while there after her passing, it seemed at one point like some of the channels on the TV were changing on their own.

S: It feels to me that this person was controlling the channels and trying to get your attention. I'm also shown that you are very open and have the ability to communicate with spirit. And "they" are telling me that you are learning well.

J: True. I'm studying away.

S: Also, I'm shown some conflict on a relationship. What about this?

J: Well, I have some conflict since she's passed due to feeling guilty for not always unconditionally loving this person and so on. And while we were together, although our relationship was pretty incredible, we were drifting apart without our even being that much aware of it—or at least without my being that much aware of it. Maybe she was.

S: So I'm seeing the conflict in you, then.

J: Probably. But she had some too, I'm sure.

S: I'm given the image of a tall man and a short woman together. Is that you and her?

J: No.

S: This may be other people. Maybe a grandmother energy.

J: Now you are on the money with somebody else. My grandmother was extremely short.

S: Now who would be the tall man?

J: Her husband, my grandfather, was extremely tall.

S: Well, your grandmother is around then, because this was a really short woman and a really tall man. They were holding hands and enjoying each other.

What Susan called the "pre-reading orientation" had concluded. Now the contact session began in earnest.

S: Now, let me move some of this emotion through. Just a second. Your grandmother is coming in first.

J: All right.

S: She has been talking to you, too. Because she shows me talking into your ear and telling you things. Does that make any sense?

J: Yes.

S: She feels like she's a guide to you and helping you in many ways. A very strong connectedness to you. She tells me she was always so proud of you. She's telling me that you are very talented.

J: Yes.

S: Now, you play the piano, is that right?

J: Yes.

This, to me, right out of the box, was pretty amazing. How could this medium have known and/or taken a guess at this? She didn't even know my last name until I paid her after the session.

S: Because she's showing me a picture of a piano. She describes your music as magical music, as it speaks to the heart and soul. And this is part of your mission in your life, to express this music to people, as it pulls out of people a deep love vibration, which helps people change spiritually. Therefore I'm being told that your work is very important. Now I'm getting the symbol of your work being connected to higher dimensional beings—star family or higher energy level—

that you are pulling down into this planet. Your grandma is again telling me that she is so proud of you for this.

J: My question is, could this be the other female or do you think it's still the grandmother energy?

S: It's still the grandmother energy. The other energy is still there though, and is more of a love who has crossed over.

J: True.

S: She will come through when she is ready, but for now it's your grandmother. Your grandmother feels like if she doesn't speak now she won't get in as the other person is very talkative and in control. Does that make sense?

J: Yes.

S: So she's allowing your grandmother to come in first. I now get an image of your grandmother and grandfather holding hands. They look really cute together and so they must have had a great relationship. And she was very short. She was also very feisty, but with a good heart—and she was a ball of energy. She's saying something else now, but I'm trying to decipher it. Give me a second, as it's not real clear yet to me. Oh, yes, she's showing me that one of the lessons you have been learning over the past couple of years is learning how to allow spirit to lead your life, rather than your being in control of it.

J: Yes, true. Rather than the Spock logical side always being in control, I'm trying to operate as a function of my higher self.

S: I'm being told that it's a little hard for you to give up control, but you're working on that, and I'm told that you're making good progress. I'm being shown that you are taking your hands off the controls and saying, okay, spirit, lead me where you want me to go, rather than I need to do this or fix that. She's telling me that you're doing a good job and allowing yourself to be in the flow of what spirit wants.

J: Makes sense.

S: I really feel like she has a lot of wisdom and she is very, very interested in your life and is acting like a guide for you. Are you aware of that?

J: Well, I wasn't aware of the guide part. We always had a good time when she was here and alive, but when she passed I didn't know our good time was going to turn into this, which is nice, by the way.

Susan's husband, Milt, was listening in on the session. He suggested that Susan ask my grandmother why she was so interested in my life.

S: Wow! Funny answer. (*laughing*) She clearly said that you are a happening person. Clearly things are happening around you and she is interested in seeing what's going on. You are one of the most awake people in your family, right? And so there seems to be a lot of activity going on around you in other dimensions and that's why she is interested in helping you, as she sees the importance of your work and she wants to be in the middle of everything.

J: Right on.

S: She's working with you because she wants to be there right in the middle of everything. She's quite a character. She's also giving me goodbye, so you must not have had good closure with her.

J: Well, she was back east in the hospital and I was in Los Angeles so I wasn't there physically.

S: Yes, I guess she means goodbye just in a physical sense. Her grand aura and personality that she had about her still exists on the other side too. Now about your girlfriend—or were you married?

J: We were married.

S: I'm feeling a lot of angel energy around her. She had that kind of aura. Does that resonate?

J: Yes, exactly.

S: The way it comes off is, if you didn't know she was a human being, you would swear she was an angel.

J: Yes, I always used to tell her that she shouldn't have incarnated because she was too aesthetically perfect for this world.

S: So that does resonate, then?

J: Yes.

S: She comes across as an angel energy. Now, why does it feel like things happened around her? Like there was a supernatural quality; things just happened around her. Like she did carry this major divine or special energy about her that was really expressed in the world through her and her personality. She does apologize for having to leave, though.

J: She does or doesn't?

S: Does. She's giving me the image of it that it absolutely ripped your heart out! Geesh! That's where the emotion is coming from!

J: Yes. Now you're on to it.

S: Whew! Whew! Now let me just work through this. I usually don't feel emotion like that, which tells me she has incredible energy about her. I'm getting that she is a very old soul.

J: Yes.

S: I still have to work through these feelings, as I'm the one now that needs to cry. Okay, now she's telling me that after her passing she was trying to get you up off your butt. Did you have a real hard time getting going after that?

J: Yes.

S: She's showing me an image of pulling you up by your collar and pushing you up by your butt to get you going again. And she's now happy that you're going again. She says that you need to be out there and you need to be doing your thing.

J: Right on the money. It took me awhile!

S: She says, you know I'm always with you.

J: Yes.

S: Now she's saying, what a great love! It even surprised the both of you!

J: (*grieving*) Right.

S: The love when you two came together—I'm now given this image of it knocking both you two reeling. Like two dynamic sparks bamming into one another, which sent you both reeling. Does that make sense, the way I described it?

J: Totally on the money! Yes, the phrase we used to use was it made us feel brand new.

S: She's a soul mate!

J: Yes. I wanted you to find that out. We were definitely soul mates!

S: Yes, I'm getting goose bumps on that! And do you know how rare that is? Whew! Whew! Whew!

J: (*grieving*) That's why it was so hard on me.

S: It's like when you come together, you have found that missing part of yourself and you could literally crawl inside the other person and be them. And that's a true soul mate.

J: Yes! Yes! Everybody around us used to admire that about us.

S: It's like a twin flame situation.

J: Yes, funny you should say that, because I started writing a song called *One Love, Two Hearts*, and she helped me write the lyrics from the other side! And the way I know this is because I'm horrible at writing lyrics and these lyrics are great!

S: That was just going to come out of my mouth. She's feeding you the lines.

J: Yes, indeed!

S: Twin flames are more than soul mates, by the way. You are from one flame that has split apart. And when they come back together, it's a very magical and powerful moment, as you have been looking for each other all your life. And so when you find them, it's an incredible spiritual experience.

J: Right!

S: Because your coming together feels like such a spiritual experience.

J: Right! But that's why it didn't make sense that we had to then go apart, at least so quickly, other than my learning a lesson.

S: Other than your learning a lesson. The way it feels like to me is that it needed to be this way, because she's kind of directing traffic from the other side in order to help you accomplish the important tasks that you have to do on this side.

J: Right!

S: The partnership is still there, by the way, but just not in physical form. But it needed this. She needed to access the divine energy from spirit, not to diminish your energy, but to send it to you for you guys to complete the task that you came to accomplish.

J: Totally! Because we used to scratch our heads as to why our careers, though doing well, hadn't exploded out the roof yet, though they sometimes seemed so close to doing so.

S: Absolutely! She's standing around with a smile and her arms crossed and is happy you got that. She acknowledges that the separation has been really difficult, especially for you. She knows you miss her and probably will every day of you life, but she is there with you and working with you. She tells me you guys are the dynamic duo!

J: Yep!

S: And what a dynamic duo to be doing this work from the other side. Wow! That's real cool!

J: Yes, it's an interdimensional relationship. Four stars!

S: She's telling me that you guys meet when you sleep. You meet in other dimensions. Do you remember these?

J: Yes. Probably not all of them. But it has already happened. I know that for sure. One time in particular was so real it was amazing. And I request these meetings often.

S: Well, you will be doing that more. Keep asking, though she's telling me this will happen when something important is supposed to happen. Then this connection will be made.

S: Right. It's not like something you can control on this end. It's like they beam you up when you're ready. And they're telling me those moments are also to help you want to still be here, still on this side. Because you don't want to be here, not really.

J: Correct. Even though I'm 100 billion percent away from anything like suicide or deep depression, the point is I would still rather be there with her.

We talked about the work I had to do here on earth with Gloria's help. Then Susan exclaimed: "Boy, did the energy really shift when they came in." It seemed "they" was a consortium of elder spirits, called "the Council" by Susan, which had just made an entrance. Did I have questions for them? I said I had some big decisions to make that I was having trouble making. They said, as communicated by Susan, that I should give myself some time, that I should keep pushing forward. Susan now asked me a question that caught me right off guard:

S: Who is the vocalist? Is she the vocalist? Because I see a microphone to her mouth.

J: Yes, she's the killer vocalist. That's why the project sort of went kaput when she left.

This was amazing, as Gloria was of course a vocalist. In fact, the logo for her book and school was her picture with a mike held to her mouth. Gloria seemed to have sent Susan that exact image. I asked myself: What were the odds of Susan's just pulling that out of a hat?

S: She sings to your heart every day. So she's going to be writing music through you also. Yes, it feels like you're supposed to be doing your musical writing—boy, I'm seeing the musical pages take wing and take flight on their own—so she's saying keep writing your music now that you have a message to give, and that it will find a way to get out.

J: Yes, I've always known that, but now after a loss such as this you're in the labyrinth.

S: She's showing me a saxophone. Most of the time to me this is symbolic of the blues. So, are you struggling with depression, or really feeling down, or something like that?

J: No, not really. I'm handling that, when it comes up, with my spiritual practice and discipline. I grew up however as a predominantly blues musician and so I channel my emotions easily that way or through that style.

S: Maybe she's just letting me know the style of music because when I see that symbol, I always think of the blues in some way.

J: We were pretty bluesy as far as our musical style.

S: Got it. She's showing me this lit candle that you light for her a lot.

J: Yes. Very true.

S: She's acknowledging it and she likes it.

J: It's lit right now. Wow! That's great!

This was another amazing comment. It's no doubt true that many people light candles for their departed loved ones. But I had a special altar for Gloria, and I would always light the candle and kneel down before the altar and talk to her. I had also purposely lit the candle before this phone reading, hoping that the medium would comment on it.

S: Well, I see it lit, and you light it all the time.

J: Yes, I do.

S: Do you light it when you write your music?

J: Not really. Usually, though, at night.

S: Well, she's acknowledging you for that and thanks you.

J: (*very emotionally*) She is welcome!

S: She says that, when you play, she's sitting there right beside you and she has got her head laying on your back and rubbing your back. Can you feel that?

J: Not aware of the back rubbing, but I can feel that sometimes she's around me hugging me from behind.

S: The way I'm seeing it is that she has her head on your back, rubbing your back, her energy is right there. But it seems to be especially around when you're playing the piano. Now it sounds like she's scolding you about eating more or better.

J: Not about eating more, because I eat a lot, but probably about eating better.

S: Eating better—it's something about eating—probably eating better, if that makes sense.

J: Is she saying anything at all about how and why she got her illness and why it all occurred? I don't want to give you any data.

S: Did her death go quickly?

J: Well, sort of, once she discovered what she had. But she did struggle for awhile, but then near the end it went too fast.

S: Why do I see you carrying her? Did you have to do a lot of taking care of her or helping her get around? I see you carrying her.

J: Yes, a couple of times that happened.

S: She talks about being so weak.

J: Yes, especially near the end.

S: Yes, and you had to take her into the bathroom and all those kinds of things too? And being sick to her stomach and throwing up? It was really nasty.

J: Yes, that's her word.

Gloria always used the word "nasty" to describe things or situations that were not aesthetically pleasing to her or things that were just plain gross. It seemed to me that she was now most likely telling the medium about the nasty side effects of the chemotherapy and of all the pain medicine she'd taken.

S: She's sorry she had to put you through that.

J: I used to yell at her though, for her thinking she was a burden.

S: Yes, but that was her thing. She hated being a weakling. Being physically weak was not her thing, because she never was before.

J: No, she wasn't at all.

S: Why does she say it was like something grabbed me by the throat?

J: Yes, in the end that's what happened.

S: Because I'm getting all choked up around the throat—like something grabbed her by the throat.

J: Yes, it did, without giving you any more data.

S: She talks about not being able to sing any more.

J: Yes.

S: And that was very difficult for her. (*grieving, very emotionally*) Because she loved to sing—whew!

J: Yes, whew!

This seemed to be truly right on the money, because, as I've previously written, the cancer impinged on a nerve connected to Gloria's vocal chords and gave her a chipmunk-like voice.

S: I know—I'm getting all choked up too. Man, the energy around my throat is incredible.

J: Yes, it was destroying me.

The session continued with small but telling details. Susan seemed to see me feeding Gloria, giving her tea. I said that we'd "done the whole alternative madness thing." Susan communicated to me that, on passing over, Gloria had experienced, first, relief, and then a feeling of great love. Gloria began talking about "a new baby in the house," apparently referring to our granddaughter Naomi, born after Gloria's death. She mentioned the flowers I'd given her; in fact I constantly replenished the flowers on Gloria's altar.

S: Did you and she talk about who would have the rougher time?

J: Yes. And I said once, I'm sorry, you're going to lose this argument if you have to go, you'll find out that I'm the one with the harder task.

S: And she is only gone physically.

J: (*very emotionally*) I know, but...

S: She tells me you look for her all the time, for a manifestation.

J: I guess the skeptical side of me still wants the more obvious manifestations, like real apparitions, to help me out when I miss her in the flesh. But I can tell she gets a little mad when I demand this too often.

S: Well, that's the human ego mind talking.

J: I've read many many stories of people seeing real apparitions and so I'm taunting her, Come on! Don't you have the chops over there? I know you can do it! But then I keep getting communications back, from either her or somebody else, that that wouldn't really help you right now like you think it would.

S: You may actually not need it, because you already know about her continued existence.

Then Gloria, as communicated by Susan, mentioned—of all things!—our mutual hair stylist. She spoke briefly of our favorite romantic vacation place. She mentioned our granddaughter Naomi, who she said would increasingly be serving as a link between Gloria and all the family back here. She mentioned my book, saying that "the whole story was not done yet" and that at this point I could not know all that it would contain. She spoke of the lesson of unconditional love that we both had to learn in our lifetimes. She told me that another lesson I was learning was how to listen to Spirit.

J: Well, they are sort of both connected, because unconditional love comes from the spirit plane and not the physical plane, not ego.

S: Absolutely! So you have to listen to Spirit and learn how to let go. Although you are doing okay with it, it's hard.

J: Well, yes. That's because the guilt still comes through that if I had already learned that lesson, then she wouldn't have had to leave.

S: Ahh. It's not your fault. She's saying clearly that it's not your fault. Let that go for sure! She was already told that she needed to be over there helping you with your work. Also, remember that guilt keeps you from remembering Divine Spirit. Anytime we hold guilt, that is a block to hearing, knowing, and listening to Spirit in our life.

J: Yes, it is a much lower, raw emotional tone level, this I know from my studies as well. It's not a very responsible tone.

S: You need to release that, because it's not true. Ask Spirit to help you release that. That's an illusion.

J: I did a tribute to her life. Stevie Wonder performed, as well as a lot of other special guests. How did she like it? Although, somehow I already know that she loved it.

S: She said that the love she felt from you and the other people touched everybody's heart. It was a real spiritual moment. It was transformational in people's hearts. It was a significant life-changing point for people.

J: Yes, that's true. Stevie Wonder, who was a good friend and one of Gloria's vocal students, said he's been at many of these kinds of events but he has never in his life been to a more spiritual awakening, even for himself, let alone for others.

S: Yes, she said there was something greater and divine going on, other than just a celebration of her life. She says it was a moment of salvation—of people experiencing an incredible love that went beyond an earthly love to a divine love which changes people's hearts and brings them to a realization of what they have within them.

J: That's exactly what happened that night, for sure! Another question is that the whole aftermath of the fight with the illness basically wiped me out financially, especially not working, the medical bills, etc. Does she have any comments about that? I know deep down that this will change and all will go into abundance, but I still wanted to see if she had any comments.

S: I'm getting that it's definitely going to be okay and just let go and allow Spirit to lead and the money will follow. Trust [that that will happen] as long as you follow your inner divine self. They say you are well on your way. Your recording projects that you are doing and going to do are going to help out a lot, and you are not going to lack for anything.

J: Except her body.

S: Yes, except that. I think that's it for now. She's a neat lady. She's an angel.

J: Yes, she is! Thank you.

Chapter 42

Contacting the Beyond: Dennis Jackson

Again, there had been so much corroboration! By now, I had come to believe in the power of mediumship. I couldn't resist searching out yet another medium. This time, I found Dennis Jackson.

The session took place February 8, 2001. Dennis said much that was new and compelling, not the least in connection with his concept of the "Placeholder"—which implied there was some chance Gloria might come back to me even before I departed this present lifetime!

D: A male or father figure seems to be coming through. In what context, I don't know. Does that mean anything to you?

J: No, not really.

D: Also, a woman is trying to come through at the same time. I have asked them to come through one at a time.

J: The woman makes more sense than the dad does.

D: Could be a grandfather, but it seems to be one generation down. It could be an uncle, too. Now, besides this man and woman energy, there's a car accident that I'm getting and also a long illness that seems to be surrounding this woman. It's long and drawn out, but at the end she seems to be passing very quickly. Is this your mom?

J: No.

D: Who is she? It's like mother energy and it's off to your side.

J: Should I answer that?

D: Well, sometimes it's good just to figure it out and keep on going. Was this person, this female, like a mother figure to you? Or would she tell you what to do sort-of-a-thing?

J: Well, more like telling me what to do a lot, I guess.

D: That's like a mother figure to me, sort of telling you what to do. There's a letter G in the name, like Grace or that kind of name.

J: That's close. It's not Grace, but it does begin with a G.

D: What is the name?

J: Gloria.

D: She's not used to this. She hasn't been over there that long.

J: Just a year, actually.

D: That's perfect. It feels like that because she's very clear and usually that means more than a year. Under a year can be very difficult and sometimes I get nothing. Man, there is a lot of love coming through. There seems to be a real strong connection between the two of you. It's a love situation for sure.

This was the third instant corroboration of the soul-mate bond between Gloria and myself. How could it be a coincidence?

J: Yes, it is a love situation for sure!

D: Not a family love. More than that. It's between two people. Was there a romance aspect to this love?

J: Yes, she was my wife.

D: Okay, but right now the connection seems a little distant. Let me ask her a little more. She now wants to talk about a child that's on the other side with her.

J: That's interesting.

D: Was there a miscarriage or an abortion?

J: You hit it right on the head.

D: Because she says there's a child there. Now, do you have children here on this side?

J: She had two children that are grown up.

D: Okay, but she's not talking about the two children. She's talking about the miscarriage/abortion with you.

J: That's exactly right.

D: Because she wants to talk about that. She says it's all okay. She was really upset about it, but it was supposed to happen that way, and the child is not angry with her.

J: Cool.

D: So, she's really okay with that. She really really wants you to know that this is okay. Everything is good.

J: Good, I got it.

Again, certainly the medium could not personally have known about the abortion. I found this data absolutely amazing, as it was the third reading where Gloria had come through with such information. I think Gloria knew this data would definitely be confirmation for me that she was okay and still with me.

D: Now she wants to talk about a small red car.

J: Wow!

D: Was there a red sports car that she owned?

J: Yes, she had a favorite red sports car that we sold reluctantly during her illness, to raise money for medicine and bills, etc.

I found this utterly amazing. How could Dennis have known this? The red Volvo sports car was very special to Gloria, and she was very upset when we had to sell it to raise money.

D: She's laughing! She says it was okay! But she was upset about it. But you've got to understand that everything is okay. "I'm having a wonderful time," she says. She wants you to know that she talks to you in your dreams a lot.

J: Yes, I'm very aware of this, as she does it a lot.

D: She comes to you—oh, wow! She says there was one night, about six months after she passed, where you woke up in the middle of the night and she was with you in bed. She wants to talk about that. Do you remember that?

J: Well, it's happened a variety of times.

D: Well, this particular time she says you actually felt her touch. Do you remember that?

J: Yes, I do! It was most real and when I woke up I remembered and I thought it was fantastic. Her hands were touching my hair even after I woke up. I felt it.

D: She says, "That really was me. Don't doubt that at all." It was really her! Don't ever doubt that. Now she's talking about a mother, yours I think, that she was really close to. Does that make sense?

J: Well, not really. I mean, she got along with my mother, but she wasn't really all that close. Maybe it was my grandmother?

D: Could be, but I get a mother energy. Anyway, she's talking about having tea, etc. She's also bringing up England.

J: Well, before I met her she lived there for awhile, and one time we went there together.

D: Okay, well, she's talking about Great Britain, about maybe going there. She's giving me a picture of her sitting in bed and you guys are talking about going on a vacation or somewhere.

J: Well, we were definitely talking about going somewhere, but—

D: It was definitely across the water somewhere.

J: Yes, we were definitely talking about going to our favorite place when she kicked her illness.

D: She said, "Go there!" Because when you go there, I go there! She's around you a lot! She is also showing me a picture of a dog. It was one of the saddest days.

J: Not sure which dog it could be.

D: She says it was a light-colored one.

J: Yes, I remember, because I felt bad too, because for various reasons that I'm also responsible for that dog was neglected in the end and we both felt bad.

D: She wants you to know that that's all right. Everything is cool. Everything is very great! Now she wants to talk about music.

J: Now you're in the right area!

D: Is she a musician?   Because she says there is one song that she was trying to get down that she couldn't. Anyway, she got it. Was she writing a song?

J: Yes, she's a lyricist and a vocalist.

D: She was writing one to the baby—to the child that was on the other side. Have you gone through her lyrics totally yet?

J: Pretty much, but not all of them.

D: Well, she's referring to the child maybe on the other side—to the loss—like she healed herself with the lyrics. She used to heal herself with writing her lyrics. (*I hadn't known about this, but I could believe it.*)

J: We wrote many songs about how we met again this lifetime and how we'd meet again and again. She never thought that this illness would actually take her out like it did. My question is, did she know during her illness that this was in the script? That she was going to have to go and thus was keeping it from me, as she knew I would have trouble with that? Or did she really fight and was surprised herself when she had to split?

D: She was very surprised. She was actually at the transition but still thought she would get through it.

J: That makes sense.

D: She was fighting right to the end, and when she felt her soul actually start to leave it was still: "No, wait a minute—I got too much to do here. I can't leave yet." Now, I want you to keep an open mind about this, because she's telling me something very interesting here. She's talking about a Placeholder. Because we know what we're going to do each lifetime, we set up agreements with people. She knew that she would leave at this time in this life before she incarnated, but, of course, once we incarnate the veil comes over and we all forget. But she says that she *is* going to try and come back to you!

J: Well, we also discussed how we would pull this off in a later incarnation, or my joining her, or whatever.

D: Hold it. Don't go any farther. Let me explain what she is telling me right now. She says she has a Placeholder, a soul this life that she had a previous agreement with, so that a few years after she has passed she will attempt to transfer to the body of this other person who is supposed to leave.

J: You mean, like a Walk-In?

"Walk-In" is a term popularized by the author and psychic Ruth Montgomery. It refers to an agreement between souls whereby an incarnate soul "leaves early" (i.e. while the physical body is still reasonably intact) so that a second soul, not yet incarnate, can enter that body and carry to full term the body's physical life. Obviously, the individual will be greatly altered by this "changing of place." Some-

thing analogous to this "soul replacement" procedure takes place in the movie <u>Heaven Can Wait</u> starring Warren Beattie.

D: Yes, but I call it a Placeholder because the "Walk-Out" actually knows they are going to leave. What happens is that suddenly their whole attitude changes and suddenly they say, "Gee, I think life is really wonderful now. I think I'll stay here!" That's because the Walk-Out has checked out and the Walk-In has checked in. Then your paths will cross again, because this soul is so important to you. This has only come up in two of my readings in the last five years.

J: Well, you're dealing with an intense twin soul relationship, so anything is possible, especially with our background and studies.

D: Yes, I know. Well, she's going to try and come back—but she first has some process to complete over there on the other side. And when you come across her on this side, you will recognize her.

J: Very cool if that happens! Another question: I'm in a dilemma regarding this wrongful death lawsuit due to my wife's medical illness. Some doctor and clinic really committed malpractice. But since spiritually this was meant to be—her having to leave, that is—I'm in a turmoil about proceeding, especially since it's a rough case and a rough ride. Does she have any comments?

D: She says that life on the other side is a spiritual life. On this side we're dealing with a human situation, and anything we go through is for experience and learning, and so going through a wrongful death lawsuit is for a purpose. Why would you want to deprive the doctors and attorneys of going through their experience that they need to go through? Your wife, by the way, is saying this tongue-in-cheek: "And why would you want to deprive them of going through all this?"

J: Yes, the *Star Trek* prime directive at work again.

D: Of course, you don't change their path just like your path. Inside, you know that you all have to go through this. She says, absolutely, do it!

J: Did she say anything about her illness?

D: Well, she didn't really talk about it. But it seemed more painful on the outside than it actually was. She wants to comment on this. The pain level was intense at times, but because of who she was and what she was involved with and where she could kind of check out to, she kind of checked out of her body and the pain was kind of eased.

J: Right.

D: Now she wants to talk about a male person. This is that male person who came through in the beginning. It's now clear that it was connected to her and not you, a relative or a favorite uncle.

J: Well, she had several people pass away in her family when she was young.

D: She says that part of the reason she was able to go through the pain was mainly because of this one man.

J: She was very close to her father.

D: Well, I wasn't getting a very clear picture of him because it didn't matter, but that's who it is. He helped her through it.

J: Another question is that, although her passing accelerated my spiritual growth to warp-drive proportions—

D: Absolutely, absolutely.

J: Because of that, I feel responsible because of our agreement. I feel she volunteered as my twin soul to hook up with me this lifetime and split like she did to help me go through this experience to have this spiritual growth, this incredible lesson which has opened my heart to the beauty of unconditional love, for her getting ill and having to go.

D: It's not so much responsibility.

J: In other words, for my lesson, she had to go through that.

D: Understand that because of your going through your part of it, she went through her part of it that she wanted to experience.

J: Exactly.

D: It was a choice. And she reiterates that the pain is how we went forward. We both had the pain, but the cool part of all this is that she is going to be able to come back in a different form and come to you again.

J: Now, in another earlier reading, she said she would be greeting me when my work was done here.

D: Well, that message was because she hadn't yet remembered everything. Some people take a while to go through the "veil of forgetfulness." And since she really really wanted to stay here on this side so much, she kept trying to come back so much that the human game and memories, the human part, lingers a lot longer. So it takes a lot longer to get clear of the human part and connect back with the spiritual dimension and remember the entire game. She's saying that she hadn't yet remembered that she had an agreement to come back again in another form. She's very strong. She comes through very clearly.

J   How did she like her life tribute?

D: She absolutely loved it—but did you have to get so personal? She's laughing about it, though. Don't worry about it.

J: Any comments from her about the rest of my path here on this side? I got wiped out financially from her illness and now not having her here to play our artistic game, well, things look a little iffy, if you know what I mean. Even though I know deep down they'll somehow work out.

D: She says there are films and movies in the future—the big screen is where you've got to go.

J: Wow, I just had a meeting with my partner regarding this.

D: Yes, about 18 months away, something you're doing will be seen. It's absolutely in the path.

J: Did she have an easy transition?

D: Yes, all except her fighting the transition. Now she's saying that there was someone standing at the foot of the bed. Seems to be her dad. He helped her move out. She pulls her energy back, but says she's with you all the time.

J: She probably gets mad at me occasionally, as I'm always demanding she visit me or that I visit her out-of-body while I sleep, etc. Or I demand that she appear to me in an apparition, and when she doesn't I get mad.

D: She hasn't mastered that yet!

J: Well, I told her that besides my personal satisfaction I need material for my book.

D: Now is the time, because it takes about a year before everything kind of cools down and the communication gets really strong. You're right at the right time where she is going to start coming through with some stuff.

J: Okay. Cool.

Chapter 43

Contacting the Beyond: George Anderson

George Anderson is one of the best-known psychics and mediums in the U.S. A book featuring many of his readings, *We Don't Die: George Anderson's Conversations with the Other Side*, by Joel Martin and Patricia Romanowski and published in 1989, was a bestseller for many months and is still selling well. George has written a number of books of his own, including *Lessons from the Light* (2000) and *Walking in the Garden of Souls* (2001).

My contact session with George, conducted by telephone, and anonymously as usual on my part, took place on January 24, 2002, almost exactly two years after Gloria's death. I'll paraphrase the earlier exchanges.

George sensed a male presence and two female presences. They seemed to be my grandfather Tom, my grandmother Rachel, and Gloria. The latter presence was a "right-to-the-point, no-nonsense lady....When she puts a symbol up, she immediately explains what the symbol is, etc. In this case a sweetheart symbol could mean that she's your literal sweetheart or that she's just fond of you."

I confirmed that both these interpretations were true in this case. George continued, "She says point-blankly that she knows it kills you that she passed on before you." I acknowledged this, with George replying that though Gloria had physically lost the battle against cancer she felt she had won it anyway. I surmised that this was because her illness had served to set up our interdimensional contacts. George went on to a description of how Gloria had felt at the end, and his description struck me as very accurate. The medium then told me Saint Agatha was being shown to him, as "the patron saint of women who have breast cancer or some form of cancer." I told him that Gloria had died of breast cancer.

George now communicated to me Gloria's feeling that "she could be a little more difficult in the marriage than you could be," affirming that "there was never any doubt that she knew you loved her, and she certainly loved you and still does, and her heart was always in the right place [, but she] wasn't the happiest person here. You were more adapted and/or adjusted than she was." She admitted "being at times very, very frustrated."

I was awestruck. "Frustrated" was Gloria to a tee. She had often been mystified as to why her career had never really gotten out the roof. It made her very anxiety-prone. George communicated to me that Gloria was very grateful for all the patience I had shown her. And she "didn't know how I had done it." I'll now continue with the transcript:

G: In some ways, she didn't have the happiest life growing up.

J: That's certainly correct from what I know of her early life.

G: Now she claims that she works with children in the hereafter. She's chosen that work because she's learning patience and to ease frustration. She does say to you that she has come to you in your sleep. This is not the first time she has communicated to you, though, as you know. She also wants you to know that dreams of anxiety are dreams of your mind playing tricks on you, while comforting visitations are communion with her. She also knows that you have kind of seen her and/or sensed her presence, that one way or another you knew she was there. She is a lot closer to you than you could imagine. She also speaks of her grandparents being there with her, so I take it they have passed on. (*Gloria also spoke of having her father there with her. Then:*) She is talking about losing a child.

J: Correct.

G: She says she had lost a child before birth. Maybe she's even saying she lost children, not sure.

J: A child before birth is correct.

I was astonished once again at the fact of the abortion's coming up in a contact session. George next alluded to Gloria's having been married before we met, which perhaps explained a couple of references she now made to her other children. Gloria communicated to me through George the frustration we both had felt that we had gotten so much karma out of the way, then met, then gotten married—and then Gloria had been taken, relatively early.

G: She said that's where your loss of her, too, becomes so dreadfully frustrating, because you finally meet somebody you are really into, and then she up and passes on.

J: Yes. How dare she!?

G: Yes, frustration was such a terrible aspect of her life here on earth, in more ways than one. And she admits that she is glad to be liberated from that feeling of frustration because, as she says, one of the most difficult things about being on earth is having feelings and not knowing how to deal with them or link with them.

J: Yes.

G: She now says to me that she was an extremely sensitive woman and that's great, but many times it became her downfall. She also says her first name is short.

J: What do you mean?

G: When souls in the hereafter tell me their name is short, I take it to mean their formal name is less than eight letters.

J: True.

G: Okay, so her formal name is less than eight letters. That's why she said it was short. She knows I interpret "short" to mean that.

J: To be frank, why bother to do this "less-than, greater-than" game?

I was expressing a frustration I often felt at these sessions: Why were the spirits so damned coy about telling us their names? Why didn't they just come out with their names, as they came out with so much else that was so much more interesting?

G: Well, I don't know, but now she's saying it's less than seven, yes?

J: Yes.

George told me that Gloria was now suggesting I should move out of the house. This might help me to better deal with the memory of her loss. He told me she wanted me to tell her children about our contacts, that she was still there for them and that she had not deserted them. Then Gloria seemed to bring up the subject of the life tribute.

G: She's talking about the support shown after she passed on.

J: Over there?

G: No, here. Something about the number of people that showed up at her funeral or something. True?

J: Yes, I did a major tribute to her life.

G: You know that what she brings up, that there were so many people that paid applause to her and saw in their subconscious the completion of her life.

J: Yes.

G: She also calls out to all of those she knew she left behind, because again she was young by today's standards, and she doesn't want people to be frightened by her death. Because she knows that some see it that she was cheated, terminated, or got short-changed on her life. She says they don't realize that it's not quantity, it's quality [in a life]. And again, no reflection on you, she says she's not disappointed now to be away from here, because certainly earth is the proving ground and very trying in its lessons, but, in the end, worth the experience.

There ensued a discussion of my career. George said that I would soon overcome my lethargy and move forward in vast new directions. Then the subject of Gloria's first name came up again:

G: She said she has a common first name, that her formal first name is short and she shows me six letters. Is that the amount it is?

J: Yes, it is.

G: But it can be shortened, yes?

J: Yes.

G: It's one of those names that you can use a nickname for, but that is not usually done, example, Brian could be Bri, but it's not usually that way. (*It seemed George felt the same irritation that I did:*) I go out of my mind with this. She comes forward and says my name is six letters, yet you can nickname it, even though it is not traditionally done. I have this experience with spirits, that they introduce another spirit and say, for example, "Hi! Linda"—or it could be Francine or Joan or whatever—"is here, and she passed on young too," but then they don't come out and say, "My name is Fred," or whatever. And yet sometimes they do. They say my name is Maureen, and I say, well, great and that's what I call service. But it's so frustrating that you just have to learn that you have to do it their way. But there must be a reason, because they somehow have to get into my subconscious mind to make the conscious mind understand what it is hearing.

J: Yes, I guess we'll both find out the difficulties when we make the jump. Besides, a name is only an ID tag, and it's what they say that's important, not the name.

G: That's true too, and I'm starting to learn that, but I've been kind of into the scorecard thing and getting those details correct. But the thing is, that's not what they're into. They're into what is needed to be heard, and that's that. She does express a thank you for the memorial and her name in memory and for the planting too. She's showing a tree growing in front of me, so that means either a tree has been planted in her honor or it's symbolic of something that has taken root in her remembrance.

J: Wow! That's 100 percent accurate.

This was pretty wild, because a close friend of mine and I had gone shopping and bought a beautiful tree with purple flowers when it bloomed (Gloria loved the color purple) which we had planted in front of our house. It's there today, blossoming constantly with beautiful purple flowers in Gloria's honor.

Next, Gloria conveyed to me through George a Red Alert concerning my health! She specified that I should get more rest, if possible worry less, and try to fight a feeling of emptiness that often came upon me now as a result of her passing. She told me, "You really have a blessed life except for this [her passing]."

G: She's now saying your name: John, John.

J: *(jokingly)* Is she saying I'm passing on soon or something?

G: *(laughing)* No, I don't think so. She's saying you're not supposed to be there yet, though the time will come when it's supposed to come. But she does say you have more to look forward to and that you are definitely not alone. Once again, as she states, she just never thought that would happen to you—not at this time, anyway.

J: Although earlier in this reading she states, if I remember correctly, that she knew.

G: Well, no. She knew she was going to pass, but that's after the point of the diagnosis. But for you she meant that everything was going fine until this happened. But at least have the satisfaction that she certainly is all right and at peace in the hereafter and totally back to her old self, and she knows that on a bad day you'll think about that and say, well, that doesn't compensate me very much.

J: Maybe.

G: She says she knows you have this feeling of isolation since she passed on, so even though you have had many contacts, there is still that feeling of being on your own. And that's why she says that in the hereafter you learn that a good soul loves impersonally, as God does, because in the end we're all on our own. And this is certainly the case here. But she states that she has embraced you from the hereafter, that you have in a sense been spiritually hugged in such a way where you actually get the chills.

J: Yes, and I'm very aware of it.

G: And that's her way of communicating to you that she is near and that she is indeed a lot closer to you than you can imagine.

J: I understand.

G: She also says you're a bit in no man's land.

J: That would be putting it mildly.

G: But she does again encourage you to go on with your life in whatever way you feel comfortable, including if you meet someone else, because she wants to make you understand that she won't think you are abandoning her. She certainly loves you unconditionally, and wants you to move on, with that said, in whatever way it takes. She knows your life for you is a little bit on hold, but shortly you will venture forth again and be out of the no man's land.

J: Yes, I agree. I'm just now getting ready to put the pedal to the metal again and resume where I was at before she became ill. Only I feel even stronger now, more inspired.

G: All she can do is encourage you to move on, but from the hereafter [she] can't fix things. All and all, we have to find the answer for ourselves, as difficult as that may be at times. Otherwise, there is no sense of accomplishment or triumph, as she puts it. But she certainly has given you evidence and signs that she is very near to you, and she assures you that will be the case until the day you meet again. She also blesses you for being good to her prior to her passing, understood?

J: (*emotionally*) Totally.

G: And she does state that you did right by her, understood?

J: Yes.

G: Because she recognizes that a lot of unpleasant decisions were put on your shoulders.

J: (*jokingly*) Yeah, a few thousand!

G: She says you did right by her, that then again in many ways your hands were tied, but you just had to do it anyway. I think that she is going to sign me off now and step back. Funny, though, she says Saint Anthony draws near to you and he is dressed in black and that is usually the sign of hearing news of a passing; but, as your wife states, you are not going to be the least bit shocked by it. Not anything of the magnitude of what you went through with her. And there is also another male coming to you in a fatherly manner. Your folks are still on the earth, yes?

J: Yes.

G: She says your folks are still here, too, but there is another male coming through in a fatherly manner so it must be another grandfather that just wants to let you know that he is near. But your wife certainly extends love to you from the hereafter, asking that you remember to pray for her, and assures you and her children and close family that she is always near. But she says she is very happy now and is glad to be liberated from the feeling of frustration which at times was a very agonizing aspect of her life, but nevertheless necessary for her journey.

J: Yes, especially the physical pain she went though at the end.

G: She states that there were so many times that you tried to do something about it, but couldn't.

J: Yes.

G: But she is saying it wasn't your job to make her happy as she had her lessons to learn, but you certainly did a very good job of bringing great joy into her life for the time she was here. So she sends her love again, asking you to pray for her along with other people in the background, from her side, that you also wanted to hear from. She's not alone and is doing well and is now well adapted and in a harmonious state until you guys meet again. And with that she steps aside, along with the others.

J: Okay. Thanks, George. (*The reading ended—or so it seemed. Then:*)

G: Just out of curiosity, as I couldn't get her name and it's driving me crazy—

J: Gloria.

G: Okay. I just wanted to find out to make sure that I didn't hear the correct name but then didn't say anything, but I can honestly say that I at no time ever heard the name Gloria. So I feel better.

J: All right, George. Thanks for your work.

G: Bye now.

Chapter 44

Contacting the Beyond: Sylvia Browne

If the great number of personal details were what particularly caught my interest in the contact session with George Anderson, it was the somewhat more cosmic scope of some of the details that emerged from my session with Sylvia Brown that really held my attention. Like George Anderson, Sylvia is a published author whose books include *Adventures of a Psychic* (1998), *The Other Side and Back: A Psychic's Guide to Our World and Beyond* (2000) and *Life on the Other Side: A Psychic's Tour of the After Life* (2001). My session with her took place on May 11, 2002. Exceptionally, this session took place at the medium's home.

Sylvia began by talking about my health, on the subject of which she was remarkably accurate (not that I have any real health problems). Next, she talked about my career, expressing great optimism about my future and even saying I would be traveling to a great number of countries. She would return to the subject of my career frequently during this contact session, but I'll merely touch upon those sections, as I believe it's the subject of my interdimensional contacts with Gloria that is truly of interest to the reader (and to me!).

When I focused my inner attention on the real reason I'd set this session up (which reason I had not yet revealed to Sylvia), a very tall man and a very short woman came into my medium's field of psychic vision. This arrival freaked me out, as my grandmother had said in a previous contact session that she knew what it was like to have a broken heart since she had lost her husband, my grandfather, all too early, spending the next 40 years plus without him. And, of course, if she had lost her husband early, you can imagine how my grandfather must have felt, having to leave her so early and so suddenly.

I asked Sylvia about making contact with my deceased wife.

S: Did she have beautiful wavy hair and gorgeous eyes?

J: Yes for sure. She was a knockout!

S: Well, she comes around you a lot. You know she's telling me that the tragedy of it was that she thought she beat it.

J: True! We really fought hard and thought we would beat it. She never thought this would be the way she was going to go.

S: But then it, the cancer, got into the whole lymph system and her lungs and everything and then it just went crazy, right?

J: Right!

S: Even with mammograms, they still don't catch it.

J: Well, that's what happened with us.

S: I know you know this: She's infusing you all of the time. She said she heard you talking to her before she went, even when she was in her coma and unable to talk at all.

J: Yes, I figured so.

S: Now, why is she talking to me about the picture that you have up that she likes so much? The one where she's three-quarter face.

J: Yes, my favorite picture of her is up in the house and in my recording studio. We also made posters of it.

S: She looks like an angel. See, the thing about all this that I'm just now picking up is, she's never going to leave you.

J: Yes. I don't want this to sound stupid or trite, but I really feel like I have a genuine guardian angel. For me it feels like the relationship is just continuing interdimensionally. I read some of your books and so I know you understand this sort of relationship. (*laughing*) Our relationship seems as if it's still continuing as usual, only she has a Romulan cloaking device!

S: You see, that's why I very rarely talk about soul mates, because everybody wants one, but you had one.

J: Yes, our relationship was special. We used to inspire others.

S: Not only that, but if you felt something then she did, true?

J: For sure!

S: It's something called "joined at the hip." Even if one goes to another dimension, they are never to go apart. You see, there are marvelous miracles—and I don't use that word loosely—that can happen with soul mates. It's sort of like the movie with Robin Williams, *What Dreams May Come*.

That hit home. Watching <u>What Dreams May Come</u> *had gotten me pretty emotional, especially the scene where Robin Williams gets upset when his angel guide tells him that he will never be able to see his deceased wife again, because she committed suicide and therefore had gone to a sort of hell/purgatory where no one could visit her. Williams adamantly refuses to accept this, insisting he will find a way to get to his wife and free her from her depression.*

At the time I was watching the movie I was feeling equally adamant about seeing Gloria again. And while I was sitting in front of the TV thinking these thoughts, some of the lights in the house went on and off. I checked for a short circuit, but could find none. I declared mentally that if this were Gloria affecting the lights, then she should do it again. At that moment the lights flickered on and off again. This mention of <u>What Dreams May Come</u> *struck me as very synchronistic.*

J: Yes, that was an unbelievable movie!

S: Anyway, she says she's glad you wrote your book, because it is a celebration of her life. And I'm sure others have said that since she was so amazing, why did she have to go? Sometimes you have to think, well, maybe that's why she did go, because it was scripted and for a good reason. Look at how many people you touched during the ordeal, and how many more you're going to touch with your inspiring performances and book. And then you see terrorists like Bin Laden still running around, and it doesn't make any sense! But she'll always be with you—always. She's not going to go into another life right away or to Outer Mongolia or somewhere.

J: I just know there's no planned reincarnation for her, at least not until we meet again here or there. The spiritual growth we both attained was planned and we were meant to always be together.

S: Correct. In a regular relationship, which we call a kindred soul relationship, this would never happen. But with a soul mate or twin soul relationship, which you guys have, if there is any way to go to hell or back or for them to come to hell and back, a soul mate can do it. That's why I mentioned the Robin Williams movie.

J: For some reason, because of her having to leave, it seems that my playing is much more inspired—as if it comes from a different viewpoint. It's as if her passing and my deep love for her opened my heart.

S: The good news is, it really did open your creative juices, not that they weren't there, but your floodgates are going crazy now.

J: She's helping me from the other side. I can feel it. I'm never been so effortless in my artistic production. I can feel things about to pop!

S: Yes, it's like she has a drill to your head. (*laughing*) Life is so transient, so passing. We'll all be together over there. We do the best we can on this bad camping trip and throw as much ripple dust as we can around, and then we go. But you do know she's going to be there, and the nicest thing about soul mates is that you'll never have to compete with anybody else. It's always going to be this cement! And I think that's a great comfort in some way, a security.

J: Right after the tragedy, I wanted to turn back the hands of time. But now, in hindsight, I've seen not only my wife's spiritual growth but now mine and, well, I wouldn't want to give that growth up. Do you know what I mean? It was a gift.

Sylvia told me that because of this gift my career was about to break loose and that I had many productive years ahead of me. I saw this as a mixed blessing: the longer I lived, the longer it would be until I saw Gloria again. I remarked that the ordeal of Gloria's illness had at least made me fearless, in that I couldn't imagine anything worse ever happening to me. Sylvia replied that when the worst happened, and you got through it, then you actually had been set free.

S: Artistic people seem to get through these tragedies the best, because of their abilities. Once your book and your projects get rolling, which they are just about to, everything will be coming to you.

On that optimistic note, our contact session ended.

Looking back on it all after these contact sessions, it seemed to me that I owed Gloria a karmic debt. Or perhaps we were even; perhaps she had owed me one. I grieved; I was devastated; but it also seemed to me that Gloria had given me an amazing gift. Our soul mate energy was still connecting us across the dimensions. Just as we had comforted and supported each other in this physical dimension, we were now doing the same thing across the barriers of the dimensions.

It now seemed to me that I had first-hand evidence of the power of unconditional love to burst the very bonds of life itself. The number and frequency of interdimensional communications and third-party corroboration, from friends, from psychics, from mediums, were too numerous for it to be possible for me to ignore them. It seemed to me that some of these proofs were indisputable.

Looking back at it all now, I'm not sure how I personally could have learned in any other way the lessons I am now learning. I'd been a tough nut to crack. I had needed a severe reality adjustment—and I most definitely had gotten one!

I feel greatly reassured in my belief—one that has now, because of Gloria, become a proven fact for me—that unconditional love is all there is, and that as long as we remain resolutely focused upon the truth of this, then everything we want will automatically follow.

I feel greatly reassured in my belief—one that has, again, because of Gloria, become a proven fact for me—that in the scheme of eternity we are immortal spiritual beings.

I am reassured in my belief that we all live many, many lives, and that, beyond those lives, there is no such thing as death. For me, death is simply a graduation. It is an awakening. It is the end of the dream of the body and the beginning of the wakefulness of the soul. It is a transition, a vacation between lives.

And, in the vast and brilliant spaces between our lives, the songs of our lives that we sing in joy are repeated, forever, and ever, and ever.

APPENDIX

TIPS FROM HEAVEN

Tips from Heaven

I call this final section "Tips From Heaven," because I believe the following principles to live by are just that, ways of handling life that are based upon unselfish love and service to others—in other words, heaven. In our, "Everybody's in the fast lane, give a little, take a lot" society (lyric courtesy of Gloria), unselfish love and service to others are all but extinct. Those few who haven't allowed the entanglements of the physical universe to corrupt their spiritual heritage are looked upon by society either as rare saints or as "do-gooders" who spoil everything for the rest of us. We're jealous of people who practice good deeds; they tend to make us extremely uncomfortable.

Of course, there's a reason why they make us uncomfortable. It's because we know deep down in our souls that the "give a little, take a lot" way of living our lives is not okay—that replacing the power of love with the love of power doesn't really make us or others feel good. It does not make for a better world. It is not the path to happiness and spiritual freedom.

Living selfishly violates the basic truth of human nature that we are all fundamentally good. When we act "badly," or even in a fashion that is "evil," it is only because we are lost in the entanglements of the physical universe. We haven't learned the correct spiritual lessons. Remember the comedy *Groundhog Day,* starring Bill Murray? Murray plays a TV weatherman who is sent to Punxsutawney, Pennsylvania to cover the annual Groundhog Day festivities. But, on his way out of town on the evening of Groundhog Day, he is caught in a giant blizzard—which he failed to predict—and finds himself having to spend the rest of the evening in what seems to him to be a small-town hell, and then having to stay overnight.

He wakes up the next morning to find it's Groundhog Day all over again, and he lives the entire day again. And then this scenario repeats, again, and again...and again! *Groundhog Day* director Harold Ramis has estimated that the Bill Murray protagonist lives Groundhog

Day over and over again 10,000 times! The hapless, bewildered weatherman is only able to get to tomorrow when he has learned complete selflessness and complete goodness in the course of these many today's. Or so it seems; one of the virtues of this wonderful movie is that it never preaches, and does not even give us a hint of what cosmic/divine forces, if any, have placed the Bill Murray character in this unique predicament.

In my opinion, each and every one of us is living his or her own "Groundhog Day," that being our life on earth with, as is my belief, its successive reincarnations. And, just as Bill Murray could not die and could not escape waking up to the same scenario every day, i.e. facing his "selfish, give-a-little, take-a-lot self," we too face a similar scenario of being reborn into a next lifetime not too different from this one— one containing the same problems as in the last lifetime because we failed to grow sufficiently in spirituality to resolve them—unless we make huge leaps forward in love and selflessness in this lifetime. If we manage to do this latter, not only will we be reborn into a next lifetime where we face entirely new challenges, but also, hopefully, we may even find we have leapt off the wheel of earthly incarnations forever!

Can we take responsibility for this process and accelerate it? I believe we can. We have free will. It is totally up to us whether our path turns out to be "hell on earth" or a smooth, heavenly ascent to our spiritual heritage through the daily application of the principles of unselfish love and action. Through the disciplined study of spiritual truths and the lessons life teaches us, I believe we can all accelerate our spiritual journey and make a difference, rather than just wake up to a next lifetime that is very much like this one.

Think of this chapter as a workshop. Merely reading these tips, these do's and don't's, won't help us very much. What *will* bring about accomplishment is sincerely and methodically applying these tips to our daily lives until they awaken that wonderful, perfect, loving being that we all have inside us. I have personally learned these tips the hard way. Did I know about most of them before Gloria's illness? Yes, in theory, I did, more or less. Did they make an impact? Did I apply them diligently and consistently in my life? In hindsight, hardly! Am I applying them now? Yes, indeed! Are they working? You bet!

My suggestion is to read and study each tip. See which ones you can benefit from, and begin honestly and patiently to apply them to your life, even if it's only one at a time. Note the results. How do you feel when you operate in this way? How do others around you react to your new mode of operation?

Note that these tips are not in any significant order. Read through them at your leisure, perhaps over and over again. Reflect on how you can personally apply them to your daily life. Think of times in the past where you didn't apply them, and recall the results. Remember, these are only tips; they are hardly commandments. They are just hard-earned advice that I would like to share with you. What's true for you is what's true for you.

As you begin applying these simple tips to your everyday life and seeing the positive and sometimes amazing results they generate, it will become easier and easier for you to operate in this way. It may take some time for you to change your old habits, so be patient. The rewards are worth the effort.

The tips are organized with the tip first, then the theory that lies behind it afterward. Finally, I give some examples from life to help clarify the nature of the tip and how it is applied.

(1) Try to forgive yourself for your weaknesses and bad deeds

Concentrate primarily on the present, not the past. Work on doing good deeds and playing from your strengths. This will eventually allow you to love yourself unconditionally. You could, of course—if you're up to it—simply forgive yourself and unconditionally love your-self, despite all your weaknesses and bad deeds; we're all unique and perfect beings, but in the rough-and-tumble, often devastating daily experience of the real world, our egos get in the way. To rise above ego is part of the learning experience that is life. Surrender your ego—which amounts to forgiving yourself—and appreciate all that you are. Unconditionally loving yourself may seem like an act of arrogance. However, if you do not love yourself, you will never have the strength to humble yourself, let alone to love others unconditionally and help them with their own lives.

a. I used to dwell on my weaknesses as a pianist and worry about them constantly. I would wonder why it was that, no matter how much I practiced, I still wasn't nearly as good as Beethoven, or Vladimir Horowitz, or Oscar Peterson, or my good friend Chick Corea. I con-stantly indulged in self-doubt and self-denial. But, at a certain point—after continually wondering if I were ever going to be satisfied with my abilities—I decided to simply forgive myself for all the so-called "weaknesses" involved in my not being as good as Beethoven or Horowitz or Peterson or Corea. I told my ego to just shut up! I asked myself, "What *am* I good at?" And I realized that I was good at playing soulful funky blues. I concentrated on that and, sure enough, I was soon playing much better—and the audience was loving it. I thought, "Wow! I just needed to love who I already was and not who my ego thought I should be!"

We are all unique, and we all have special ways in which we can perform services for others. It's worth the time and the effort to find out what those ways are. We can start by forgiving ourselves and unconditionally loving who we already are.

b. When Gloria lost her battle with cancer, I blamed myself for practically everything: all the times that we'd fought, that I'd put her in the wrong, that I hadn't been with her because I was too busy working—all the times that I'd taken from her instead of giving to her. It required a lot of unconditional self-love on my part to finally forgive myself for all these shortcomings. And, when I'd finally done so, I turned my attention to my strengths, such as composing and playing and writing and lecturing. I completed the solo CD Gloria and I had been working on. Then, inspired by her courageous fight, I set out to write this book. I don't think I would have recovered from all that had happened to us if I hadn't sought out my strengths and applied them.

(2) **Never take a loved one for granted**

Never, never, never! Love them as if today were the last day you were ever going to see them. Having lost my spouse, I can't begin to tell you how important this is. There's nothing more important than expressing your love for a beloved. Nothing! When that loved one is gone, it's too late to express your love. The following examples are written as if they were from husband to wife, but with a little thought they can be adapted to a from-wife-to-husband situation or indeed to any relationship.

a. Buy your wife flowers and tell her she means the world to you.

b. Every night before you go to bed, ask her if there's anything you can do to improve the relationship. Accept each and every answer she gives you and make a real effort to deliver on what she wants.

c. Handle all disagreements with lots of empathy and understanding.

No disagreement is worth a heated fight. If you think you'll have a problem doing this, then ask yourself the following: "If today were her last day on earth, would I still express my anger in this manner?" Probably, you wouldn't.

d. Thank her for all the little things she does, like making dinner, watering the plants, shopping, taking care of the kids, providing sex and romance, bringing in income, planning a vacation, having bright ideas and supporting your own bright ideas, marrying you, smiling her precious smile, loving you with devotion—and just "being her." I can't tell you how important this last is. When loved ones go, the real hurt is exactly this, that all of a sudden you realize you can't thank them anymore for just being who they are—and, boy, does that hurt!

e. Do some investigating and occasionally (though not on her birthday or Christmas) surprise her with a gift that you know she really wants, if for no other reason than to show her that you love her. The gift doesn't have to be expensive, but, if it is—all the better!

f. When she wants you to go with her to visit her folks—your in-laws—do it willingly and actually have a great time. Really care about her folks and take an interest in their well-being.

g. Never go to sleep when you and your spouse are angry with each other.

h. Hug your spouse every day. Let her know she's the most important person in your life.

i. Write down significant days—birthdays, anniversaries, the first time you met, etc. Do something special on each of these days—flowers, a card, a special dinner, something really nice.

(3) Never be too busy for family

a. Call your elderly grandparents for no reason at all and ask them how they're doing. Better still, pay them a surprise visit. Nothing brightens up the day of an elderly person more than a surprise visit from a grandchild. We "young" people are usually too busy enjoying life to remember our elders. But, ponder this: One day, if you are lucky enough to reach that same old age, wouldn't you appreciate a visit from one of your own grandchildren?

b. Your employer is demanding that you work overtime tonight, but you promised your wife you would go with her to a special party. Instead of politely bowing out of the party because of work obligations (you hate parties anyway), put your work on hold—if possible; you'll have to clear this with your boss, as sometimes overtime work really is necessary—and go to the party and have a great time!

(4) Perform a daily act of kindness

a. In the grocery store line behind you, you see someone in a hurry and stressed out. Tell that person it's okay to go in line in front of you.
b. You've just landed from your flight and the elderly lady in front of you is having trouble getting her bags out of the upper compartment. You're in a hurry to get off the plane, as you need to make another connection. Lend her a hand anyway.
c. You're driving down the road. The weather is stormy. You see an obviously distressed stray dog. Pull off the road and see if you can help the dog. See if it has a collar and an ID tag. Either take it home and give it a good meal and a shampoo and call its owner, or put an ad about it in your local newspaper's lost-and-found column, or take it to the nearest animal rescue center. So what if your car gets dirty and you have to clean it up afterward? Imagine if it were your own family dog that was lost. Helping animals is a very special act of kindness. It'll make your day.

(5) Patch up a broken relationship

a. Make a list of all those things you really like about the person with whom you have broken off the relationship. Concentrate on these qualities until you feel better about the person. Then call the person up.
b. Call up a family member, friend, or business associate with whom you have an unresolved situation. Apologize for the upset, even if you think it is not your fault. (This is usually the problem with a broken relationship, anyway: both parties think they're right!) Offer to get back into communication, to meet for dinner—and of course, in the case of the latter, offer to pick up the tab!

(6) Live every day as if it might be your last

You cannot go after your dreams, prosper, do good deeds, make the world a better place to live in, without an all-out assault. Don't take it for granted that you'll be here tomorrow! Be, do and have now everything you are capable of dreaming of.

a. You're thinking of starting your own business, but you're afraid it might fail. Start it anyway! Declare affirmatively that, "My business is successful!"

b. You're a jazz singer, but everyone tells you that to make a living you should sing in a more commercial style, e.g. rhythm and blues. But you love jazz and you're good at it. Follow your heart! Declare affirmatively, "My debut jazz CD is Number One on the jazz charts!"

c. You've always wanted a new 740 BMW. However, it's a little beyond your means. Should you give up your dreams? Hell, no! Declare affirmatively that "I now own a black brand new 740 BMW!"

(7) Make it your *"modus operandi"* (method of operating) to affirm your goals and purposes

An affirmation is a personal statement of fact. In other words, in your mind it's a done deal. True, it may not have happened yet in the physical universe, but the fact that it is affirmed in your internal universe actually impinges on the external physical universe. Although we can't possibly understand all the factors involved in the creation of reality—and although at the same time as we affirm that something will happen, we must act decisively in the real world to make that desired end come about (that is, we mustn't just sit around dreaming about what we want to have happen)—still, our thoughts do effectively create reality. Here are some examples of affirmations:

(a) My next CD will sell a million copies.

(b) My headache is gone.

(c) I have lots of good friends.

(d) I have won the lottery.

(e) I am spiritually free.

(f) I am a great artist.

(g) My book is on the bestseller list.

(h) There is no more criminality on planet Earth.

(i) I've won the Olympic gold medal in the men's 100-yard dash.

(j) I have landed the starring part in the movie I just auditioned for.

Remember, again, that affirmations do not work unless at the same time you yourself make a colossal personal effort, through your actions, to bring the desired event about. Here, the old kabbalic dictum applies: "Pray as if everything depended on God. Act as if everything depended on you."

(8) Say a prayer for a loved one, departed or not

My wife passed away after a long battle with breast cancer. I say a daily prayer that in the afterworld she do well in her endeavors.
a. If someone you know is fighting a serious illness, say a prayer to God that he or she will speedily recover.
b. If a friend tells you about a pet that is recovering from an operation, say a prayer that the pet will make a speedy recovery and be quickly reunited with its family.

(9) Look for the good in people, not the bad

Whenever you find yourself thinking critical thoughts about someone, or talking critically about that person behind his or her back, find something positive to say about that person, and say that instead. If you can't find say anything good to say about a person, try silence. If you could get back all the time you've wasted criticizing others, you might be surprised to find out how much time you have on your hands with which to do something good. Besides, if anyone has made a strong enough impression on you that you waste your precious thought processes coming up with critical things to say about that person, you can bet that he or she is mostly reminding you of your own faults.
a. In conversation, a friend starts putting down a mutual acquaintance. Though you partially agree, you exercise self-discipline and restrain from joining in. After your friend is finished, you either make it clear to that friend that you heard what was said but you add no critical comments of your own, or you point out some good trait in the person under discussion. Or you could just say, "Stop! I don't want to be exposed to any more of this negative energy."
b. You know someone who really isn't coping very well. Instead of criticizing that person to others, you set up a meeting with him or her and actually help the person to get his or her life together. You could also declare affirmatively that the person is doing well. Whichever one you choose, it's better than spreading around the fact that that person is not doing well. The latter action has no value whatsoever and can even make matters worse.

c. You discover you're feeling very critical of a friend of yours. Instead of wasting your time with these negative thoughts, you recall a time when you and your friend were getting on well together. You think of the good times! Better yet, you try to identify what bad deed you might have done to that person. Trust me: If you're really feeling critical of your friend, the bad deed is there, and you must acknowledge it and take responsibility for it. Now, call your friend up. Arrange for the two of you to go out to dinner together, and have a great time. What do you have to lose but your critical thoughts?

(10) Handle all worries—money, career, health, etc.—with love

Yes, that's what I said—with love, true love/unconditional love. Now how, you ask, can one love a worry, a problem, an illness, an argument, a death? My answer is that worry, apathy, fear, anger, grief, all such feelings are negative in nature and therefore useless in arriving at constructive solutions to problems. Besides, there are lessons to be learned from our difficulties. Love, affection, liking: these are all positive states of being and are therefore useful and effective in solving our problems. Once you get to these latter places of serenity and positivity, then all kinds of magic can and does happen. Here are some examples of handling "negative" events in useful and constructive ways:

a. Let's say you have a real bad flu. Notice all the incredible attributes of this flu: its cold chills and its high fever, how quickly it came on, your upset stomach, etc. Appreciate the unique and incredible nature of these qualities. Like, this flu is a really tough character! What an amazing fever and cold chills! Absolutely amazing!

b. You've had a terrible argument with your spouse, the worst you ever had. It's over now, but you're beside yourself, stressed out, and very worried about the repercussions of the argument. You're very angry with your spouse. Well then, quite purposefully and consciously think of that terrible fight in the most positive terms possible: How incredible your spouse was during it all, how brilliantly and effectively—and painfully!—she took off your head! What a terrific sparring partner she is! And look at how much influence you two had that you didn't even know you had: your shouting woke up the neighbors!

c. You've just totaled your new car. Luckily, you weren't that badly hurt. But your car is a catastrophe! However: Instead of worry, regret, anger, grief, blame and all those other negative and non-constructive emotions that have no positive effects, you decide to go directly to your higher self and shower the whole incident with love. You look at your car and think, man, did I total that! Look at that mess! It doesn't even look like my car anymore. An amazing accident! And it's amazing to think that I'm still alive! Wow!

(11) **Plan weekly meetings to review your relationship**

This works wonders for keeping a relationship fresh. When both parties know there is a pre-designated time when they can not only air their differences, problems, worries, and concerns, but also discuss their goals, suggestions, wins, and so forth, there's no need to have unscheduled scrapes during the week that disrupt the relationship and separate the two of you from each other.

a. Your wife's parents unexpectedly pay you a visit. You had planned on a nice, quiet, romantic evening at home; now, in your eyes, they've ruined it. When the parents leave, instead of going on about them to your wife, tell her what great parents she has, since it is they who brought her into the world in the first place. You wouldn't have her without them, would you? Then go on with your romantic evening. However, if your in-laws' visit really wasn't okay, bring this up at the weekly meeting (though in a nice way). Your wife will probably agree with you and figure out a way to handle this in the future.

b. You get an audit letter from the IRS! This causes you some upset and you feel like railing against the IRS to your wife. Doing this will, of course, upset you even more and also upset your wife. A better way to handle things is: (1), call your accountant or tax attorney and make an appointment; and (2), bring the audit letter and its contents up at your weekly meeting. When you do this latter, do it calmly and tell your wife that you have already routed the letter to the accountant and that you have a meeting scheduled with the accountant for next week.

(12) **Don't take more than you can give**

This tip reminds me of the following story: A man is walking down the street and a brick from a building falls on his head. "Ouch!" he groans. He gets mad and starts blaming everything and everybody for the incident. A second man walks down the street and a brick falls on his head, too. "Ouch!" he exclaims. "Ow! That was pretty incredible! What are the odds of my being hit on my head with a brick? Amazingly remote! Why did *I* cause that brick to hit my head? I must be trying to tell myself something."

The former victim of the falling brick is taking no responsibility for the incident, while the latter is taking full responsibility. Which attitude do you think will produce the more positive results?

The first time this datum was really brought home to me was when I heard a song by Dave Mason in which the lyrics go,

> *"Shouldn't have took more than you gave,*
> *'Cause you wouldn't be in this mess today!"*

The truth of these lyrics was slammed down my spiritual throat when my wife Gloria made her transition. All the times I "took more than I gave" reared their ugly head big-time—because I no longer had the chance to give enough to make up for what I'd taken. I can personally testify that there is no getting away from the overwhelming sense of guilt you feel when you get in the kind of situation I did.

Don't abstain from such unethical activity—taking more than you give—because of the fear of its boomeranging in your face. Although I guess that would be a step up from taking more than you give, it's still a far cry from simply giving freely, without any expectation and any taking. This is real unconditional love. Whether it's a matter of a relationship, a career, sports, a hobby, or whatever, giving freely, exchanging in abundance, giving more than is ever expected—that is the secret to real success in anything. Try it and see for yourself.

a. You're upset with your spouse because she didn't do your laundry when you needed it done. Time out! How many times has she done your laundry without your ever saying thank you, without your ever asking her if she needed any help, without your ever volunteering to give her a break while *you* did the laundry? What is probably really upsetting you is that, way down deep in your spirit self, you know that you owe her—you know that you've taken more than you've given. And here's the solution: You say, "Honey, don't worry about the laundry this week. I'll do it!" Be careful, though; she might have a heart attack from sheer surprise, and then you'll be in a real jam.

b. You get asked by a friend to play at her wedding (you're a pianist). Not only do you do this, and free of charge—as a wedding gift—but you also write the bride and groom a special piece of music for the occasion. And they're thrilled!

c. It's your mom's birthday. You don't live at home any more and you usually send flowers and a card. For this birthday, you fly home and surprise her. You even throw her a surprise party—but the real surprise is *your being there* to help her celebrate this special occasion.

(13) Disconnect yourself as much as possible from all media

That's right! I said *all* media, especially TV, newspapers and radio. Sure, you can catch the occasional show that is uplifting. But most of the time you have to make your way through dangerous terrain. To awaken the sleeping perfect being within yourself, you have to operate on a pretty refined level—and I guarantee you won't find that level in the crass entertainment manipulation that constitutes 99 percent of what the media sends out. Most of the material you tune into with TV, newspapers and radio is pablum, and sometimes vicious pablum at that, and it dulls your soul and leads to an inactive, sedentary life that will make you physically and spiritually obese.

The longer you stay media-free, then the more you disengage yourself from the chaotic, media-propagated feelings that bring you down and provoke stress and anxiety and fear within you. When you spend a lot of time listening to or watching the media, to that degree you cut yourself off from the wealth of information that is available within yourself. Also, you prevent yourself from communicating with your friends and loved ones, from reading a great book, from exercising your imagination, from coming up with bright ideas, from your own dreams—from the very essence and vitality of life itself! Wake up! You're asleep, which is exactly the state that most of the broadcast material is designed to put you in, as the highest goal of the media is to keep you occupied and asleep so that they can use and abuse you.

If you don't believe me, try the following experiment: Give up TV, newspapers and radio cold turkey for an entire week. You'll find this very hard initially, because, trust me, you have no idea how addicted you are to these entertainment devices. But after a few days you'll find yourself beginning to create and explore other entertainment options. You'll become more relaxed and less frantic about life. You'll sleep and eat better. Tensions will begin to dissipate. Your mind and body will wake up and smell the roses. Dreams, goals, purposes and ideas—all of these will begin to surface. You'll begin to get excited about life, and in a very wholesome way.

a. You've come home beat from your nine-to-five job. This is a problem in itself, since if you were doing a job you loved you wouldn't be beat in the first place. Anyway, you've come home and you're beat. Your normal procedure is to grab a beer (another dampener of awareness), turn on the tube, and watch another sitcom or movie—or, worse still, a talk show (though Oprah's talk show is in general an exception to the rule). You make yourself some fast food (another mistake) and watch the TV to help you wind down—that's exactly right, "wind down"—and then, due to the numbingly negative sensations that have been bombarding you on a subliminal level, you fall asleep.

Instead of this soul-enslaving ritual, why don't you try the following: Coming home, making great food, reading a good book, talking about the day with your loved one or a roommate? Or getting on the computer and starting to decisively imagine your future; or making plans for moving forward with your special dreams; or going and working out; or telephoning your mom or dad; or taking your dog for a much-needed jaunt in the park; or, best of all, inventing something or authoring a book that will help humanity to survive.

b. You've just gotten up, and normally you have a cup of coffee (drugs are another mistake); anyway, you have that cup of coffee, and you reach for the newspaper—and, whoops, you've flunked already! The emotional vibrational level of any newspaper runs from fear up to chaos. The message of all newspapers is that the world is a dangerous place and you should be really careful and afraid in it.

Newspapers never give you solutions; they just present problems with no solutions. So be careful! Crime, disease, drugs, financial disaster, war, corrupt politics and violence—this is all utter chaos. Stop! Get up, have a great breakfast, maybe do some deep breathing exercises, read a little of that good book you bought, go over what you intend to accomplish for the day, hug your spouse, and then go off to work with a smile on your face.

c. You're in your car and you've just turned to one of those chaotic radio shows where the hosts are convicted felons, perverts, retired politicians or psychiatrists! Stop! By the time you reach your destination, you'll be totally riled up by the bad odor of the concepts, images and words you've heard being disseminated and debated on the air and passed off as entertainment.

True, what you hear might interest you and might even entertain you, but there is no way that it will uplift you, i.e. put you in a place closer to your higher self. You'd be better off not listening to anything and spending your time with yourself, your imagination and your dreams, or putting on some very high soul-tone classical music or jazz.

You don't have to like classical music or jazz for them to raise your emotional tone level. This is a much better result than getting caught up in chaotic political controversy, or a discussion of abortion or of straights versus gays or of religion or of child molestation, etc., etc. You don't want to arrive at your destination a Typhoid Annie for all the bad vibes you've just picked up! You know how it is: You get to work and then you begin telling everyone at the office about this woman who's abused her two-year-old baby by beating him every day and stuffing him in a drawer at night. You're perturbed about this—and now you're spreading this sickness to others, and for what good purpose?

Remember that these are tips for you to try out of your own volition—that is, only if you yourself are willing and nobody else has told you to try them. They won't work if you don't make a conscious effort to incorporate them into your daily life. It may take a while for them to become second nature—but, trust me, it's worth working at incorporating them, since making this so will add a little heaven to your "this life."

(14) Appreciate the little things in life

One day during her illness, Gloria looked at me and said, "Boy, do I wish I could take a shower, or go for a walk, or eat a good meal, or brush my teeth, or go to the bathroom by myself, or go to the gym and work out, or teach a vocal lesson, or pay some bills, or just sing a song!" I immediately began crying uncontrollably. Here I was, worrying about life and death and money problems, and all Gloria wanted was to be able to appreciate all the little things in life that the cancer had taken from her.

So, instead of worrying about the big things—finances, business, career, taxes, and so on—wax enthusiastic about the little things in life. Don't take them for granted. They make up such an important part of life. You *can* do this, because it is you yourself who are the creator of your thoughts and feelings. If you don't believe me, just try such a creation. Next time you're in the doldrums over some money issue or whatever and you're worrying yourself sick, start becoming enthusiastic about some small thing in life, like the beauty of the roses in your backyard, or your new pair of shoes, or your family or pet, or whatever. You'll quickly find out that it's actually *you* who is in charge of how you feel.

a. You're taking a shower. Instead of worrying about the day's events, enjoy the warm, soothing water. Ah, doesn't it feel great, the water running down your body and making you tingle all over? What a luxury! Totally enjoy the moment.

b. You've just gotten up, and immediately you start worrying about whether you'll be able to close that big account at the office today. Instead of continuing with that train of thought, you take a nice long stretch and really appreciate how good that feels. Wow! Then you notice it's a wonderfully sunny day, 75 degrees with blue skies. Appreciate that! Go outside and feel the warm and friendly rays of the sun on your body. Bask in all this richness, and say to yourself, "Wow, what a fantastic day to be alive!"

c. You're driving home and you run into God-awful traffic, bumper to bumper—the worst! You start getting angry and frustrated and you worry about being late. But then you change your mind and your behavior. You decide to test the hypothesis that *you* create your own feelings. You scan the radio for a favorite song and begin listening to it. You marvel at how good the new sound system is that you recently installed in your car. You allow your body to vibrate to the beat and your mind to get engrossed in the lyrics. You totally immerse yourself in this experience, and you think how great it is to be able to listen to and enjoy a great song. You start feeling so good that now you look at all the cars and their drivers as your friends and not your enemies. You even let a few people cut in front of you in order to help them out. You're amazed at how good you feel; usually, in a situation like this, you're totally upset for the rest of the day. You arrive home refreshed, even though you're 45 minutes late. Wow!

d. You begin opening your mail, and after a few minutes you are totally worried about all the bills and how you're going to pay them. You decide to change your viewpoint. You say to yourself, Wow, I have created all these wonderful bills to pay. What a game! I caused all these bills—little old me! I'm healthy and alive and all I have to do is make some money and pay them.

Besides, all these bills are things that contribute to my incredible life—mortgage, power, gas, the vacation, the new suit and computer that I charged on my credit cards, the flowers I bought for my wife. You appreciate all of them for they greatly contribute to your life. They are part of life, and they are a part that you created. You think: Why deny myself? I'll go out and make some more money and create some new bills, and in the process I'll have a great time! Bills are cool, they're part of life, and I'm alive! I think I'll go out and have a great meal and create another bill!

Now, by no means have I exhausted the possibilities here regarding applying these tips from heaven. The possibilities are infinite. Don't get discouraged. If applying these tips were easy, you'd be living a "heavenly" life right now! But you're not. Besides knowledge, it takes clear purpose, discipline and perseverance to incorporate these tips into your daily life. In actuality, it may take years. But what is in front of you is eternity, your eternity. And I can guarantee you that the more of these tips you apply to your life, the more your eternity will be heavenly.

About the Author

JOHN NOVELLO was born in Erie, Pennsylvania, and has lived in Los Angeles since 1978. An author, composer, and producer as well as a keyboardist, he has performed around the world with numerous groups and artists including Chick Corea, Mark Isham, Andy Summers, Ramsey Lewis, Manhatten Transfer, Carl Anderson, Donna Summer, Edgar Winter, A Taste of Honey and Ritchie Cole. In 1985, he published the industry-standard textbook and instruction methodology *The Contemporary Keyboardist* (Hal Leonard). He composed the score for the film *Au Pair* and served as consultant and coach for the film *Red Hot*. His company, Lunatek Music, a partnership with Alan Howarth, writes music for CDs, feature films, TV commercials, theme parks and special venues. In 1995-96, Novello co-founded with Billy Sheehan the progressive jazz rock fusion group Niacin, with himself at Hammond B3 organ, Billy Sheehan on bass, and Dennis Chambers on drums. Their latest CD release is *Time Crunch*, from Magna Carta.

John Novello's mailing address is John Novello Productions, P.O. Box 5252, North Hollywood, CA 91616. He may be contacted through the following websites: www.keysnovello.com (personal site); www.lunatek.tv (film site); and www.niacinb3.com (Niacin site). The Gloria Rusch-Novello life tribute CD *Tightrope* is available through the website www.cdbaby.com.